The House at Zaronza

A Tale of Corsica

Vanessa Couchman

Photography: Jean Cliclac
Design: Crooked Cat
Editor: Sue Barnard

The House at Zaronza: 978-1-909841-82-6

First Blue Line Edition, Crooked Cat Publishing Ltd. 2014

To Per

Puss och kram

The Author

Vanessa Couchman has lived in southwest France since 1997. She works as a freelance writer, offering copywriting services to international clients and writing magazine articles on French life and the art of writing. She is a member of online, ex-pat writing group Writers Abroad. She has also been a Writers Bureau tutor.

Vanessa is passionate about French and Corsican history and culture, from which she draws inspiration for much of her fiction. Her short stories have been published in anthologies and on websites. She has also won and been placed, short-listed and long-listed in creative writing competitions.

The House at Zaronza is Vanessa's debut novel.

Acknowledgments

I owe thanks to many people. My writing colleagues at Writers Abroad provided pertinent and constructive comments on early drafts. Fellow-members of the Parisot Writing Group were almost as pleased as I was to know that the book would be published and have keenly followed its progress.

Lorraine Mace has given consistent help and encouragement in so many ways. Steph and Laurence Patterson at Crooked Cat Publishing had faith in the story and took me on. The judicious comments and eagle eye of my editor, Sue Barnard, saved me from many howlers. And my husband has been endlessly patient, supportive and tolerant.

My cat did nothing, but no doubt thought he was indispensable.

The House at Zaronza

Chapter 1

Zaronza 2010

The ruins of the château forked into the sky above Zaronza as Rachel arrived late on a September afternoon. The sun was already dipping towards the horizon, wreathed in skeins of crimson and purple. A small knot of anticipation formed in her stomach. This was where her grandmother might have lived as a girl.

Zaronza was a popular tourist spot, even that late in the season, and Rachel had difficulty finding a space to park her hired Golf. The café thronged with day-trippers taking an apéritif before heading back to Bastia or Santa-Lucia. All the way up the coast she had to press the car almost into the mountainside as another coach full of holidaymakers loomed around the improbable bends. The road was not designed for that volume of traffic, and she was not used to driving on the right. She was exhausted by the time she eased the car into an opening that was barely long enough.

Straightening her screaming back she took her overnight bag from the boot and set off up the hill towards the village. The absence of pavements and the insouciance of the Corsican drivers didn't make for easy progress. She wondered what Zaronza must be like in the high season but as she crossed the main square the noise of traffic ebbed away.

The house was one of the most imposing in the village, at the end of an alleyway. A typical Corsican house, it was foursquare and without ornament, almost severe. With its narrow windows, it resembled a fortress. A rocky pinnacle sheltered it from the sea breezes and rose up steeply to the ruined château and an eighteenth-century watchtower. Rachel felt a strange affinity for the place.

She unlatched the gate from the alleyway and approached the front door, which was solid and studded with iron bolts, matching the severity of the rest of the house. She raised the knocker (in the shape of a clenched fist) and let it fall. After a few moments, a smiling, thickset figure emerged around the corner of the house.

"Excuse me; I was outside on the terrace. I am Pascal Respighi. You must be Madame Swift. We were expecting you. Please come this way."

They shook hands.

"I'm sorry I'm a little later than planned, Monsieur Respighi." Rachel gestured back towards the road. "It takes longer to get here from Santa-Lucia than it appears on the map."

His eyes twinkled and he raised a finger. "Here on Corsica, Madame, we don't trust maps or signposts. We never talk about what distance it is from one place to the next but about how long it takes." He grinned, his teeth gleaming white against his tanned skin.

He pushed open the heavy door, which grated on the uneven flagstones. They entered a cool, dark hallway furnished with a long-case clock and a polished oak buffet. It had that smell of damp stone and wood ash that is the trademark of old houses. The walls were bare of decoration, except for a single faded sepia photograph. Taking Rachel's bag, Monsieur Respighi gestured towards the broad staircase and they went up to the second floor. Black-framed pictures hung on the walls, but as they walked along the corridor she saw they were not pictures but pages of handwriting. There was no time to look closer. Monsieur Respighi flung open a door at the end of the passage, flooding it with mellow evening light.

"Here we are," he said. "This room has one of the best views in the whole house. You can see the village from here as well as the bay. I hope you'll be comfortable."

He looked at her more closely. "Excuse my curiosity, but your French is excellent. I would even say you look a little Corsican. Do you have relatives here?"

Rachel smiled. "You're very kind – and very observant. I teach French at a university. I'm English, but I discovered recently that my maternal grandmother, whom I never met, was Corsican. It's possible that I still have relatives in Corsica but I'm not sure. And I understand my grandmother had connections with Zaronza. That's why I'm here."

He raised his eyebrows. "We Corsicans always recognise each other. We must talk more about this. But now I expect you would like to rest. Please don't hesitate to ask if you need anything. You'll normally find us in the kitchen or on the terrace at the back."

He placed her bag on a chair and closed the door behind him. His footsteps receded along the passage and down the stairs. The front door grated on the slabs again.

Rachel crossed to the window that had been left open to air the room. Placing her elbows on the wide stone sill, she took in the view of the village. In the foreground, on the opposite side of the square, stood the church. It was surprisingly small and intimate, and was painted a faded apricot that reflected the glow of the sinking sun. The bell in the separate *campanile* was striking eight. The hills, covered with scrub and silvery-green olive trees, reared up straight behind the village. Apart from the occasional tourist coach that surged in front of the church, the view must have remained unchanged for centuries.

She moved to the other window, the one which overlooked the sea, and opened it. A salt-laden breeze wafted in. For a moment, the sight of the purple-tinged mountains on the other side of the bay made her hold her breath. The sun's lengthening rays tinted the sea with red and gold. Another scent prickled her nostrils, aromatic and dry like sun-baked mud. She closed her eyes and breathed it in. This was the unique aroma of Corsica, that many Corsicans claim they can detect miles out to sea: part of the magic of the island, the Circe that had enchanted many a traveller before Rachel. A feeling of coming home washed over her.

The room was comfortable, if not luxurious, with well-polished furniture and a double bed covered with a white counterpane. A framed picture on the massive chest of drawers drew her attention. Like the pictures in the corridor, it was a page of handwriting. The paper was yellowed and spotted with age and the ink was a faded brown. She picked it up and held it to the light.

My lovely Maria,

Why are you so harsh to me? You accuse me of flirting with other girls but you know I only have eyes for you. If I look at another girl it is only to compare her with you – and you are incomparable. I have never been unfaithful to you in thought, word or deed.

The letter continued in this vein but was unsigned. The author wrote in an elegant, flowing hand and was clearly lettered and educated. Rachel's pulse quickened. Her grandmother's name was Maria. But then, she reasoned, many girls in Corsica were and still are called Maria.

She unpacked and shook out her creased clothes. Her growling stomach reminded her she had scarcely eaten all day, apart from an unappetising airline sandwich. The Respighis did not provide evening meals, so she would have to find somewhere to eat. As she walked along the corridor, the framed pages caught her attention again. When she pressed the *minuterie* button a faint light came on. They were letters, like the one in her room.

Adorable Maria, the first one read. *Imagine my dismay when I arrived back in Zaronza and found that you had been ill. If only I had known that your life was in danger, I would certainly have come back to Zaronza without delay.*

All the time I was with my family I missed you: your violet scent that would enable me to pick you out among a thousand women; the light touch of your fingers on my arm; your mellow voice; your kisses like the wing of a butterfly brushing my lips; but above all your rippling, raven hair that flows like a dark waterfall when you untie it.

The note stretched over two pages in this florid style. Rachel wanted to read on but the *minuterie* went out and the rumbling in her stomach grew more insistent, so she went downstairs and outside into the passageway. The terrace behind the house was built right into the rock. Above it stretched an ancient arbour. A gnarled vine of great age twined along it, its thick stems heavy with bunches of grapes. Cactus plants with sword-like leaves grew straight out of clefts in the rock face. Below the terrace, squat yellow lemon-like fruits bowed down the branches of a cedrat tree. The late September sun was hot, even though its rays were lengthening as evening drew on. Monsieur Respighi and a dark-haired woman were sitting at a solid table in the shade of the vine.

"My wife, Angelina," he said. They shook hands.

"Could you recommend somewhere to eat?" Rachel asked.

"Certainly. And it's not far away. A friend runs the restaurant in the castle ruins up there." He pointed to the rocky mound above the house. "You'll eat well there and the prices are correct. You just follow the path opposite our gate."

"Thank you." She hesitated. "I noticed the framed letters in my room and on the walls. I'd like to hear more about them if possible."

He smiled.

"I'd be happy to tell you the story, but I suggest you eat and sleep first. You must be tired after your journey. Let's talk about it tomorrow."

"It's a long story and he loves to embroider it," Madame

Respighi added, tapping him on the arm.

By the time Rachel reached the top of the hill, the sun had almost disappeared, but the path to the castle was well lit. Coloured lighting played over the crumbling walls, softening the jagged angles. As she ate fresh seafood and pungent Corsican cheeses overlooking the ever-changing bay, she resolved to return and explore in daylight. Regaining her room, she slid between crisp, cool sheets and fell into a deep sleep.

***

Fingers of sunlight edging through a chink in the shutters woke Rachel the next morning. She looked at her watch. It was already nine o'clock. Showering and dressing fast, she sought the kitchen where Angelina was making coffee.

"Good morning, Madame. I hope you slept well. I'll serve your breakfast on the terrace. There's a table with one place set for you."

A few other guests, all couples, were breakfasting under the vine. She greeted them and found her table. Angelina, swathed in a multi-coloured apron, her hair piled on top of her head, brought a tray groaning with croissants, crusty bread, butter and home-made fig and plum jams. Pascal plonked down a *cafetière* and a plastic sleeve containing a sheaf of papers.

"I've brought these for you to read when you've finished your breakfast. But I'll tell you the story before you start on them."

He moved between the tables, chatting with the other guests, joking and winking as he went. Here was a man who enjoyed his work. Ravenous despite the copious meal of the night before, Rachel devoured the bread and croissants, savouring the fig preserve, a taste redolent of Corsica. Angelina came and took away the tray but left Rachel's cup and the coffee pot. Pascal pulled up a chair and served her more coffee before filling his own cup. He placed his hand flat on the sleeve of papers.

"Who was the Maria in the letters?" Rachel asked. "I was

wondering if she might have been my grandmother."

"I regret to say that it seems unlikely, Madame. The letters I'm going to show you date back to about 1900."

Her heart plunged. Grandmother Maria was born around 1911.

"Let me start at the beginning and then you can tell me your story." He paused for dramatic effect, looking at the house.

The church bell chimed ten o'clock. Rachel waited.

"Angelina and I bought this house more than ten years ago from a Corsican who lived on the mainland. We were looking for a big village house that we could convert into a guesthouse. We fell in love with it at first sight, but the place had been empty and shuttered up for many years, so it was desperately in need of work. Tasks like painting and decorating we could do ourselves, but some of the jobs required specialist help."

Rachel nodded and sipped her coffee as Pascal got into full flow.

"One of our projects was to turn the attic into a bedroom, so we called in a local builder, Pietro. He had a reputation for being a good worker. We could see that a niche in the attic had been blocked up and we decided to put a small built-in wardrobe in there. Pietro's first job was to remove the stones blocking the niche. I was painting the ceiling of the bedroom right underneath and I could hear Pietro cursing and spluttering as he hacked away. It was a hot and dusty job. Rather him than me." He smiled at the memory.

Another guest signalled to him.

"Excuse me a moment," he said. "I have to see to their bill."

Rachel swallowed her impatience. He returned a few minutes later bearing a fresh pot of hot coffee.

"Where was I?"

"Pietro was working in the attic," she said.

"Ah, yes. Above my head, the stones thudded onto the floor as he prised them out. He was a good worker but a bit ham-fisted. Anyway, after a while the chiselling and thumping stopped. I thought he'd decided to have a break and then I heard him coming downstairs. He found something to grumble about at least once a day, so I thought it must be complaints time. But I didn't mind too much. My arm ached from the painting and I was glad of a breather.

"He came into the bedroom and held out a metal box. 'Look what I've found,' he said. 'It was in that niche, covered up with an old piece of sacking.' I asked him if he'd opened it.

"'Well, yes,' he said, not looking me in the eye. 'But there's only some old letters and a few seashells and pebbles by the look of it. No gold. Not even any coins. Worthless.'

"I did wonder if he'd have been so forthcoming if there *had* been anything valuable in the box. Corsicans have always hidden their savings, you see: never trusted banks and paper money. They would wrap gold coins in sacking and stow them in a well. Or they would lever up a tile at the corner of the hearth and dig a hole beneath it. These hoards still turn up sometimes during restoration work. That's what Pietro was hoping for, of course, when he found the box."

"And the box contained the letters that are now on the walls?" Rachel asked, hoping to short-circuit the description.

Pascal nodded. "Exactly. When I opened it there was a bundle of a dozen or so envelopes, tied up with a black ribbon, along with some notes written in pencil, probably by a child, and the other bits and pieces Pietro had mentioned. I picked one of the envelopes at random. The paper was very flimsy and yellow with age. I could see at once that these were love letters written some time ago. Pietro lost interest, muttered something about never finding anything useful, and tramped back upstairs." He paused.

"What did you do with them then?"

"I took them down to show Angelina. She wasn't entirely pleased at the interruption since she was trying to light the old range to heat the water. We were working against the clock to get the house ready for our first guests. But as we went through the letters, her interest was tickled."

"Were they all written by the same person?"

"Yes. They're all unsigned, but they're in the same handwriting and rather florid style. They start on a date in October but there's no year. The final one is dated February. They are all addressed to Maria."

"So do you know who she was?"

"I did a bit of digging around when I had time – which wasn't a lot in the first few years. It turns out she was a young woman who lived in this house at the end of the nineteenth century, the daughter of a bourgeois family, the Orsinis. We've never been able to discover much about the writer of the letters, except that he might have been the village schoolmaster. The style they're written in would seem to support that."

"It sounds a fascinating story. What happened to them? Do you think they got married? Or were they a pair of star-crossed lovers?"

Pascal shrugged. "I haven't been able to find out, although it would have been unusual for bourgeois parents here to allow their daughter to marry a humble schoolmaster – who was probably a socialist and an atheist besides. In any case, the letters stop suddenly. And what were they doing in the niche? Surely you wouldn't hide letters your husband had written to you while you were courting? It's a mystery. There's no one left alive now in the village who remembers her, although there is a vague story about a husband leaving Corsica to go to the West Indies. Mind you, a lot of people did that at one time."

He patted the packet of letters. "One of our previous guests read these letters and reckoned that their relationship was pretty turbulent and maybe not entirely proper." He grinned. "Now, before you read them, tell me about your grandmother. What's her link to Zaronza?"

Rachel spread her fingers and looked at her hands. "There isn't much to tell, because I know very little about her. She died in the late 1970s, a year or so before I was born. Her husband, my grandfather, was an RAF pilot who was killed much earlier, during the Second World War. He was English, and I'd always assumed she was too."

"You said you found out only recently that she was Corsican."

"Yes. My mother died recently. She and my grandmother never got on, and my mother rarely mentioned her until shortly before her death. I didn't ask too much about it since I guessed she didn't want to talk about it. She regretted it, I suppose. It turns out my grandmother was a doctor. That must have been very unusual at the time, especially for a Corsican woman..." Rachel made a small grimace of apology but Pascal waved it aside. "It appears she came to England when she married my father. My mother said she had lived at Zaronza for a while as a girl."

"What was her maiden name?"

"Maria Colombani."

Pascal pursed his lips and shook his head. "Colombani is quite a common surname in Corsica, but I don't know anyone in Zaronza with that name. I can ask around if you like."

Rachel's face brightened. "I would be very grateful if you could. I'd like to find out as much as I can about her, although I realise that my chances of doing so after such a long time are limited. Perhaps your letters might provide some clues?"

"You never know. Here they are, anyway. I transcribed them onto the computer since they were so flimsy. There's the odd word I couldn't decipher, so I had to make some guesses. I'll leave you to read them. They're in date order."

She pulled the letters towards her and was soon engrossed in them. Her coffee grew cold. A story began to unfold; a relationship that was both passionate and stormy.

But the correspondence was one-sided, and Rachel could only guess at Maria's replies.

The final letter concluded,

Now you truly believe that I am yours and yours only. I cannot wait for Friday, when I will prove it to you once and for all and we will be together forever. Take care, my darling Maria, until then.

Leaning back in the chair, she steepled her fingers and started to think. The story of Maria and her unnamed lover had captivated her just as Corsica had done already. Who was he? What happened to them? Did they have any connection with her grandmother? How could she find out more?

Chapter 2

Not wanting to get under the Respighis' feet, Rachel decided to explore Zaronza. It was still too early for the tourist hordes to arrive, so she had the place almost to herself. Why, she thought, do French villages – including Corsican ones – always look deserted? Most of the shutters were closed and some of the houses appeared empty. Apart from a small grocery store and the café, the tiny village had no shops. She moved the car closer to the house so she could transfer her suitcase to her room later on. After that, she could sightsee in peace.

The church glowed even more brightly in the morning sun than it had the previous evening. But inside it was dark and quiet, with the musty odour of crumbling prayer books and ancient stone. There wasn't very much of note, just the usual images of Madonna and Child and rows of votive candles in glass holders flickering before the altar. As she advanced up the aisle, Rachel noticed a small, black-clad woman on her knees in the front pew, her face pressed to her clasped hands. She decided not to intrude and, on tiptoe, sought the heavy door and emerged into the blinding sunshine.

Where to go from here? Since it had been almost dark when she'd gone up to the château-restaurant the previous evening, she had not been able to see much. So she crossed the square towards the guesthouse again but, instead of unlatching the gate into the passage, she turned right up the steep and stony path. At the top, one pathway went to the château, while the other led to a flat esplanade. The square, forbidding watchtower stood beyond.

The place was deserted, but, from there, she had a panoramic view of the purple hills across the bay. Shadows of clouds played on the mountainsides as the sun dipped in and out, so the view was ever-changing. Rachel went up to the rail around the edge of the esplanade and looked over. The hillside stretched downwards over jagged rocks to the beach below, its strange dark sands also deserted. She turned back to the watchtower, foursquare and unadorned, standing sentinel over the bay as it had for more than two hundred years. She tried the door. Locked. She noticed that a large, flat stone had been placed as a bench next to the tower's entrance. So she sat down and leaned with her back against the wall, hugging her knees to her and gazing at the rugged view.

The same feeling – of coming home – that she had experienced the evening before, flowed through her. Did Maria and her unnamed lover meet up here by the tower? Or would that have been too dangerous? Fragments of the letters she had read that morning came back: *"your hair like a dark waterfall… why are you so cruel to me?…now I am yours and yours only…we will be together forever."* But they didn't seem to have been destined for a happy future. The letters stopped, and their tantalising story was like something seen through a patchy mist. It was all so long ago. Nobody knew of them any more, and no one could be alive who could tell their story. Even so, Rachel had the conviction that, even if this Maria was not her own grandmother, the two Marias were somehow connected.

She had come all this way, hoping to find out more about Grandmother Maria, whom she had never known, and about her own Corsican ancestry: to piece together the family history that was still only partial. Instead, she had found a mystery to which no one seemed to have the key. It was like catching a glimpse of a secret, walled garden through a gateway, only to have the door slammed in your face.

Rachel shook her head as if to dispel these thoughts and then stood up and stretched, her body stiff from the stone bench. Well, now she was here she might as well explore beyond Zaronza and make the most of her time. Glancing at her watch, she noticed it was almost midday – lunchtime in Corsica, as in the whole of France. She made her way down the hill towards the village, passing a fig tree from which the dark purple fruits were falling onto the path. She picked one up, turning it over to make sure no wasps were lurking in it, and then sank her teeth into it, the soft flesh contrasting with the tiny, crunchy seeds. She had eaten figs before, but none like this, fresh from the tree.

Her appetite whetted, Rachel crossed the square to the small café opposite the church, which served snacks, and ordered a goat's cheese salad.

"On holiday are you?" asked *la patronne*, as she brought the order to the table. Apart from an old man in blue overalls and a beret, sipping a glass of red wine, Rachel was the only customer.

"Yes. I'm staying at the guest house over there." Rachel nodded back over the square.

"Nice couple, the Respighis. Not from here, of course. Not everyone in the village likes strangers moving in but I think the place needs a bit of life apart from the tourists. They've done up that old house beautifully. It needed it, that's for sure. No one had lived in it for years. It brings me a bit of extra custom, so I'm not complaining."

The woman sat down opposite Rachel, glad of the opportunity to chat.

"Are you from Zaronza?" Rachel asked.

"Oh yes, born and bred here. But, of course, like everyone else I left when I was young and went to the mainland – Marseille."

"But you came back…"

The woman sniffed. "I never cared for the place. Oh, it was the big city and quite exciting to start with. I got married there, had a couple of kids who now live in Paris, and then my husband died. So I came back here. I always missed Corsica, anyway. Most people do, whatever they might say."

Rachel tore off a piece of bread and wiped her plate. "Monsieur Respighi talked to me about some love letters they found in the attic. Do you know the story?"

La patronne shrugged. "Oh, those. Of course, I've seen them but I don't know much more than that. I was born years and years after those letters must have been written. I remember Granny talking about a family that lived in the house in the twenties and thirties. But she was always close, Granny, and didn't say much. Always good at keeping a secret."

Rachel's face fell.

"And I suppose your grandmother wouldn't still be alive now."

"Oh yes, she's still going strong. Outlived all her children. Ninety-five last month and pig-headed as ever."

Rachel's heart started to beat faster. She leant forward. "And does she live in Zaronza?"

"Not since she was a girl. She married a fisherman and went to live in Santa-Lucia. She still lives there all on her own. Her other grandchildren, my cousins, who live down that way, keep an eye on her. I see her sometimes – she's family, after all – but she and I never really got on."

"Do you think she might be prepared to talk to me?" Rachel gave *la patronne* an edited version of what she had already explained to Pascal Respighi.

The woman sucked her teeth and grimaced. "Hard to say. Granny can be pretty difficult, and you won't get anything out of her if she doesn't feel like it. She doesn't like strangers, so she didn't want to talk to Respighi when she heard he had bought the house. You can try, but I don't guarantee you'll get a result. I suppose the fact your granny is supposed to have lived here might help. And you do look a bit Corsican."

"Perhaps I could phone her up and arrange to see her."

La patronne laughed. "She's not even on the phone! She says she can't be doing with all that modern stuff. And she's getting a bit hard of hearing so it wouldn't be much good to her, anyway. No, you'll just have to turn up and hope she's in a good mood. Morning is the best time to go. She has a siesta in the afternoon and then she goes to bed about eight."

She wrote down the address and gave Rachel directions. Rachel had to swallow her impatience. She had hoped to go and see the old lady that very afternoon. But it sounded as if she had to be treated with kid gloves, so it would just be counter-productive to turn up at the wrong moment. Instead, she paid and wandered out into the sunshine. Since it was a Monday, there were fewer people around than the previous day. Even so, a tourist bus was heaving up the hill towards the village and knots of people were making their way up to the watchtower and the château.

Rachel spent the rest of the afternoon looking around Zaronza. Walking downhill from the village she found a long flight of stone steps leading down to the beach. An arrow pointed to the shrine of Santa Giulia. She picked her way down the crumbling staircase and arrived at the shrine. It was a cave in the rock with a neo-classical façade, flanked by two large urns. One was cracked and the decorative swags had broken off. The shrine itself was protected by a locked grille, but Rachel could peer through it and see the small altar with a statue of the saint in a niche above it. Nothing indicated who the saint had been or what her story was, so she made a mental note to ask Pascal about it.

The beach didn't look particularly appealing, so, having exhausted the sights in the village, Rachel wandered back up the hill and climbed the alley on the opposite side of the square from the guest house. The path went around another large, stern-looking house, shuttered up and empty. The cobbled lane petered out after a hundred yards or so and became a rough track winding up into the hills above the village. Having little else to do, Rachel continued along the track, wondering where it led and taking note of landmarks in case she got lost.

The path looped up the steep hill between olive trees, rosemary and cistus bushes. That sun-baked, aromatic scent rose up again and Rachel breathed it in. How different all this was from London: another world. Sweating hard now, she stopped for breath by a pile of stones. A couple of rotting joists stuck out of the rubble. The ruined building was too small to have been a house. Maybe a shepherd's hut? She sat down on a block of stone and looked at the toy town village far below, framed in the curve of the bay and the mountains beyond, now glowing amber in the strong afternoon sun.

Again, she felt as if a veil were hiding the truth from her. But her pulse quickened at the thought of the interview to come with the old lady in Santa-Lucia. She prayed she wouldn't turn her away. That would be too much, having come this far.

Rachel sat there for a long time, turning over in her mind the little she knew of Maria's story. As the sun's rays lengthened, she got up, brushed her shorts down and started off down the hill. Going any further uphill wouldn't be a good idea. Her skin prickled from the sun and her shins were covered in dust from the dry path. A shower and then dinner up at the château again beckoned.

She unlatched the gate into the passage and pushed open the heavy front door, which caught, as usual, on the flagstones. A natural anti-burglar device, Rachel thought. Sure enough, a door opened and Pascal appeared.

"Had a good day?" he asked.

"Yes, fine, thank you. I had a good look around the village and I've got a number of questions to ask you about some of the sights. But that can wait, since I'm sure you're busy."

"Yes, good idea. Breakfast is usually the best time."

Rachel decided not to mention her proposed visit to the café owner's grandmother the following day. After all, the old woman had refused to have anything to do with him for her own reasons and she didn't want to offend Pascal. If he asked, she would just say she was going to Santa-Lucia for the day.

***

Pascal was even more voluble at breakfast the next day and Rachel was itching to get away. But he had promised to answer her questions about the village, so she couldn't complain. Even so, she swallowed her coffee as fast as possible and cut off some of his longer descriptions, looking at her watch and explaining that she was hoping to spend the day sightseeing.

The drive down to Santa-Lucia was not quite as hair-raising as the journey up to Zaronza the previous Sunday. Rachel began to get the hang of driving on the switchback Corsican roads and appreciated the scenery, if not some of the other drivers' disdain for the dangers of overtaking on blind corners.

Pascal had told her she mustn't miss the Cathedral of the Nebbio, one of the only Pisan cathedrals on the island, with its embalmed Saint Flor on show in a glass-fronted coffin. It was not in Santa-Lucia itself but down a narrow country lane a mile or so outside. But that could wait. She drove into the centre of the town and parked at the yacht marina. Once a port, Santa-Lucia was now a haven for pleasure-boats, whose jumbled masts rose up like the trunks of some blasted forest.

With a dry mouth and a tingling in her stomach, Rachel made her way up the busy main street towards the citadel and the old town, passing the thronging tourist cafés and the clusters of chatting residents. At the citadel she stopped and consulted the rough sketch map the café owner in Zaronza had drawn for her. It would be all too easy to lose herself in the muddle of backstreets that straggled down the hill towards the old port. Even so, she had to ask directions from an unsmiling young man with black hair and an almost Moorish face. He pointed towards one of the narrower alleys, festooned with washing slung on lines between the balconies. It reminded Rachel of streets she had seen in parts of Italy. Two elderly women sat on rush-seated chairs on the pavement, not conversing, just watching the world go by. Rachel bade them good morning as she walked past. They nodded and smiled, gap-toothed.

Number fifty-four was at the other end of the street, a tall, narrow building with a row of buzzers beside the door. Taking a deep breath, Rachel pressed the one marked Santoni and waited. Nothing happened but she figured that it might take the old lady some time to get to the door. She pushed the buzzer again. Still nothing. Her heart plummeting, she looked around. At the next house, a woman in a flowered apron-cum-dress was washing her front step.

"Excuse me, Madame, I'm looking for Madame Santoni. I've tried the bell but there's no reply."

The woman stood up, easing her back, and looked Rachel up and down.

"No, well, you've just missed her. She's gone out to do her marketing. She still does it all herself. But she should be back in about half an hour. I should give her forty-five minutes or so. She doesn't like being rushed."

Rachel thanked her and set off back along the street. She had noticed a small café in another side street on the way and decided to wait there, rather than go back to the crowded and overpriced tourist cafés overlooking the harbour. Settling herself at one of the small tables outside on the street, she waited for someone to come and serve her. What seemed like a violent argument was going on inside the café with raised voices and hands slapping table tops. A small, dark man came out and noticed Rachel's unease.

"Don't mind them," he said. "They're just commenting on today's news."

He brought her a small coffee in a chipped cup with a couple of paper-wrapped sugar lumps in the saucer. It was bitter and very hot. She sipped it, checking her watch every couple of minutes. Why does the time always drag when you want it to do the opposite? Rachel thought. Her coffee finished, she left some coins on the table. The men inside were still arguing. She was a little early but couldn't wait any longer.

She retraced her steps along the street where Madame

Santoni lived and stopped again in front of the door. This time, after a minute or so, the door opened a crack. A wizened face peered out and then opened the door wider.

The old lady put her hand to her throat.

"Maria," she gasped.

Chapter 3

They regarded each other for a moment.

"I'm sorry to have startled you," Rachel said. "I think you must be mistaking me for someone else."

Madame Santoni shook her head. "Yes, I'm sorry, you couldn't possibly be Maria. She would be nearly a hundred now. What do you want, anyway? You're not selling something, are you?" She peered at Rachel.

"No, I can assure you I'm not selling anything. But I think you might be able to help me to find out about my grandmother, who used to live in Zaronza. Your granddaughter at the café there thought you might be prepared to talk to me."

The old lady's face closed up and she pursed her lips. Rachel's heart stopped.

"She did, did she? Always pushy and taking liberties, that one. Always telling other people what to do." She paused. "Well, you seem honest. And since you look like Maria, you'd better come in. We can't stand here nattering on the street. Don't want to give *her* anything to gossip about." She jerked her thumb at the apron-clad woman who was still washing the step next door, pretending not to take any notice of them.

Madame Santoni turned and Rachel followed her into a dark passage, closing the door behind her. The old lady was so bent that she was almost doubled up, but she got along well enough with the aid of a cane. She opened a door into a bright, comfortable room, furnished with a massive *buffet* cupboard and several easy chairs. A solid table stood in the centre, surrounded by upholstered dining chairs. Madame Santoni lowered herself onto one of them with a sigh and gestured to Rachel to do the same.

"I must admit, you gave me quite a turn when I first saw you. I thought it was a ghost. We Corsicans are renowned for seeing ghosts at every turn. But you're quite obviously flesh and blood. You have to allow a very old woman the odd quirk. But I'm all clear up here." She tapped her forehead. "Not like some."

"Whose ghost did you think it was, Madame?"

"Oh, someone I knew a long time ago. But it doesn't matter now. Tell me what you're here for."

Rachel told her what little she knew of her grandmother.

"What was her name?"

"She was called Maria. I think her maiden name was Colombani but I can't be completely sure. As I said, she married an Englishman and then she took his surname, which was Gordon."

Madame Santoni chewed her lip and thought for a while. She nodded.

"I thought so," she said, looking at Rachel.

"Thought what, Madame?"

"The resemblance was so striking, it just had to be. The Maria I knew was your grandmother."

"How can you be so sure?"

The old woman's eyes flashed. Despite her sunken face, she must have been a formidable beauty in her youth.

"I know what I'm talking about, young woman. It all fits. There can't have been two."

Rachel leant forward, almost afraid to breathe. "Please tell me," she said.

Madame Santoni settled herself in her chair. "Pour me a glass of myrtle wine and one for yourself," she said, gesturing at a bottle on the *buffet*. "I don't normally drink, but I have a feeling this might be the day for one."

Rachel placed a glass of the ruby liquid in front of Madame Santoni and sipped her own. It tasted like the distilled scent of the hillside vegetation, the *maquis*.

"I didn't know your grandmother all that well. I was born in

1915 and she must have been about four years older. She wasn't born in Zaronza but somewhere in central Corsica, in the mountains. They came to the village when she was about eight years old. Colombani, the family was called. She was very clever and had all sorts of notions about women being just as good as men and capable of doing the same professions. Well, you can imagine how that went down. Corsican women are supposed to run the home and look after their menfolk, not try to change the world."

She looked into the middle distance, a smile playing on her lips. Rachel waited for her to continue.

Madame Santoni took a sip from her glass and cleared her throat.

"I was always a little bit in awe of her. She could be rather fierce. Four years makes a lot of difference when you're that age. Now we'd just be a couple of old biddies together." She wheezed with laughter. "Anyway, she continued to get top marks at school. The woman she called Tante Maria and another woman who lived in the village – can't remember her name now; she was the mayor's daughter – had a lot of influence over her. When she was about fifteen, I suppose – must have been in 1926 or '27; I would have been eleven or twelve – she managed to persuade them to send her to the mainland to continue her education. That was unheard of at the time. But she was a very determined young woman. Said she wanted to become a doctor. That was unusual, too: a nurse, maybe, but a doctor was quite another thing for a woman."

Rachel nodded. "That fits. My grandmother Maria was a doctor."

"I never saw her again. She didn't come back to Zaronza while I lived there. Anyway, I married at sixteen and moved here to Santa-Lucia, where I've been ever since. I never went back very often, since my family and Nicolas, my husband, didn't get on all that well. That's all I can tell you, really."

"You've already told me much more than I already knew.

Whereabouts did she live in Zaronza? Since I'm staying there, it would be nice to see her former home, even if only from the outside. I wouldn't want to be a nuisance to the present owners."

Madame Santoni smiled. "You won't have to look far. That guest house you're staying in – that's where she lived. With her mother, two brothers and the older woman they all called Tante Maria."

Rachel stared at her. "This older woman, what was her surname?"

"Orsini. Maria Orsini."

Rachel's mouth fell open. She had wondered if there might be some connection between her grandmother and the Maria in the letters but now she had confirmation. Maria Orsini and Tante Maria were the same person.

"What can you tell me about Maria Orsini? I've seen some love letters that someone wrote to her. I have a feeling that there's quite a story there."

"Yes. That Respighi chap wanted to see me to find out more about it all. But I refused. I didn't think it was any of his business. He didn't have any connection with the village. Just bought that house. He was a stranger."

"And what about me? Surely you regard me as a stranger, too."

She shook her head. "You have more of a connection than he does. Much more."

Madame Santoni thought for a moment, then continued. "You came to Corsica wanting to find out more about your grandmother and your family history. Well, I've told you about her, but there's more. And nobody knows about it now but me. All the rest are dead."

"What do you mean?"

"Wait a moment."

Leaning on her cane, she heaved herself up from the chair. She opened a door into an inner room, where Rachel could hear her rummaging about. She returned after a while bearing a cardboard box.

"Here. You should have this."

"What is it?" Rachel opened the box. A whiff of musty paper rose from it. She peered inside and saw a thick sheaf of yellowed sheets bearing elegant handwriting.

"Maria Orsini wrote all that. I think you should take it away and read it. And then come back and I'll tell you the rest."

"How did you get this?"

Madame Santoni waved the question aside. "Read it first, and then I'll answer that. You have more right to this than anyone else. I've just been its keeper all these years. I never thought anyone close enough would come back."

Her face closed in again. She looked pale underneath her nut-brown skin and very old.

"Now I'm tired and I need to lie down. See yourself out and come back tomorrow or the next day."

She pushed herself up from the table again, tottered towards the inner door and closed it behind her. Rachel sat for a moment with the box in her hands, then laid it on the table and replaced the lid. She put the two empty glasses back on top of the *buffet* and let herself out of the front door.

***

I'm starting to drive like a real Corsican, Rachel thought as she sped up the coast road again towards Zaronza. A tourist coach lumbered along in front and, as soon as she could, she accelerated past, earning her a couple of blasts on the horn from the driver. The mummified Saint Flor in his cathedral forgotten, and with no appetite for lunch, she had decided to return and find somewhere quiet to read the bundle of papers.

Heart thumping, she arrived back in the village – but the tourists had got there before her, and she had to park the car down the hill, some way from the guesthouse. She sat in the driving seat for a moment, wondering where she could go that would be peaceful enough. Pascal's well-meaning curiosity would be too intrusive. He would ask why she had come home so early, when she had said she would be at Santa-Lucia all day. And it would be difficult to conceal the box. She wasn't sure if she was ready to tell him about it – not yet. The stone bench up at the watchtower would no doubt be overrun with day-trippers. What about the ruined shepherd's hut up the hill? She doubted if the sightseers would make it that far. It was a steep climb and a hot day. And there wasn't much to see once you got there, except for the view.

Rachel climbed out of the air-conditioned car and the heat struck her. She had better take some water and something to eat if she was going to spend the afternoon on the hillside.

"Well, I was just about to close," the shopkeeper said, looking at her watch. "It's already one o'clock. I normally close at twelve-thirty." The bell in the campanile chimed the hour.

"I won't take a moment, I promise," Rachel said.

"Well, all right. But I'll put the closed sign up anyway. I don't want anyone else coming in."

Rachel packed her picnic in the plastic carrier bag and laid the box on top. The shopkeeper looked at the box but said nothing, and then locked the door behind Rachel. She walked up the hill towards the square as fast as the midday heat and the heavy bag would allow. Turning into the alleyway opposite the guesthouse, she marched up the cobbled lane past the house that was shuttered up and onto the rough track. The sun beat down as she laboured up the steep slope and she was glad of her hat.

Reaching the ruins of the hut, she laid the carrier bag under a spreading fig tree and sat down, fanning herself with her hat. For a moment, she took in the ever-changing view. The midday light polished the mountains across the bay into high definition, so that she could almost reach out and touch them.

Taking a deep breath, she delved into the carrier bag and took out the box. Lifting the lid, the dusty smell of old paper arose again. She settled the pile of papers on her knees, peeled off the first page and began to read.

PART 1 – AWAKENING 1899-1900

Chapter 4

May 1899

My life changed that day, although I didn't know it. Papa was in a very bad mood. It was probably to do with business. I knew very little about the wine trade then – and cared less – but even I was aware that it was taking a long time to pick up after the *phylloxera*[1] scourge. At least Papa had branched out into olives and citrus fruits. But he often sat at the dinner table, scowling, staring into space.

Just the sight of me annoyed him. I crept about the house like a mouse, trying not to attract his attention. And Maman seemed more worried than ever, as she always did when Papa was difficult. Even Annunciata snapped at me for walking on her wet floor.

"Why do you have to be so grumpy, Annunciata?"

She looked at me coolly, hands perched on ample hips.

"I've known you for twenty years, since you were a tiny baby, Mademoiselle Maria, so if I have to wash my floor again because you walk all over it I have every right to get cross."

I said nothing but marched out of the house and unlatched the gate onto the alley. Should I cross the square and go to see Sophia, or should I climb the hill to the château? I thought for a moment and decided on the château.

The way up was steep and stony but I didn't care. It would stop anyone following me, although I would be able to hear Maman calling me from the garden. I stopped to catch my

---

[1] A vine weevil that devastated the French (and Corsican) wine trade in the late 19th century.

breath on the flat esplanade at the top. A little further on, the ruined château and the watchtower raised their granite fists to the sky. When I was little I made up romantic stories about maidens kept prisoner in the tower.

"It's unlikely any maidens were ever locked up here," Sophia told me. "It was only built in the last century as a lookout post."

The sun was setting. I have always loved this moment best but it lasts only a short time. That evening, the sea was like molten gold. The mountains over the bay were hazy, almost ghostly.

I went close to the edge. Maman always told me to take care. It was a sheer drop to the rocks below. But I liked the quiver of danger that ran up and down my spine and I never went close enough to fall. A little adventure in my life would have been nice but that seemed unlikely. I would live quietly with Maman and Papa, the well-brought-up daughter of a respected family, until they found someone suitable for me to marry.

Sometimes a ship ventured up the strait to Santa-Lucia but mostly they went to Bastia or on to Calvi. Very few people had any reason to come up Cap Corse as far as Zaronza – certainly none that would interest me.

"I thought I'd find you up here, Maria." I instantly recognised Sophia's soft voice and turned around, smiling. Despite her club foot, she had managed to sneak up on me.

"What are you doing?" she asked. "Daydreaming as usual, I suppose."

"Well, there's no harm in that. I have to have something to brighten up my life."

Sophia shook her head. "Dreaming about princes and maidens again. It won't do you any good, Maria. Life is simply not like that, above all not for women. Our lives are mapped out for us. We do as we are told, we marry the men our parents choose for us, we bear children, some of whom might live to become adults. We have no choice, no will of our own. Do you know, I heard a story about a woman in a village near Corte whose husband allowed her to leave their house only three times during their marriage? Can you imagine it? Being a prisoner in your own home with your husband as gaoler!"

I sighed. I had heard all this before. Sophia always seemed older than her twenty years. Sometimes I felt much younger, although she was a few months my junior. Perhaps she appeared more mature because her mother had died when she was very young. Growing up in a household of men, she must have missed a mother's love. Goodness knows, my own mother was not always affectionate or tender. Mostly she took Papa's side against me. She had little choice; my father could be very stern. But at least I had both of my parents. Sophia's father was a kind man and had always taken care of her but that couldn't make up for not having a mother.

She was not beautiful, although her smile lit up her whole face. It was a pity she didn't smile more often. And she was very intelligent – head always in a book when she didn't have household duties to take care of. I was not sure if husbands cared for intelligent wives: men always expected to have the last word.

All this flashed through my mind as I looked at Sophia and then she smiled, that quick, elusive smile that was gone almost as soon as it appeared.

"But that's not what I came to talk about," she said. "I've got some news."

That was better. I hoped it was something interesting. "Oh, what is it?"

Sophia walked closer to the edge, stumbling a little because of her foot, and peered over the cliff. I moved towards her in case I needed to hold on to stop her falling.

"Well, I might tell you…or I might not." She faced outwards over the bay, closed her eyes and held her face up to the breeze.

"Sophia!"

She turned around, with the little dimple in her cheek that always appeared when she was making fun of me.

"Well, I suppose I might as well tell you. You'll find out soon enough anyway."

I leant forward, hungry for any news that might relieve my dull life.

"As you know," she said, "Monsieur Catarelli is retiring at the end of the school year and moving back to Ajaccio."

I waved my hand, brushing this information aside. I knew all that already.

"Well, a new schoolmaster will take up his appointment from this coming September."

"And? What about him? Is he old, young, married, single, handsome, ugly?"

Monsieur Catarelli was a small mouse of a man and his wife was like a long, dry, old stick. Their appearance together was so absurd that the schoolchildren sniggered at them behind their hands.

Sophia laughed, a small pealing sound like an angelus.

"You're so predictable, Maria. Yes, I believe he's young, although I don't know his exact age. No, he's not married. He comes from a village in the central mountains somewhere east of Corte and trained to be a teacher in France. His first post was in a place near Marseille but he has managed to get himself posted back to Corsica."

As mayor of the village, Sophia's father would have known this, since the new schoolmaster would be secretary at the town hall by virtue of his post.

"And I have absolutely no idea what he looks like. I believe teachers are appointed for their professional qualities, not for their appearance." The dimple reappeared.

"Is that all you can tell me? What's his name?"

"I believe it's Monsieur Colombani. But now you know as much as I do. Don't be so impatient, Maria. We'll find out soon enough what he's like."

Soon enough? It was only the end of May and he wouldn't arrive until early September! I would have to wait three whole months. But at least it was something to look forward to. So few people came to or left Zaronza that even a travelling pedlar was news.

"Maria." A faint voice floated up the hillside. Maman.

"I must go, Sophia. If I'm late for supper Papa will be cross and he's already in a bad mood today."

Sophia stumbled and I took her arm to help her down the steep path. When we reached the bottom, I kissed her quickly on both cheeks and then opened the gate. I turned to watch her hobbling across the square, her tiny figure purposeful as she went to see to her father's supper. Sometimes, I regretted that I was not more like her: more thoughtful, less hasty. But then it passed and I pushed open the heavy door into the dark hallway. It grated on the flagstones as usual.

"Where have you been, Maria?" Maman asked as I entered the kitchen. "I needed your help. You know your father likes his supper on time."

"I'm sorry, Maman. I was with Sophia and we were talking."

"You young women," my mother exclaimed. "Heads always in the clouds. And Sophia should know better. She has to keep house for her father. She has more important things to think about than frittering away her time in idle gossip."

I sighed and said nothing. It was no use trying to argue with Maman. She was just repeating what she had heard from Papa, anyway.

"Now, help me," Maman said. "Take the soup tureen into the dining room. Your father is already waiting for his supper."

Taking the steaming bowl I pushed open the dining room door with my hip and placed the soup on the table. My father was in his place at the head, watch in hand. He was a stickler for time keeping.

"Good evening, Papa."

He nodded, a sign that he was no longer in quite such a bad mood. But I had to be careful not to provoke him or it would flare up again.

Maman came in bearing the bread, which she handed to Papa. He cut slices from it while Maman ladled soup into our bowls. We ate in silence. Maman never sat at the table with us but served Papa and then ate her own dinner at the corner of the hearth, like so many women in our village. She sat with us only if we had guests for dinner, which was very rare. On those occasions, Annunciata came in from her little house to wait on us, grumbling as she did so but secretly enjoying the chance to hear any interesting "gentry gossip," as she called it.

The news about Monsieur Catarelli's replacement was like a hot cinder burning in my chest. I couldn't resist it any longer.

"Sophia told me something very interesting today," I blurted out.

Maman's eyes widened. Papa raised his head slowly. His face was like stone. I should have recognised the warning signs but carried on like a cart careering downhill out of control.

"A new schoolmaster has been appointed. He trained on the mainland, his previous appointment was in Marseille, he is young and not married and he's going to start in September." It came out all in a rush.

"And what's that to you, Maria?" my father asked.

I bowed my head. "I thought you might be interested to know, Papa," I said in a small voice.

"Why should it interest me that a young upstart is coming to teach the village brats? And he's no doubt a socialist and an atheist, as all the young ones are these days. Putting ideas in people's heads about improving their station and upsetting the social order. What end does that serve? Eh? Tell me that."

"I don't know, Papa."

Maman adopted that wrinkled brow and hunted look that she always did when she feared I had upset Papa. But she remained silent.

"You don't know? Then I'll tell you." He pointed his spoon at me, reinforcing his words. "These arrogant young idiots have their heads stuffed full of nonsense at the teacher training colleges. They come and spout it out to children who don't know any better, and no end of damage is done. Oh, they're clever, no doubt, but they gnaw away at the very fabric of society. No good will come of it. Men like that are not fit company for you, Maria. Do you understand?"

"Yes, Papa."

My father raised his spoon to his lips, a sign that no further discussion would take place. My heart felt like lead. I had hoped that my parents might invite the new schoolmaster to our home and that our social life would become a little more interesting. But it seemed that his arrival would make no difference to me; things would just continue as before.

Unless I took them in hand. But how?

Chapter 5

Monsieur Colombani – his first name was Raphaël, Sophia said – arrived a few days before term began, in order to prepare for the coming school year. I was longing to know more about him, so I crossed the square and walked up the alley to the mayor's house above the church. I unlatched the gate and went around to the kitchen rather than use the massive front door with its heavy brass knocker. The kitchen door was ajar since it was still September-hot. I peered in and saw Sophia with her back to me standing at the oak table rolling out pastry.

I crept up and tickled the back of her neck.

Sophia jumped, then turned her head and smiled.

"Oh, it's you. I thought it was Orso. He's always playing around and teasing me when I'm trying to get things done."

"Your brother's a little too fond of practical jokes. Is he here?"

"He'll be here soon, that's why I thought you were him."

Orso used to pull my hair when we were little. He said it was a joke but it hurt, so I didn't find it as amusing as he did. Now he worked in Bastia for a friend of his father who ran a shipping company. He came back every weekend, bringing his dirty linen for Sophia to wash and expecting to be fed and looked after. He didn't pull my hair anymore, but he didn't speak to me much either. In fact, I didn't think he liked me, since he always avoided me. It was nothing to me; I didn't find him appealing, anyway.

"Are you very busy?" I asked.

"Well, Papa insisted on my making Orso's favourite cheese and herb pastries for lunch today. I need to get on with them."

Orso was the apple of his father's eye: his only son. His father and sister spoiled him terribly. That was another thing in his disfavour, as far as I was concerned.

"Can I just sit here and talk while you work? Or perhaps I could help you?"

Sophia chuckled. She knew my cooking skills left plenty to be desired, despite the efforts of Maman and Annunciata.

"No, just stay there and look pretty, as you always do."

I settled down at the end of the table and we didn't speak for a few minutes while Sophia rolled out her pastry. She was an excellent cook and made delicious pies. She bit her lip and frowned, as she did at school when puzzling over a difficult sum or a grammatical problem.

I traced a pattern with my finger in some spilt flour on the table. But after a while I couldn't bear the suspense any longer.

"I was wondering how Monsieur Colombani is settling in."

"Oh, quite well, I believe." She kept her eyes firmly fixed on her work but the dimple appeared at the corner of her mouth.

Why did Sophia always have to tease me like that? She knew I was burning with curiosity. I took a deep breath.

"Where's he going to live?"

"In the little building next to the schoolhouse. The house that Monsieur and Madame Catarelli rented in the village is empty now they've gone back to Ajaccio. But it's too big for him."

It was like squeezing tears from a rock. The watchtower itself would have been more forthcoming.

"Wasn't it in poor condition, the little house by the school?"

"It must have been. No one's lived in it for years. Monsieur Colombani had to clean it all himself, as he isn't married."

I looked at her, wide-eyed. "Himself? Couldn't he have hired a woman from the village to do it?" I had a sudden vision of Papa on his hands and knees scrubbing the floor, and stifled a giggle.

Sophia smiled and looked into the distance. "I expect he didn't want the expense. He has plans for the schoolroom, too.

Do you remember how old-fashioned it was, Maria? Monsieur Catarelli was a nice man but he never did anything to brighten it up. It still has just a map of the world on the wall and a bust of Marianne, like it was when you and I were there. I liked it best in winter, when Madame Catarelli lit the old stove and sometimes let us roast chestnuts on it."

I drummed my fingers on the table. I didn't want to dwell on memories of our schooldays. "Have you met Monsieur Colombani?"

"Yes, of course. He'll be secretary at the town hall, as you know, so he's been to see Papa several times to talk about it."

"And what's he like?"

"You'll find out for yourself shortly. Papa is going to invite a few of the village notables, including your father, and their families to meet him."

My heart flipped over. "Oh, when?"

"Next weekend. But you'd better not say anything to your parents until Papa has invited you properly." Sophia wiped her floury hands on her apron. "And now it will soon be lunchtime and I must finish these pies. If I keep on chatting with you I'll never get them done."

Sighing, I rose from the table and kissed Sophia. As I went out of the door, Orso was coming in. He stood aside to let me pass. He was dusty from his journey from Bastia and carried a bundle under his arm: his dirty linen, I supposed. He looked down and brushed his jacket with his hand.

"Good morning, Orso."

"Good morning, Maria." He avoided my eyes, looked over my head and his face opened up as he saw Sophia.

"Hello, little sister. Making my favourite pies, I see." He put the bundle on the table, took a handful of stuffing from a basin and crammed it into his mouth. Sophia tapped him on the hand with the rolling pin.

"If you eat all that now there'll be nothing left for the pies. Go and see Papa, he'll want to know you're here. You know he always likes to hear the news from Bastia."

Chuckling, Orso bent and kissed Sophia on both cheeks and then went to find his father.

I turned away and retraced my steps across the square to our house, hugging the secret about the party to myself. This time, I resolved to say nothing at the table.

***

"Hmm. I'm not sure about this," Papa said on receiving the mayor's invitation. "I don't see why the arrival of a socialist firebrand in the village is something to celebrate. I can't say I welcome it."

I held my breath. Please don't turn down the invitation, I thought.

"I don't know, Antonio," Maman said quietly. "If we don't go, I'm afraid we will insult Monsieur Franceschi, and he is one of your oldest friends. It's only for an evening, and you don't need to have anything to do with the schoolmaster after that if you find you don't like him."

Papa considered her for a moment.

"Very well," he said. "Just this once. I don't want to offend Franceschi. But this Colombani had better not start spouting his socialist nonsense in front of me."

To conceal my joy, I bit my lip until the blood almost ran.

***

All day I agonised about what to wear to Monsieur Franceschi's party. My mother wanted me to wear the deep violet dress and, while people said I looked pretty in it, I thought I would look better in the black one. It was more fashionable and made me appear more serious. I didn't want Monsieur Colombani to think I was frivolous. And it went so well with my jet-black hair. But my mother's mouth turned down.

"Black is not a colour for a young girl. There'll be plenty of time for that later on in your life."

I always wished Maman could be a little happier, but she seemed bowed down, crushed by something. At the time, I supposed it was because Papa was so demanding. Nothing ever came up to his standards. I was not a very good cook, but when I had made some *canistrelli* biscuits especially for him a few days previously, he had just said, "I prefer them less burnt." Being an only daughter was not easy. When I saw Orso with Sophia, I was sorry that I had never had at least one brother. My parents must have regretted it, too, although they never talked about it. Perhaps that was why Papa was so stern with me. I was not the son he had really wanted.

But I had to forget all that and think about how I was going to behave that evening. Monsieur Colombani was an intellectual, I was sure, and I needed to think of things to say that didn't make me look stupid. Sophia would find it easy, of course. She had read so many books and knew so much. I could never have competed with her in that sense.

"Are you ready, Maria? It wouldn't do to keep Monsieur Franceschi waiting. And your father will be getting impatient."

To please Maman, I put on the violet dress. My hair was in a simple bun and I was wearing the single strand of pearls my parents had given me for my eighteenth birthday and the bracelet that was a christening gift from the Franceschi family. Maman held me at arm's length and nodded her approval. As always, she was in black, but in honour of the occasion she had added a silver brooch to her dress. Her figure was still good, but her face was lined and her once-black hair was peppered with grey. In a sudden rush of affection I hugged her. Fleetingly, she returned my hug, then patted my arm and said, "That's enough now. We must go. Papa is waiting."

As we emerged from the alley into the square, Papa offered an arm each to Maman and me and we walked across to the mayor's house. This time we entered by the grand front door and Monsieur Franceschi showed us to the salon, where the buzz of conversation and the tinkling of glasses revealed that the party had already started.

Papa stood back to allow Maman and me to enter first. I held up my head and my gaze swept the room. I knew everyone there except for a tall young man, who I assumed must be Monsieur Colombani, standing near the fireplace talking to Sophia and Orso. A slight flush highlighted Sophia's cheeks and her eyes sparkled. For her, too, this party was a rare pleasure. Orso glanced at me, scowled and looked away as Monsieur Colombani continued to explain something, his hand outstretched.

Monsieur Franceschi crossed the room and touched Monsieur Colombani on the arm. He led him across to us.

"Let me introduce you to Monsieur Orsini, an old friend. The Orsinis are among Zaronza's oldest and most respected families."

"I'm honoured, sir," said Monsieur Colombani, bowing to my father. He was slim, almost willowy, and his thick black hair curled in a wave around his temples. His clothing was plain and simple but neat and clean. His only ornament was a signet ring. My father nodded, a little curtly I thought, and extended his hand.

Monsieur Colombani bowed and raised my mother's hand to his lips. She nodded.

"And this," the mayor indicated me, "is their daughter, Mademoiselle Orsini."

I bent my head and Monsieur Colombani took my hand. He looked into my face and his eyes widened. They were chestnut brown beneath a broad forehead. My heart raced. I caught the scent of something sweet and spicy. Did he perfume himself? I smiled at him, but not too much.

"Which part of Corsica do you come from, Monsieur Colombani?" Maman asked.

He looked into my eyes a little longer, then switched his attention to Maman. "From the Bozio, Madame, east of Corte. Our tiny village is perched on a hill and the view from there is magnificent, especially in the autumn when the trees turn. You can see as far as the Aiguilles de Bavella. My parents still live there but my sisters have married and moved away. My father has his own smallholding and owns part of a chestnut forest as well."

"I understand you taught on the mainland," Papa said.

"Yes, sir, in Marseille. It's a wonderful city but, being the son of simple peasants, I was glad to return to Corsica."

"Hmm. And while you were there, I suppose you spread the educational and political theories of the day."

My cheeks flamed as I recognised the danger signals. Surely Papa was not going to start an argument here.

Monsieur Colombani hesitated. "Naturally, sir, I attended the *école normale* in Ajaccio for my studies. We were taught to uphold the beliefs of the French republic, which I have always tried to pass on to my pupils."

"And now you're here I suppose you think that filling their heads with republican nonsense is the way to solve Corsica's problems?"

My blush spread to the roots of my hair. Oh, Papa! I thought, why do you have to be so hostile? Give the poor man a chance.

The schoolmaster's eyes widened and his jaw tightened.

"I believe that universal education is the only way forward, if Corsica is not to remain mired in the Middle Ages."

Papa's colour heightened and he opened his mouth but before he could speak the mayor interrupted. He knew his friend well.

"Monsieur Colombani already has some excellent ideas for our school here, which I think even you would approve of, Orsini. Now, what do you think of our Muscat de Patrimonio, Monsieur Colombani?"

Papa bristled beside me, but remained silent.

"It's very pleasant. I've never tasted it before, although I admit that I rarely drink alcohol. Where I come from we make a chestnut liqueur, which is also very agreeable. Allow me to bring you back a bottle, Madame, next time I visit my parents."

My mother nodded.

"Now, let me introduce you to Monsieur Agostino. He also spent some time in Marseille, and I'm sure he will be very keen to compare notes with you."

Monsieur Franceschi steered the schoolmaster away. I was partly relieved, partly disappointed.

"Arrogant young upstart," muttered my father, before turning to talk to Père Allegri, the village priest. I suppressed a smile as I wondered what the priest and Monsieur Colombani would find to talk about: they could hardly have very much in common. My mother turned to greet Père Allegri as well and I took the opportunity to escape and find Sophia. She was still standing by the fireplace, talking to a female neighbour while Orso looked on. I joined them. The neighbour and Orso moved away. I couldn't imagine why Orso had to make it so obvious that he was avoiding me.

I kissed Sophia. "It's a lovely party. I'm so glad your father invited us. But what's the matter with Orso? I have a feeling that he dislikes me."

"Oh no," Sophia replied. "You're mistaken – it's quite the opposite. He just feels shy in your company."

"Orso? I don't believe it. Anyway, never mind that. Monsieur Colombani seems very nice but it didn't take long for him and my father to annoy each other. I must say, he's very handsome. I'm surprised he's not married yet. Perhaps he's broken a few hearts along the way."

Sophia flushed. "I doubt it. From what I know of him, he's an honourable man and wouldn't lead a woman to think he was in love with her if that weren't the case."

"How would you know? Have you had much to do with

him?"

"Certainly not. That wouldn't be proper. But of course I see him when he comes to talk with my father about council business. He's a very educated man and was apparently one of the top students in his year, although he's too modest to say so himself. Father found that out. He has promised to lend me some books from his own collection. I'll enjoy that, since I've read all of my own several times."

I turned a little so that I could see Monsieur Colombani out of the corner of my eye. I felt that he was watching me in the same way, although he appeared to be giving his full attention to Monsieur Agostino, who could have bored even a Marseillais with his memories of their city. Monsieur Agostino had the habit of tapping men on the lapel as he talked: to make sure they were listening, I suppose. Not allowing himself the same familiarity with women, he just raised a finger to hold their attention. I felt sorry for Monsieur Colombani stuck with such a dull man. If I had been him I would have wanted to jump up and down and scream. But I didn't see how I could interrupt.

All of a sudden, I was aware that Orso was watching me from the other side of the room. He had the strangest expression, almost as if he were angry, his thick eyebrows knitted together. Why did he always seem to be annoyed with me? Ignoring him, I turned back to Sophia.

She and I chatted a little longer and village acquaintances came to greet us. I didn't have the opportunity to talk to Monsieur Colombani again and, soon afterwards, he approached his host to say that he must leave. He no doubt had his classes to prepare. My heart sank but I couldn't do anything. Our eyes met briefly as he left the room. I looked round to make sure Papa hadn't seen but he was still deep in conversation with the priest.

Not long afterwards, the party began to break up. We thanked Monsieur Franceschi and Sophia. She still had colour in her cheeks and a light in her eyes. I hadn't seen her look like that for a long time. Orso had disappeared.

We crossed the square to our house and Papa closed the heavy door behind us, barring it with an iron rod as he always did. I couldn't imagine who he thought would try to break it down. Zaronza was not exactly Marseille.

He turned to me and Maman.

"That young man is going to cause trouble here. I can see it now. And don't let him turn your head, Maria. I would never allow my daughter to marry a man like that. He's not good enough for you. You have quite a different future in store."

"Yes, Papa."

I bowed my head. What did Papa mean? That he and Maman would arrange a marriage for me, I supposed, with someone they deemed "suitable." My heart constricted inside my ribs. Climbing the stairs to bed, I wondered when I would see Monsieur Colombani again. As I laid my head on the pillow and closed my eyelids, I saw his ink black wavy hair and shining chestnut eyes.

Chapter 6

After the party, a fortnight passed but I didn't see Monsieur Colombani again. The new school year had begun, and Sophia said he had been busy preparing his lessons and getting to know his pupils. I found excuses to visit her, especially on a Wednesday afternoon when there was no school. Perhaps I would see him as I crossed the square. Sophia didn't say much about him, even when I asked her, so I assumed she hadn't seen him very often.

"You've been visiting Sophia a lot recently – even more than usual," Maman had said the previous day. She noticed everything, and always caught me out if I didn't tell the truth.

My face glowed. "Have I? I hadn't really noticed."

"Well, I suppose there's no harm in it provided you're here when I need you. Sophia is such a sensible girl."

The following afternoon, I had a good excuse. My dressmaking was as poor as my cooking, but Sophia sewed like an angel, and she had promised to alter my violet dress to make it more fashionable. Zaronza was not Ajaccio, but I felt that was no reason to look like a peasant. Returning across the square, I saw Monsieur Colombani coming up the hill from the schoolhouse. My heart quickened. Catching sight of me, he walked faster and we met by the fountain.

He bowed slightly. "Good afternoon, Mademoiselle Orsini. It's a beautiful day, isn't it?" The sun shone with the mellow warmth of September. This reminded me that I hadn't been up to the château recently to see the sunset and I had a sudden longing to go there.

"Yes it is, Monsieur Colombani." I couldn't think of anything else to say and perspiration beaded my upper lip.

What a fool he must have thought me. Sophia would have thought of something clever or witty, or at least interesting, to say in reply.

"Although I've been in Zaronza for several weeks I haven't had the chance to get to know it. I was wondering if you might have the time to show me around the village? I'm sure there's plenty to see, but I need someone who lives here to point it out to me. Since it's Wednesday, there's no school this afternoon and I'm ahead of myself in my preparations for my classes."

I hesitated. The square was deserted but I was afraid someone might have noticed us. It was a good thing Orso wasn't there during the week since he'd have been sure to appear at that moment. No doubt he would have disapproved, as always. I knew I shouldn't really be seen alone with Monsieur Colombani. What would Maman and Papa have said if they had known? My heart shrank as I imagined my father's reaction, but I asked myself, what harm we would be doing? After all, I was being kind to a newcomer to the village. I couldn't see how anyone could object to that, especially if we stayed in public places.

"I'd be delighted. Where would you like to start?"

"What about your lovely church, since it's close by?"

I nodded and we turned to look at the church. I saw it almost every day when I crossed the square, and of course we went every Sunday, so I barely noticed it. But he was right. It *was* beautiful. Painted a faded apricot colour it gave out a warm glow even in the depths of winter. It was small, simple and welcoming.

"This is the church of Santa Giulia," I said. "She was a saint who lived in the fifth century and became a martyr. She's also the patron Saint of Corsica." Oh dear, I sounded like a history textbook. He must have known the history, anyway. I hoped he wouldn't ask me to say any more, since the legend said that her breasts were cut off and flung down the hill. Two springs gushed from the place where they landed, and were still there.

He said nothing, simply looked at me and nodded. I sensed that he wasn't really listening.

"Would you like to go inside?" I asked, and then wished I hadn't. Of course he didn't go to church, which hadn't gained him the approval of either my father or Père Allegri, the priest. "But we don't have to," I hastened to add.

"Oh, I would find it very interesting. Studying Corsican church architecture is my hobby, and I've visited many churches on the island. Some of them are now in ruins, unfortunately. But one of my favourites is a Pisan thirteenth-century church at Murato, which is still in good condition. It's built of green and white marble, like a chequerboard, and has some fine stone carvings with biblical scenes and mythical beasts." As he warmed to his subject a slight flush rose in his cheeks and his eyes shone. He must be an inspiring teacher, I thought: I could listen to him for hours.

He paused and glanced at me. "I'm so sorry," he said. "I'm taking over what was supposed to be your guided tour. Once a teacher, always a teacher." He shrugged and smiled with a little twist of his mouth. I wondered what it would be like to kiss him. I blushed, swallowed hard and looked down.

"There's no need to apologise, Monsieur Colombani. You know so much more than I do. I'd be surprised if I could tell you anything about Zaronza that you don't know already."

"Ah, but it's so much more satisfying to hear it from you than from a guide book. It takes someone who lives in a place to understand it."

I turned aside so that he couldn't see my deepening blush and walked towards the church entrance. We stood at the back just inside the open door. I dared not go further in. In any case, Madame Contarini was on her knees in one of the front pews as usual, having just lit a candle for her son who drowned at sea. I didn't think she had noticed us. Since there wasn't much of note to see inside the church, I pointed to the door, raising my eyebrows. We paused at the top of the steps. Fortunately, no one was around.

What else could I show him? Zaronza is such a small place. The only other things were the ruined château and the watchtower. But to get to them you had to go right past our garden gate, and I didn't want to risk meeting Maman or, worse still, Papa. So I pointed them out to him from the church steps. He was very interested in the watchtower and I told him the story of a Corsican captain, who held out there single-handed against the French troops, pretending that he had a whole army with him. He gazed at me and his eyes took on a faraway look, no doubt thinking I was foolish and uneducated. But would he have preferred an intellectual? I didn't know. I stammered to a halt.

"There's very little else to see in the village, except the shrine to Santa Giulia, which is down a long flight of steps that leads to the beach."

"I'd like to see that very much, Mademoiselle Orsini. Would you be kind enough to show it to me? But only if you have time, of course." He leant towards me. His sharp, citrus scent wafted over me and I stepped back a pace, a little giddy. The clock in the *campanile* struck five. I blinked several times and the spell was broken. Provided I was home by six, I would be able to stay out of trouble. I had told Maman that I would be with Sophia most of the afternoon. I nodded and smiled.

We picked our way down the steep and uneven staircase cut into the rock. The springs still flowed as strongly as they are said to have done when Santa Giulia met her terrible fate. I shivered.

"Are you cold, Mademoiselle? I'm sorry, in my enthusiasm to see Zaronza I've forgotten my manners."

"No, excuse me. I was just remembering the time I slipped on the steps coming down here as a little girl, when it was raining. I still have the scar on my arm." I would have been terribly embarrassed if he had known I was thinking of the legend of Santa Giulia's breasts.

"I'm so sorry to hear about it, Mademoiselle, but at least

your accident wasn't more serious." A furrow appeared between his eyes.

To change the subject I asked him about his life in Marseille.

"I have never left the island," I said. "In fact, the farthest I have ever been from home is to Bastia on rare outings with Papa."

"First, I did my teacher training at the *école normale* in Ajaccio," he replied. "We had to follow a strict daily routine and study hard. You can't choose your first post. I would much rather have stayed in Corsica but I saw that I needed to widen my experience. So I was appointed to a large elementary school in a suburb of Marseille. It was demanding work but I found it rewarding seeing my pupils develop. I didn't have much spare time but whenever I could I learnt about the city and its long and fascinating history. Being an important port, it's teeming with people of all races and colours."

His lively description made the city come alive. I could hear the hubbub, smell the spicy scents. I longed to explore the alleys and taste the fresh fish in the Vieux Port. I gazed out over the sea towards the mainland and wondered if I would ever have the chance to go there.

He told me of the people who walled themselves into a neighbourhood of Marseille when the plague came in the eighteenth century. They pretended they weren't there for fear of becoming victims of the disease themselves. The children had to play in silence, and families had to live without fires for fear of raising suspicions. He was a very good storyteller. I could see why he had become a teacher.

"Many Corsicans have moved to Marseille because they can't find jobs here," he said. "And, like most of them, I started to pine for home. Interesting and exciting as I found Marseille, I decided to come back.

"The authorities disagreed. They had predicted a bright future for me, even suggesting that I might become the director of a Marseille school one day. But I felt there was more I could do in Corsica than on the mainland. I believe that education is the road to prosperity, and I wanted to give other Corsican children the opportunity to get on in the way that I had. So, in the end, they let me return."

"Don't you miss your friends in Marseille?"

He smiled. "I had very little time for friendship. And most of my school colleagues were married with families. They didn't have time to socialise out of school. And not being married myself, I didn't quite fit in." He shrugged. "I just didn't meet the right woman while I was there." He clearly had high standards. He held my gaze a little longer than necessary, and the treacherous blush rose.

He turned to look at the shrine again. It occupies a cave that goes back into the hillside and has a façade like a tiny church. In fact, it looks like the church up in the village, painted the same apricot colour. It has two niches on either side of the entrance, each of which contains a large urn. I showed him a slot at the back of one of them. Sophia and I found it when we were children.

"One of our games was to hide notes here, even though we only live across the square from each other. Sophia had trouble with the steps because of her foot, but she's always tried to ignore it." Yet again, I could have bitten off my tongue. I should never have drawn attention to Sophia's foot in front of Monsieur Colombani. She would have been livid if she knew. However, he didn't seem to have heard. Instead, he was very interested in the hiding place.

The church bell chimed six o'clock, its clear notes ringing out above us. The hillside beyond the village returned the echo. I had stayed too long and would have to hurry or Papa would be angry as usual.

"Let me walk you home, Mademoiselle Orsini."

"That's very kind of you, but I think it's better if we go separately. People in Zaronza gossip at the slightest opportunity. And I don't think my father would approve." I looked down, wondering if I had said too much.

"I don't want to cause you any trouble and, of course, I must respect your father's views. I know he doesn't approve of me: it was obvious when we met that our opinions differ. I won't provoke him any further. But thank you for your company. It's a long time since I spent such a pleasant afternoon. I hope I can do so again soon."

He shook my hand with a firm, warm pressure. My heart lurched and I drew my hand away. I prayed that no one had seen us. I hurried up the steps, dry-mouthed, holding my skirt above my ankles. As I reached the top, I looked back. He was studying the shrine but lifted his head and waved when he saw me. I raised my hand and set off quickly across the square.

My heart beat fast as I opened the front door in case it grated on the uneven flagstones. I tiptoed up the wide wooden staircase to my room on the top floor, where I flung myself on the bed, gasping. It took several minutes for my heart to calm down. A flushed and feverish face looked back at me from the mirror. I bathed my cheeks with water until the blotchy redness disappeared.

My mother looked up as I entered the kitchen. "Ah, there you are. What did Sophia say about the dress?"

"Oh, it will be easy enough for her to make the alterations I asked for. I wish I could sew as well as her."

Maman pursed her lips. She obviously agreed. "You were with Sophia for a long time. And you look a little flushed. I hope you're not sickening for something."

"I'm sorry, Maman. When we talk we don't notice the time passing. It was rather hot in Sophia's kitchen; she was baking. Can I help you?" I hoped she wasn't going to press me further.

"You can stir this soup while I chop some onions."

I took the spoon and dipped it into the cauldron but I longed to get up to the château and be alone. I had plenty to think about.

Chapter 7

Maman needed my help for several days after that to make fig and walnut jam, so I couldn't get away. I never wanted to see another walnut again. My fingers were brown from the shells. And the cedrat juice stung a cut in my finger. The kitchen was a furnace. At the end of each day I was sticky and damp. But at last it was all bottled, labelled and stacked away in the store cupboard.

One afternoon, Papa had gone to Santa-Lucia on business and Maman was lying down in her darkened room with a headache. I slipped out of the house shortly after lunch and toiled up the hill. It was the end of September but the sun was still white-hot. The wild figs were so ripe that they burst open when they dropped onto the path. Their rich, fleshy scent hung in the air, and wasps and black lines of ants clustered around them.

I sat on a flat, warm stone with my back against the wall of the watchtower, my knees drawn up, and gazed over the bay to the mountains beyond. They were blue and hazy, as if seen through gauze – a sign that the good weather would continue. If they were clear and sharp it meant rain within a day or so.

I considered some of the things Raphaël – that was how I thought of him – had said last Wednesday during our tour of the village. Could he have been interested in me? He must have met far more stylish and clever women in Marseille. I had led such a sheltered life. Zaronza was a country village on a small island, and I was an ignorant young woman. If only I had Sophia's brains.

Footsteps stumbling on the stones broke into my daydream. Sophia? I sighed. I didn't even want to see Sophia; I wasn't yet ready to let her into my secret.

As the footsteps approached, I said without looking round, "You can stay and talk for a while but this afternoon I'm thinking."

"So I see," a deep voice replied.

I leapt up and spun round. Raphaël was standing on the esplanade, pink-cheeked, slightly out of breath. He had taken off his hat and the breeze had ruffled his hair. His dark eyes shone. A warm glow flooded my chest.

"I…I'm sorry," I stammered, then laughed. "I thought you were Sophia. Sometimes she comes to find me up here. This is one of my favourite places. I like to look at the mountains and think."

"In that case, I hope I'm not disturbing you." I shook my head vigorously. He stepped towards me and I retreated and sat down on the stone again. "I can see why you like it. The view over the bay is magnificent, and you have quite a different perspective of the village. When you told me the story about the tower, I was intrigued and decided to see for myself."

He moved closer to the edge.

"Do be careful," I said. "There's a steep drop."

He smiled. "Don't worry: where I come from the hillsides are even steeper than they are here. I'm as sure-footed as a mountain goat."

Even so, he moved away from the unprotected drop. Without warning he came and sat next to me on the stone. We weren't touching but his closeness was like an electric charge. I sat up straighter and edged away a little.

"Mademoiselle Orsini – or can I call you Maria?"

I nodded, holding my breath.

"In that case I wish you would call me Raphaël. I was hoping to see you today, Maria. When we talked at the shrine the other day, I told you that I hadn't met the right woman yet." He looked down at his hands and spread his tapering fingers. "That isn't true."

My heart plummeted. He was going to tell me he was in love with someone. The prospect occurred to me in a flash. Maybe it was Sophia? After all, he saw her often enough at the mayor's house.

"I hope you won't think I'm too bold if I tell you that the first time I met you at Monsieur Franceschi's party, I felt something that I have never experienced before. Although we've known each other for only a short time, those feelings have strengthened each time I've seen you. Forgive me for being so direct but I can't hide it from you."

The blood drained from my cheeks. I opened my mouth but couldn't make a sound.

His eyes searched my face and he held up his hands. "I have great respect for you, Maria. I wouldn't dream of insulting you."

My heart pounded against my ribs and I buried my head in my hands.

"I'm sorry; I've gone too far and offended you," he said, making to stand up.

I put a hand on his sleeve then withdrew it as if stung. "No, please stay…Raphaël. It's just that this is so unexpected." I took a deep breath. "But I feel like that, too."

The frown smoothed away and his lips curved in his crooked smile. He took my hand and kissed it, then put his arm around my waist and drew me to him. It was all going much too fast, but I didn't care. For a while we were silent, enjoying each other's warmth and closeness and gazing out over the view. His citrus scent enclosed me. He shifted and held me away from him, looking into my eyes.

"I'm well aware that your parents would strongly disapprove of this. I don't want to cause you any difficulties; that would be as painful for me as for you. So I need to be sure that you want to continue seeing me."

I smiled and nodded. "I'm quite sure."

"For the moment, then, we have to meet in secret until we see what happens. Since I'm so busy at the school we can't see each other very often. But perhaps, for now, it's better if we don't attract people's attention."

"Yes, but where can we meet? It would be too risky to come up here. You have to go right past our garden gate. We're lucky that Papa is away on business today and Maman is feeling ill."

"What about Santa Giulia's shrine?"

I shook my head. "It's too close to the village. And other people go there to pray to the saint."

After a moment it came to me. An abandoned shepherd's hut stood on the hillside well above the village. Very few people went up there, and no one would see us from Zaronza. I didn't think my parents would suspect anything. I often went for walks on my own and could usually make some excuse to get away.

We decided to meet there the following Wednesday afternoon. If one of us couldn't make it, the other would wait for half an hour and then leave.

"In the meantime, may I write to you?" Raphaël said.

"Yes, I'd like that very much. But you can't send letters to my home. I rarely receive any, and my parents would notice strange handwriting. My father's bound to open them. We must find a safe place where we can leave notes for each other and collect them without anyone noticing."

I racked my brains but couldn't think of anywhere. A slow smile crept across Raphaël's face.

"You remember the secret place at the shrine, where you and Sophia hid your notes when you were children? That would be perfect."

I pursed my lips. "Yes, provided some of the village children haven't also discovered it and play the same game."

"In that case, we'll leave our letters unsigned. It will be safer that way. I can't write often but I'll think about you all the time. And now, speaking of schoolwork, I'm afraid I must leave you and go back to it. What a lucky chance that you were here today."

He bent his head and kissed me on the cheek. My skin tingled from the touch of his lips. He crossed the esplanade, turning to wave at the top of the hill. I raised my hand and he disappeared down the stony path. I listened to his receding footsteps until they had gone. Pulling my shawl tighter around my shoulders, I pressed my hands against my chest to hold in the secret that I wanted to shout out loud. I sat down on the flat stone again and pushed my back against the wall, which reflected the afternoon warmth. The sun was dipping towards the horizon and veins of red and purple streaked the sky by the time I decided to go home.

***

I waited a few days before checking our hiding place. I couldn't keep running up and down the steps to Santa Giulia's shrine. Someone would notice and Maman would wonder why I kept going out. And I couldn't use Sophia as an excuse all the time. So the days dragged by. The minute hand crept like a drowsy snail around the face of the grandfather clock in the hall.

Maman asked me to go to the village shop and I took the opportunity to go down the steps to the shrine. I felt around in the slot behind the urn and paper crackled under my fingers. My heartbeat quickened as I drew out an envelope. Nothing was written on it but a sheet of paper was inside. My heart shrank a little when I saw that he hadn't written more but he did say he was very busy at school. At least he had covered both sides. I was burning to read the letter but decided to keep it for later. I unbuttoned my cuff and pushed the envelope up my sleeve. After that, I went to see to Maman's purchases. All the while, the paper rubbed against my skin and a delicious thrill tingled in my stomach.

***

I had to wait several hours before I could read Raphaël's letter. Maman wanted my help in the kitchen and then Annunciata and I had to carry the rugs out onto the terrace so she could beat them. Finally, we had lunch. My father lingered over his cheese, chewing each mouthful countless times before selecting another morsel. I couldn't leave the table until he had folded and put away his knife. The temptation to leap up and dash upstairs was almost irresistible, but that would have annoyed Papa. So I sat looking at my empty plate and wrung my hands in my lap. The meal over, Papa went to his study while Maman settled down to her sewing.

"What are you going to do this afternoon, Maria?" Maman asked.

"Oh, I thought I might go across to see how Sophia's getting on with my dress. It's taking longer than she thought because she had to order the right thread from Bastia."

Maman sighed. "Well, don't stay too long."

I pulled the heavy door closed behind me and the echo rang in the empty hallway. Instead of crossing the square I climbed the hill to the château. Since that side of the house had no windows, Maman wouldn't see me going that way. I sat down on my usual flat stone. It was a little cooler, the beginning of October, and I pulled my shawl around me.

The letter was burning a hole in my dress. I reached into my sleeve and took it out. I sniffed the envelope and inhaled the faint, now familiar citrus scent. Fumbling with it, I pulled out the single sheet and unfolded it.

My dear Maria,

I can't begin to thank Providence enough for bringing us together. When I came to Zaronza I never thought I would find a beautiful woman who is everything my heart desires. Nor could I dare to hope that she would return my feelings. It was with the greatest joy, then, that I left you on Wednesday – although leaving you was hard, I admit.

I admire everything about you: not only your beauty but also your modesty and your good sense.

My heart trembled but I wondered if this was really me he was describing. Maman always said, "I wish you were more practical, Maria, like Sophia." Papa just shook his head and sighed. A wisp of doubt clouded my thoughts. I didn't want Raphaël to put me on a pedestal. Even so, it was nice to be treated like a grown woman for a change, instead of a naughty schoolgirl.

I read on. His handwriting was flowing and elegant and he expressed himself well.

He ended,

"Until we meet again, time itself is suspended and I can't wait to see you. In the meantime, let me assure you of my honourable intentions. Your devoted X."

I read the letter over until I knew every word by heart and then I replaced it in the envelope and put it back in my sleeve. I needed to write a reply, although I couldn't hope to match his eloquence. Again, I wished I had Sophia's wits. Thinking of her, I realised that I had told Maman I was going to see her this afternoon and I was curious to know how she was getting on with my dress. I was burning to tell her about Raphaël, but something told me it would be better to wait. It was still too new and unexpected and I wanted to put my thoughts in order. I stole past the garden gate and across the square.

***

When I returned from Sophia's house, a new problem presented itself. Where could I keep Raphaël's letters so that my parents didn't find them? Annunciata cleaned my room and put my fresh linen away in the wardrobe. I dared not hide the letters in there. Knowing her, she would have found and read them and then no doubt she would have told Maman.

Looking around my bedroom, my gaze rested on my jewellery box – an old cash box that Papa no longer needed. It had a removable tray, in which I kept my jewellery – although I didn't have very much: just my pearls, the christening bracelet and a plain gilt necklace. Underneath, I stored my childhood treasures and keepsakes: the perfect place. I took the envelope from my sleeve and kissed it before putting it in the box. I locked it and threaded the key onto the gilded chain, which I looped around my neck under my dress.

Sitting at my little table at the window, with a view over Zaronza, I composed a reply.

Chapter 8

From then on, one of the sweetest and most blissful, but also most frustrating, periods of my life commenced. Raphaël and I met at the shepherd's hut every Wednesday, which was his free afternoon during the week. One Wednesday, however, we couldn't meet, since it was teeming with rain. The ruined hut provided little shelter against the weather and, while we had been blessed with a radiant autumn up till then, we couldn't expect it to stay fine throughout the winter. I wondered what we would do.

I sat in my room at my little table by the window, chin in my hands, watching the rain sluicing across the hills and imagined Raphaël doing the same at his lodgings. Now we would have to wait another whole week before we could see each other again, although sometimes I caught a glimpse of him in the village. Sundays were impossible since we went to Mass in the morning and my parents expected me to stay at home with them in the afternoon. In any case, on Sundays Raphaël had to mark his pupils' work and prepare his lessons for the coming week.

To pass the time I wrote him a letter, taking care to have a shawl to hand so I could conceal it if Maman came in. My new-found passion for writing might have surprised her, so I had a book at my elbow ready to take up if I heard her coming upstairs. Raphaël's letters were a delight. I loved his elegant, flowing hand and his eloquent way of expressing himself. Now I had five that I had tied with a black ribbon and stowed away in my jewellery box. He must have found mine rather dull by comparison, but he said, "Your letters are enchanting, full of freshness and innocence. It's a great joy to me every time I find one at the shrine."

I had more time for writing than he did and some weeks he had time only to pen a short note. I would have liked to receive more letters from him but I knew he was conscientious and hardworking. That he also had a natural aptitude for teaching I had no doubt. He was a marvellous storyteller and passionately interested in the history of Corsica. He taught me about the turbulent history of the island: of the various foreign occupations, of King Theodore and his hapless and short-lived kingdom, of the visionary leader of the republic, Pascal Paoli, and of Napoleon Bonaparte.

I learned more from Raphaël in a short time than I had ever learned at school. But, then, people considered that educating women was a waste of time. Women had to know how to run a house, to do household accounts, to sew, to cook, to raise children – above all to be content with their lot and never complain. Although Sophia's views on the subject could become a little tedious, I began to sympathise with her. When I considered what the future held for me, it was with no great enthusiasm.

Raphaël and I took great precautions when we met. It would not have done for anyone to see us and tell Maman and Papa.

"Even so, I can't see what we're doing wrong," I told him. After all, we exchanged only chaste kisses and sometimes he put his arm around me. Mostly we walked about on the hill and talked or sat on a rough stone bench outside the hut and watched the ever-changing light over the sea.

He sighed. "Ah, but you see, Maria, first we're of different social classes. Your parents no doubt have a better future in mind for you than a simple schoolmaster can provide. And, of course, your father and I don't agree on a number of matters. That much was clear from our first, brief meeting."

A chill rose up my spine. I remembered my father's ominous words the night we came home from the mayor's party.

Raphaël and I had not spoken of marriage. Even I could see that it was too soon to consider such a step. We had known each other for little more than two months and sometimes I feared that it was all going too fast. We were rushing towards a chasm that would swallow us up. Who was it who said, "*The hottest love is the soonest cold*"? But I couldn't help myself. Raphaël claimed to worship the ground I walked on, but I wasn't sure that I wanted to be worshipped, however pleasant it might feel at the time. Would he grow tired of me? Would he desire a woman who was more his intellectual equal?

***

The next morning the sun had returned and it was as if the rain had never been, except that wisps of mist rose over the hills and there was a definite touch of autumn in the air. From my window, I saw the hillside turning to flame and ochre.

I had not yet shared my secret with Sophia, and a strange reserve held me back. When we were children we had no secrets from each other. To me she was like the sister I had never had – as I was to her. It was unlike me to hold my tongue for more than five minutes at a stretch. But this was different.

Realising that I hadn't seen so much of Sophia in recent days and had been neglecting her, I decided to go over to her house. I often used her as an excuse to visit our letters' hiding place, about which she didn't know anything yet. If the mood seemed right I might even tell her about Raphaël.

Unlatching the gate I walked down the alley towards the square. As I emerged, I saw Raphaël on the other side by the church. He had his back to me and didn't see me. Who was that he was talking to? Lucia Ferrano. Even from there I could see that she was blushing and coy and bent her head to one side as if she were being paid a compliment. I withdrew into the shadows. Raphaël leant towards Lucia a little and then he raised his hat and walked off towards the schoolhouse, still unaware of my presence. Lucia lifted her head and looked after him for a few seconds, and then she turned away, a secret smile lighting up her face.

I raised my hands to my chest and pressed them to my breastbone. Unable to breathe, I struggled to take in what I had just seen. Raphaël flirting with another woman? And in public? This couldn't be true. After everything he had said to me. Maybe the reason he had never married in Marseille was that he preferred to break women's hearts instead.

My visit to Sophia abandoned, I rushed upstairs to my room and threw myself on the bed. A short while later, Maman came to find me.

"I'm sorry, Maman, I have a terrible migraine. Please may I be excused lunch?"

Maman suffered from frequent headaches herself. "Pull the curtains, then, and lie down properly. I'll soak a handkerchief in lavender water and place it on your brow."

The lavender water had a calming effect. As the afternoon wore on I began to think I might have been a little hasty. After all, he would hardly have flirted with Lucia in public. I reflected further. That was what he had done with me, though. Or had he? I recalled every word of our conversation when he asked me to show him around the village. Nothing untoward occurred. He was the model of politeness and respect. That's how it began, anyway. It didn't take him long to reveal his feelings for me. Was his haste indecent?

In the end, I didn't know what to think. My thoughts twisted around in my head like a nest of snakes. I decided to wait and see how he behaved towards me next time we met.

***

The following Wednesday I had received another letter from Raphaël since I saw him talking to Lucia. But I couldn't detect anything different in its tone. If anything, it was even more passionate than his previous notes and told me of his longing to see me again. After reading it several times, I added it to the bunch in my box and retied the black ribbon.

After lunch, I toiled up the hill towards our meeting place, a dull ache in the pit of my stomach. His letter gave nothing away but maybe he would tell me today that our relations couldn't continue. Bitter tears welled up and clouded my vision.

He was there first, as usual, and came to greet me, enveloping me in his arms as if nothing were any different. "It seems an eternity since we last met. I've missed you so much. Did you find my letter?"

I nodded, sighing and dashing the tears from my eyes. They had turned from those of bitterness and dread to those of relief. He stepped back.

"But what's the matter, Maria? Has something happened? Not your parents…"

"No, it's nothing. I just have a headache, that's all. And perhaps it's the strain of having to continue to meet like this in secret."

He took my hands and bent his head a little to look into my eyes. "I find it difficult, too, not seeing you when I want to and having to take precautions just so that we don't provide meat and drink for the village gossips. We have to support each other, knowing that our love will win in the end."

I resolved not to say anything about Lucia and we were soon talking as we always did. He was as warm and solicitous as ever. Perhaps my fears were groundless. Even so, the dull ache didn't quite disappear as I made my way home later.

***

A visit to Sophia was well overdue. I persuaded Maman to allow me to go, even though it was a Sunday afternoon. Papa was away from home and I suspected Maman would be glad to get rid of me for a couple of hours since I had been pacing around the dining room like a caged wild beast.

"Whatever is the matter with you, Maria? You're so full of

energy that it gives me a headache. Perhaps a visit to Sophia will knock some sense into you. She's such a sensible girl." The implication was that I wasn't, although I found it a little unfair. After all, I had managed to bottle up a great secret for weeks. No one, not even Sophia, knew.

I kissed Maman and made for the door, pausing to pick up my shawl from the back of my chair.

How many times in my life, I wondered, as I crossed to Monsieur Franceschi's house, have I taken this route? And how many more times will I?

As ever, instead of going to the forbidding front door, I made my way around to the kitchen door. As I approached, the muffled sound of voices floated on the air: Sophia's low tones and a darker, man's voice. I assumed it was Orso, home for the weekend, so I advanced quietly, knowing he didn't like to see me. Perhaps if I waited a little, he would leave the kitchen and then I could talk to Sophia alone. It was unusually warm for mid-November and the kitchen door was ajar. Two people were sitting at the table with their backs to me. One was Sophia, and she was talking with animation. But instead of Orso's unruly chestnut curls, the head close to hers had midnight black hair. He chuckled and stretched out over the table to reach something. Raphaël.

For the second time in the space of a week, I couldn't catch my breath. They were so engrossed in one another that they were unaware of anything else. My hand pressed to my side, I stumbled back along the passage and somehow made it across the square without meeting anyone else. Thank goodness for Sunday afternoon. The hot tears were already stinging my eyes but, instead of making for my room and raising Maman's attention, I plunged up the hill towards the château and the watchtower. At that time of year, I was unlikely to be disturbed. Collapsing onto the flat stone by the tower, I gave way and sobbed until I had no more tears left.

As the sun slid towards the horizon, a chill air rose from the ground and I realised that I had to go home. As I got up from the stone, my limbs numb, a flare of anger passed through me and pushed away my misery.

How dare he do this to me? How dare he tell me he loves me and flirt behind my back, first with Lucia and then, even worse, with my best friend? What does he think I am – one of the women of easy virtue whom he no doubt came across in Marseille? I'll show him that I have more pride than that. And I might be ill-educated, but I'm no fool. I'll show him.

I straightened my dress, shook my skirts and brushed them off. Gathering my shawl around me, I stalked down the hill, kicking the stones that littered the path out of my way. As I entered the hallway, Maman emerged from the dining room. I took a deep breath; I had to conceal my dismay.

"Ah, there you are, Maria. How was Sophia?"

"Very well, Maman. She sends her best regards to you and Papa."

Maman smiled. She had always liked Sophia. "And Orso, was he there too?"

"I didn't see him, Maman. I expect he was talking with Monsieur Franceschi."

I wished she wouldn't question me anymore. One day she would find out from Sophia that I hadn't been to visit, and then I would be hard-pressed to explain what I really had been doing.

"Would you excuse me, Maman? I have a slight headache and I would like to be quiet in my room for a while to stop it getting worse."

"Very well. Your father is not yet home but I don't need you for the moment. I'm concerned that you seem to be developing a tendency for headaches. If this carries on we must consult the doctor. You look a little flushed – I hope you're not going down with something."

"Oh, it's nothing, really, Maman. I shall be down again shortly."

She nodded and continued along the passage to the kitchen. I climbed the stairs and threw my shawl on the bed. Sitting down at my little writing desk I took a sheet of paper and started to write furiously.

Despite what you say, it appears that you are not faithful to me. I have seen you recently on two occasions flirting with other women. You claim that you love me but you show little respect for me by your insulting behaviour. I would never so much as look at another man, but you appear not to feel bound by the same sense of commitment. I feel as if I have been thrown down from a mountain and left broken on the rocks below. How could you do this to me?

Folding the letter, I pressed hard along the creases with my thumbnail. There. That would teach him to treat me lightly.

I ran downstairs and met Maman coming from the kitchen.

"Oh, Maman, I realise I left my shawl at Sophia's house. I'll just run across the square and fetch it."

"Go quickly, now, I expect your father home soon. Your headache seems to have improved."

"Yes, I feel much better, thank you."

I ran along the alley and out into the square. But instead of going straight ahead towards Sophia's house I walked along the road to the stairway that led down to the shrine. When I got there, I hesitated, pushed the letter into the slot behind the urn and ran back home quickly. Now we would see how he explained himself.

Chapter 9

Although it was agony to me, I waited until Tuesday to visit the shrine to see if he had replied to my note. Sure enough, a new envelope was tucked into the slot. I tore it open, unable to wait until I got home.

My lovely Maria,
Why are you so harsh to me? You accuse me of flirting with other women but you know I only have eyes for you. If I look at another girl it is only to compare her with you – and you are incomparable. I have never been unfaithful to you in word or in deed and never shall be. My initial joy at receiving your letter soon turned to dismay when I read its contents. I have racked my brains and cannot think of any occasions when I might have offended you. For me, there is only you. I can think only of you, I even dream of you. I am convinced that all this is a misunderstanding that can be quickly and easily resolved. I am sure I have done nothing wrong but beg you to forgive me all the same. Please give me the opportunity to clear up this mystery and to prove my continuing and constant love for you. Meet me at our usual time and place. Until then, I am in torment.

I folded the single sheet and replaced it in the envelope and hid it in my sleeve as usual. His distress seemed genuine and his confusion sincere. But who knew? Maybe this was how a womaniser behaved. He wormed his way into a woman's confidence and then betrayed her behind her back, doing the same thing to several other women at once. How would I have known? I had so little knowledge of the world and so few weapons to defend myself with. I was taking as much of a risk as he was in meeting in secret. If he *was* unfaithful, he was doubly shameful for exposing me to those risks while he courted other women at the same time.

My heart divided and my brain in turmoil, I climbed the steps and made my way home. I didn't know if my inner disorder was visible in my face or behaviour. If it was, then it wouldn't take long for Maman to notice. She saw everything. Oh, being in love was sweet, but it was bitter at the same time. Nobody ever told me that. I was discovering that it was something you can only experience for yourself.

***

Part of me couldn't wait for Wednesday; part of me dreaded its arrival. But now it had arrived and I had to confront him. I needed to know if he was true to me but I wasn't sure if I could believe what he would tell me.

It was a true November day: dank, grey and chilly. The clouds that covered the hilltops in the morning had not risen. They even seemed to sink as if they would swallow up the village. How fitting to my mood!

Nonetheless, I made an excuse to get away and climb the hillside to our meeting place. He was always there before me but, then, I had to wait for Papa to finish his lunch before I could get away. Raphaël was free to do as he liked. How I began to envy men their freedom!

He came and stood before me. Normally, we embraced but his expression was downcast. I said nothing but stood with my hands on my hips, my head inclined slightly to one side, questioning.

"I want to hold you, Maria, but I don't know if I dare," he said.

"There won't be any embracing until you tell me what you were doing with Lucia Ferrano and then with my best friend, Sophia. I will *not* be taken lightly. Do you think I'm a fool?"

He shook his head. "But I'm not sure I even know this Lucia Ferrano. And Sophia I can explain very easily."

"Do you deny that you were flirting with Lucia Ferrano, *in the street*? That, I could just about tolerate but I can't bear that you could make love to my best friend!"

"Now her name comes to mean something. If it's the young lady I'm thinking of, her parents kindly invited me to dinner at their house. Don't forget that little Sampiero Ferrano is one of my pupils, and it's natural that his parents wanted to find out about his progress. It's also natural that his elder sister was at the dinner. She made a *fiadone* cake for dessert and I was simply thanking her. I also asked her to give my compliments to her mother for the delicious dinner. Now surely that can't be defined as flirting? Is that why you were so preoccupied one day up here on the hill?"

His eyes flashed. A flush rose up my cheeks.

"If you describe it like that, who am I to contradict you? All I can say is that from where I stood it looked distinctly like flirting."

"Maria," he said and spread out his arms in an "I'm an honest man" gesture.

I began to feel foolish but ploughed on. "Never mind Lucia Ferrano. What about Sophia? I was coming to see her on Sunday and I saw both of you together in the kitchen through the open door. You seemed very happy in each other's presence. She was lively and you were sitting very close to each other."

Raphaël smiled. "Do you really believe that Sophia can hold a candle to you?"

"But…but she's so much cleverer than I am. How could you not prefer her to me?"

"I'll tell you why not. Sophia is an intelligent young lady. She's well-read and has a thirst for learning that I have rarely come across. It's stifled deplorably in young Corsican women. I've loaned her some of my books, although I have only a small collection myself. She also expressed a desire to learn Italian so that she can read Dante in the original. Although I'm by no means perfect in the language I felt that I could at least teach her its basic principles. That's what we were doing when you stumbled upon us on Sunday."

I bit my lip. "But you clearly don't think I'm intelligent enough to treat in the same way."

He sighed. "Maria. Trust me. How can I persuade you that I love you and no one else? I feel a warm friendship for Sophia but I have never considered the idea that it could go beyond that. She's a worthy person, but she's not for me. And don't tell me that you aren't intelligent. You have an imagination and a way of looking at things that could have taken you far if you had been a man. Alongside that, and the two things are perhaps surprising together, you have a practical bent and a capacity for endurance that make you mature beyond your years."

I almost laughed out loud. I couldn't imagine my parents or Sophia – or Orso for that matter – describing me as mature. But then I thought again. Perhaps he does know me better than I know myself. Is that what love means?

"Those qualities are charming enough in themselves," he continued. "But when they're combined in someone with your beauty and distinction, how could I help but love you?"

My eyes smarted and my lips quivered. I had never thought about myself like that. Could I really be such a paragon? He held out his arms and I threw myself into them and pressed my face against his chest, my tears wetting his waistcoat.

"But how would you have felt if you had seen me talking to a young man in the way you talked to Lucia and Sophia?"

"I would have assumed that you had a good reason for talking to him and I should have thought no more about it. I trust you, Maria."

What strange beings men are! I almost felt affronted that he wouldn't be as jealous as I had been. But his explanations of his behaviour were sound and consistent. How could I have doubted him? Of course, as the village schoolmaster he would have to meet with the families of his pupils. Of course, as the secretary to the town council he had to cultivate Monsieur Franceschi and his family. I couldn't help feeling a twinge of jealousy about his relations with Sophia, but he assured me that he didn't find her attractive.

Perhaps everything would turn out all right for us after all.

***

Feeling lighter at heart than for some time, I picked my way down the steep hill. The clouds were so low that they were almost like mist and a chill was in the air. I wondered how much longer Raphaël and I could go on meeting at the shepherd's hut before it became too cold, but I put that thought out of my mind. We would find some way to see each other.

As I crossed the square I saw Sophia on the other side carrying her shopping basket and making her way home. I quickened my pace to catch up with her. She smiled her elusive but warm smile and I kissed her on both cheeks. She seemed a little washed-out but I put that down to the onset of winter. We all needed the sunshine.

"I haven't seen very much of you recently, Maria. What have you been doing?"

"I know. I've been rather busy and Maman very often wants my help. But there's another reason and I really want to tell you about it."

She raised her eyebrows and tilted her head to one side.

"A secret, then? It's most unlike you to keep a secret to yourself, so it must be something important." I caught the gleam in her eye. She was teasing me as usual.

"It *is* something important, the most important thing that has ever happened to me. But we can't stand here in the square. You must be getting cold."

She shivered a little under her shawl. Poor thing, she was so small and frail.

"Come up to the kitchen," she said. "The fire is lit and it's warm in there. Papa is out at the town hall and won't be back until after six. We'll have plenty of time for you to unveil your important secret." The dimple appeared in her cheek again. Why, she almost looked pretty when that happened. I felt a surge of affection for her and wanted to look after her.

Sophia placed the basket on the great scrubbed oak table in the kitchen and we sat down. I looked down at my hands, not knowing how to begin. Sophia didn't hurry me. If our positions had been reversed, I would have been burning to know her secret and impatient to prise it out of her. How different we were!

Still looking down at my hands, I started to tell her everything about Raphaël. How it began, the secret letters and our hiding place, how my love for him had grown. I was careful not to tell her about my jealousy or about seeing Raphaël with Lucia and with her. Halfway through my tale, I looked up. Sophia was staring at me wide-eyed, her face ashen and her mouth slack. She wrung her hands.

"What is it, Sophia? Are you unwell?"

She closed her eyes and didn't reply. I shook her arm a little.

"What's the matter?"

She took a deep breath and opened her eyes, first turning her gaze to the window and then switching it back to me. "Maria, you're making the most terrible mistake."

An icy hand gripped my stomach. "What do you mean? I thought you would be happy for me."

"I would be happy for you if I thought there were any future in it. But there isn't. Listen to me, Maria. You aren't right for each other. Never mind the fact that your parents are most unlikely to agree to such a match. Can you really see yourself as a schoolmaster's wife? He is educated, an intellectual. You, you are…" For once she was lost for words and sketched a vague gesture with her hand.

"I'm an ill-educated, ignorant young woman who knows

nothing of any importance. That's what you mean, isn't it?"

"I wouldn't have said it like that. But think about it carefully. Now you're carried away with the idea of being in love. Do you really think that your love can last? Do you really think that Raphaël will be satisfied? Will you be satisfied with the life he can give you? I repeat: you are not suited to each other, not at all."

"But we love each other. Surely that's enough."

Sophia shook her head. "You're being very foolish, Maria. Especially when there's another person who would be honoured to make you his wife and who would be much more suitable for you. That person is Orso."

"Orso?! I can't believe it, Sophia. He doesn't even like me. He makes every effort to avoid me. How can you say that he'd want to marry me?"

"Orso has his ways, I know. He's a little rough and ready and doesn't know how to speak to a pretty young woman. Believe me; I know what I'm talking about. Don't you think I understand my own brother?"

So that was why he had always behaved so oddly to me since we were grown up. Even so, all this was beside the point.

"But I don't love Orso, Sophia. I never could. I love Raphaël and, what's more, he loves me."

"You're both being very silly, then, and I can't answer for the consequences. I thought that Raphaël, at least, had more sense and knew where his own best interests lie."

My heart contracted. "You wouldn't tell anyone else…? My parents…?"

"Of course not. But I wouldn't like to be in your position when they find out, as they certainly will. Your father won't take this kindly. He doesn't care for Raphaël. He has even had words with my father, whom he accuses of giving preferential treatment to Raphaël, asking his opinion and treating him like an equal. Papa likes Raphaël and sees what an asset he is to the village, what a fine man he is. Your father does not."

Sophia flushed and the pallor of her face made the rush of crimson stand out even more.

"You're just like Maman and Papa," I spat out the words. "Everyone's always telling me what to do, how to behave, that I'm not clever and must give in to other people's decisions all the time. I thought that you, at least, would understand, Sophia. But I see that you don't. I thought you were my best friend, but now I'm sorry I confided in you."

I stood up and Sophia did nothing to keep me back. She sat, her hands folded on the table in front of her, and looked at me as if I were a stranger. I pushed past her and slammed the kitchen door behind me. As I emerged from the alley onto the square I bumped into Monsieur Franceschi, on his way home from the town hall.

"Maria, where are you going in such a hurry? You almost bowled me over."

My cheeks burning, I replied, "I'm sorry, Monsieur Franceschi. I'm late and was rushing to get home."

Shaking his head, he continued towards his house. I turned my steps towards our house, my heart like a stone. Why was everyone against me? Even Sophia. I was so alone, apart from Raphaël, who understood me so well. I thought of the future but could see only a swirling mist. What would happen to us? How would all this end?

Chapter 10

So we continued in limbo, Raphaël and I, after my argument with Sophia. He knew, of course, that she and I were friends, but I didn't say anything to him about our quarrel – most of all, because I would have had to say what caused it. Oh yes, I could have invented some trivial excuse for our falling out but that would have made him think badly of me. And while I was quite sure that Sophia was mistaken when she said that Raphaël and I were not suited, I didn't want to give him any cause to question his love for me.

Sophia and I had not patched up our quarrel. We had seen and greeted each other at church and she had returned my violet dress with the alterations beautifully done. Even so, it was as if a sharp frost had settled on our former warm relations. I hadn't been to see her. What could I say? And she hadn't sought me out, either. It wouldn't take long for Maman to notice. But what could I do?

We were fortunate that the weather had stayed fine and it was even quite mild some days. Raphaël and I continued to meet on the hillside every Wednesday and sent each other letters via our hiding place. We took great care to avoid discovery. But maybe we hadn't been quite careful enough. One day as I was emerging from the staircase up from the shrine, I met Madame Paoli. The eyes and ears of the village, everyone called her. Tell her something and it would be common knowledge in the blink of an eye. I always wanted to run away when I saw her dusty black dress heave in sight like a ship in full sail.

"Now, Maria," she said, wagging a finger at me. "You have a secret."

Time stood still. I couldn't breathe. Her sunken face, like a fallen plum, thrust itself at me, waiting for an answer. She plucked at my sleeve. My God! Please, I thought, don't let her feel the envelope that's hidden in there. I pulled it away from her grasp.

"Good afternoon, Madame Paoli. I'm afraid I don't know what you mean."

"Come, now. I sometimes see you going up and down to Santa Giulia's shrine. And I know what you're doing there." She nodded to underline her words. "You are praying for a husband. I know. I used to do the same when I was your age. And Santa Giulia answered my prayers."

Relief flooded through me. Poor Monsieur Paoli. I think he died just to get away from her. Not only was she ugly – and it was difficult to believe she could ever have been anything else – but she was also poisonous.

"Yes, you're right, Madame Paoli. She hasn't yet answered mine but I'm sure she will soon. After all, it did the trick for you."

My comment lost on her, she gave me a gap-toothed grin.

"It wouldn't surprise me if you were married within the year, if what I have heard is correct." She tapped the side of her nose and set off in the direction of the church.

A cold wave surged over me. What had she heard? From whom? I looked around me, expecting to see spies behind every tree or shadowy figures in every window. Raphaël and I would have to increase our precautions. The school Christmas holidays had begun, and Raphaël had to leave Zaronza the next day for a few days to visit his parents in the Bozio. While I couldn't bear the idea of him not being near me, it was perhaps for the best and might help to still wagging tongues.

When I got back, Maman told me that Papa had gone away from home again.

"He has gone to see your cousin Vincentello. I think there'll be some interesting news about him soon."

I couldn't imagine anything about Vincentello that would interest me. The only son of my father's late brother, Vincentello inherited his father's property when Uncle Orsini died a few years previously. The two families were never close, and I had seen Vincentello only a few times in my life, even though he lived only in the next village. When I had met him he always struck me as arrogant and lacking in charm. I was told he was intelligent, but as far as I could see he was lacking in application. He was handsome enough but had thin lips. That was always a bad sign as far as I was concerned.

I shrugged.

"If it's about Vincentello, it would have to be something quite remarkable to arouse my interest." As soon as the words were out of my mouth I wanted to bite them back. But the encounter with Madame Paoli had set my nerves on edge.

"Maria! You are not to speak ill of your cousin. Look how young the poor boy was when his father died. He had to take over his father's lands and business and has made a fine attempt at it."

I frowned at the word 'attempt' but replied, "Yes, Maman. I'm sorry."

My mother looked at me, her face rigid. "You'd better come and help me in the kitchen. You father will want his supper as soon as he returns."

***

There was no explanation of Maman's cryptic comments for a couple of days. Then, towards the end of lunch one day, Papa announced, "Maria, I'd like to see you in my study after you have helped your mother clear the table. She already knows what I want to tell you."

My heart skipped several beats and my eyes widened. What did he want to tell me? Normally, he asked me into his study only if he wanted to reproach me for some small error. Had someone found out about me and Raphaël and informed on us? Sophia? No, surely not. Although we had fallen out about Raphaël, I didn't believe she would give me away to my parents. Madame Paoli? She was the more likely suspect, but even she didn't appear to know the truth; if she had known, she wouldn't have been able to resist hinting at it more obviously.

So what was it?

Speculation was useless. Still, my hands were shaking so much that I clattered the plates about. Maman gave me a reproachful look but said nothing. I couldn't put off the moment any longer. Standing outside the door to Papa's study, I smoothed my skirt and rubbed my perspiring palms together. I took a deep breath and knocked at the door.

"Ah, Maria," Papa said, looking up from his papers. "You can sit down."

This was a good start. If I did something wrong I had to remain standing while he lectured me from his desk. I was even more astonished when he stood up, walked around the desk and sat in the chair opposite me.

"I have some good news for you. News that I know any young girl of your age would wish to receive." He paused. "You'll know that I have made several visits recently to your cousin Vincentello. Although his father and I never got on very well, I have a fondness for the boy. He was very young when my brother died and he had to take over as head of his family. Not only that, but he was pitched into running the business."

I wondered what all this had to do with me, but at least there was no mention of Raphaël.

Papa went on, "Your mother and I have the deepest affection for you, Maria, as I hope you know."

I nodded, although sometimes their coolness made me question the depth of it.

"However, I won't conceal from you that it has been a great sadness to us that we didn't also have a son who would carry on the family name. It wasn't to be. We have taken great pains to bring you up to be ladylike and accomplished, so that when the time came you would marry well and be a credit to the family honour."

Where was he leading me with all this? Wherever it was, I was certain that he wouldn't have considered a marriage to Raphaël in those terms.

"Vincentello and I have had a number of discussions. He agrees that you are a most attractive and desirable young lady. A marriage between you would achieve several objectives. First, you bear the same name, so any children you have would continue the family name. Second, the addition of Vincentello's lands and business interests to my own would make a substantial concern while having the benefit of keeping the possessions in the Orsini name. Third, he's a distinguished and respectful young man who would treat you as a daughter of mine deserves. I think you'll agree that this be would a most advantageous match for everyone concerned."

He sat back smiling, elbows on the arms of his chair, his fingertips pressed together in a steeple, awaiting my reaction. For a moment or two, I had none. The weight of his words had not yet struck me. Numbness settled on my limbs and I couldn't think. The meaning of what he said finally became clear. I raised my hands to my mouth. I was cold all over, and my stomach lurched.

"But…but, Papa…"

He raised his eyebrows. I pressed my palms together hard.

"I don't love him. I don't even like him. We've met only a few times and I didn't find him agreeable. Please tell me that this isn't true. I can't marry him if I don't love him."

"What are you talking about? Do you realise what a naïve and ignorant girl you are? People of our station don't marry for love. Family interests come first. This is how it must be. Do you think your mother and I married for love? No. Our marriage was arranged and we met only a few times before the ceremony itself. That hasn't prevented a deep respect and affection from growing between us over the years."

I didn't reply but stared at him, unbelieving.

"You are scarcely in a position to know what's best for you," he continued. "As your father, I have both your interests and those of the family at heart. And, believe me, it is in your interest to marry your cousin. You will be comfortable, secure and respected. What more could a young woman wish for?"

His colour was rising and he leant forward.

I swallowed.

"I'm sure Vincentello has no regard for me but sees only the financial benefits of marrying me. And I won't marry a man whom I don't love and who doesn't love me."

"You will do exactly as you're told." Papa rose from his seat, his face brick red, and poked his finger an inch from my nose. "Put all this romantic nonsense out of your head, Maria. You know nothing of the world. I know what's best for you and you'll thank me for it later on. It's decided. You will marry Vincentello. He has agreed and the contract is already drawn up."

I gasped and gripped my face in my hands. Papa tutted and expelled his breath. He strode to the door and called down the passageway, "Colomba, come and talk some sense into your daughter."

She hurried from the kitchen wiping her hands on a cloth. "What is it, Antonio? Have you told her?"

"Yes, I've told her but she seems to have difficulty recognising her good fortune. As far as I'm concerned there's nothing more to be said. It's all settled. I have business to attend to and can't spend more time on her absurd objections. But you will speak to her and impress upon her that she must be welcoming to Vincentello when he comes to spend Christmas Eve with us."

All the while, I sat there, unable to believe what was happening. Oh, Raphaël, what could I do? When my father had decided upon something it was impossible to make him change his mind. And Maman always supported him. I was so alone.

My father stamped down the corridor, his heels ringing on the flagstones. The front door stuck and grated as usual on the uneven floor. The knocker banged on the door, such was the force with which Papa slammed it.

Maman sank down into the chair opposite me. She looked at me for a moment and a fleeting glimpse of something crossed her face. Sympathy? Understanding? I couldn't tell, but it seemed unlikely. She sighed.

"Maria, you know your father always does what's right for you, for us all, for the family. You can't expect to love your husband at first, but it will come. Papa and I married because our families agreed it was in everyone's best interests. I have never regretted it, even though…even though I have never been able to have any more children."

She glanced away for a moment. Despite my own problems, I glimpsed the sadness behind the façade.

"But, Maman. You and Papa talk as if I were goods to be parcelled up and sold, like a barrel of olives. As if I had no will or wishes of my own. What about my feelings? I can't love Vincentello. I never will. When I marry I want it to be to a man I love and have chosen myself."

"Maria, stop being so unrealistic. You're a woman. Women have little choice in these matters. And you know that once your father has made up his mind he won't change it. You would do much better to reconcile yourself and prepare yourself for your marriage. So that you and Vincentello can get to know each other a little better, we have invited him to spend Christmas Eve with us. Your father and I expect you to be hospitable and agreeable towards him."

Christmas Eve! But that was only two days away. What was I going to do? I had to get a message to Raphaël in his village. But how? The posts were unreliable at the best of times.

"And now," Maman said. "I'll leave you to think about all this. I must admit that your father and I find your response to this good news very disappointing. I hope that, on reflection, you'll realise your good fortune and thank your father for having your best interests at heart."

She left me and went back to the kitchen.

Interests, interests. That was all anyone could talk about. What about love? What about feelings? Was life just to be reduced to a series of financial transactions? I thought of Vincentello and his thin, cruel lips. Papa said he would respect me. I wasn't so sure. I had heard the stories about the way he treated his mother and sisters after his father's death. His sisters got away by marrying, his mother by following his father to the grave. Why hadn't Papa heard about these things? Or maybe, in the family's "interests," he had just shut his mind to them.

I dragged myself upstairs, heavy as lead. I didn't have the energy to fling myself on my bed but sat down on the edge of it like an old woman, worn out. Even the tears didn't come, just a cold numbness that weighed me down. Now the mist that obscured my future had cleared away and I saw it stretching before me. But instead of a warm, sunny prospect, a stony, frozen wasteland spread out without end.

Chapter 11

Christmas Eve dawned, and with it a sense of dread that lay heavily on my stomach. Since Papa's revelation I had been in an agony of indecision. I wanted to contact Raphaël but didn't know how to go about it. He wouldn't return until New Year's Day. Maman had press-ganged me into helping in the kitchen. It seemed that Vincentello was to be regaled with a feast that evening and I had to help her prepare it. If I had had poison I would have added it without qualms to the wild boar stew and then eaten it myself. Even Annunciata was in a state of expectation as she dusted and mopped and scrubbed. She winked at me once or twice but I pretended not to notice. It appeared that everyone was aware of my fate – and everyone except me thought it was a great privilege.

As the day wore on, I had a headache – a real one this time. I put it down to the stress of the past few days. My parents had been severe with me but I hadn't given any quarter myself. The strain of having no one to confide in was almost unbearable. If only Sophia and I hadn't fallen out. But there would have been little time to visit her, anyway, since Maman had considered my presence indispensable.

As I went upstairs to change – the violet frock, at Maman's command, although I felt much more like wearing black this evening – my temples throbbed and I had gooseflesh. In my room, I put my hand to my forehead, which was burning. But I climbed into my frock and put up my hair. My face was flushed, no doubt from the heat of the kitchen. As I went downstairs, my limbs were as if made of rubber.

I went into the salon, a room we rarely used except on important occasions, and seated myself next to the fire.

Vincentello had arrived an hour or so before, but Annunciata showed him to his room so that he could change. Despite being next to the fire I was shivering and my mouth was dry. After a while, Maman came in, dressed in her best black with her relieving silver brooch. Today, I was aware of how she had aged. After her came the men. I was to be on my best behaviour.

"Here is your cousin Vincentello. Wish him a Merry Christmas," Papa ordered.

I dropped into a curtsey, my head swimming. Vincentello crossed the room, took my hand and pressed it and then raised it to his lips. How different from my meeting with Raphaël only a few months ago! Vincentello was wearing a new jacket and looked quite handsome, but I saw the hardness in his mouth and lips. When I looked at him I felt nothing.

The evening passed in a haze. I had no appetite and couldn't eat much. Vincentello, on the other hand, who was seated next to me, wolfed down everything he was offered. Maman pressed him to seconds of each course, which he accepted without hesitation. His table manners left something to be desired, but my parents appeared not to notice. We exchanged few words. My headache had worsened and I couldn't bear even the light from the candles.

Approaching eleven o'clock, we put on warm clothing and made our way across the square to the church of Santa Giulia for mass. Papa offered his arm to Maman and made it quite clear that I should take Vincentello's arm. My cousin's solicitous but doubtless insincere attention was revolting.

This had always been one of my favourite times of year. I loved the midnight mass when we all came together to remember the humble birth at Bethlehem. Raphaël said it was all superstitious claptrap and I never contradicted him. Even so, there was something magical about it. That night, however, my headache was so bad that I had difficulty remembering the responses. Sophia was there with her father and Orso, who, as usual, looked like thunder and eyed Vincentello up and down as if he wanted to plunge a knife into him. I wished he would. Somehow I got through the service but, to this day, I remember little of it. When we arrived home I could barely stand. Maman had prepared a light meal for us but I had no appetite.

"Maman, please excuse me, I don't feel well at all. I have a blinding headache and I want to go to bed."

"A headache again?" She put her hand on my brow. "You do seem feverish. Perhaps it *would* be a good idea if you went to bed. Your father will be disappointed. And so will Vincentello. But since he is going to spend tomorrow with us as well, it would be better if you were feeling well by the morning."

I undressed by candlelight, the fire in my room not enough to warm my limbs. I clambered into bed and fell into a slumber broken with dreams where I was sliding into a chasm. Raphaël tried to pull me back but my hand slipped out of his. And in the background Vincentello's narrow mouth smiled but not his eyes.

***

After a fitful sleep I awoke on Christmas Day and could barely move my limbs. If anything, my headache was even worse, I had a raging sore throat and I shivered and burned by turns.

When I tried to swing my legs out from under the sheets, my head swam and I couldn't raise myself up. Falling back on the pillows, I was seized with fatigue and could do no more than lie there, dozing from time to time.

After what seemed like aeons, someone knocked at my bedroom door.

"Maria, why aren't you yet up? It's already nine o'clock," Maman called from outside. I tried to respond but nothing emerged from my mouth except a faint groan.

Maman opened the door and peered in. The curtains were still drawn and she had to accustom her eyes to the gloom.

"What's wrong, Maria? Why aren't you out of bed? Are you ill?"

She came into my bedroom and pulled back the curtains of one window. The glare was unbearable and I shielded my eyes with my arm. Maman pulled the curtains again and moved across fast to my bedside. She sat on the bed and put a hand on my brow.

"Why, child, you're burning up with fever. What on earth can this be?"

"I feel very ill, Maman. I can't get up," I croaked.

Maman soaked a handkerchief in lavender water and placed it on my forehead. The cooling sensation was comfortable against my scorching brow. Maman asked me to open my mouth and peered in.

"Your throat is quite red and sore. I don't like the look of this. We must ask the doctor to come and see you."

Maman brought me some water and held me up while I tried to drink some but it felt like thorns scouring my throat as it went down. I lay back, exhausted and fell into a troubled slumber. Again, I had the dream where I was falling into a chasm and no one could help me. Again, Vincentello was watching without sympathy in the background. I cried out and woke with a jolt.

Soon afterwards, Maman brought Doctor Molinari into my room.

"I can't thank you enough, Doctor, for interrupting your Christmas Day to attend to Maria. But I'm very worried about her."

The doctor sat on my bed. "Now, Maria, let's find out what's the matter with you."

He placed a hand on my brow, then asked me to open my mouth and examined my throat. Finally he opened the top button of my nightdress and listened to my chest with his stethoscope. Was that rasping noise really coming from my lungs? He redid the button and pulled the coverlet over me.

Signalling to my mother they went into the corridor but left the door ajar.

Only snatches of their conversation came to me through the door and through my fever.

"Can't yet venture a precise diagnosis...possibly diphtheria... even a meningitis...keep her warm...plenty of liquids...dose with powders...on no account must she be distressed...come back this evening." I heard my mother's low voice in reply, but couldn't make out what she said. I passed in and out of consciousness.

After that, I moved into a twilight world where I couldn't distinguish between nightmares and reality. When I awoke from one of my terrible dreams the sense of relief was quickly replaced by terror as the walls and ceiling of my bedroom closed in on me and threatened to crush me. Sometimes, I was aware of another person in the room with me. They leant towards me and their face fragmented into a million pieces which I couldn't piece together again into a human form. A hand pressed into my back and pushed me forward. Strong fingers prised open my lips and poured in a hell-draught of bitter gall. I gagged but they hold my mouth closed. Were they trying to poison me? I struggled but the weakness in my limbs prevented me from fighting my tormentors.

Sometimes I had a moment of lucidity and I saw Maman keeping vigil by my bedside, her sewing in her hand. When she saw I was awake she smiled and held me up so I could drink some water to ease my parched throat. But soon after I had lain back on the pillows the nightmare started again and I couldn't tell if I was awake or asleep. I wasn't aware of time passing. It could have been a few seconds or epochs. As I twisted in my sweat-soaked sheets, wars could have been fought and lost, empires grown and crumbled and oceans dried and filled up again.

All of a sudden, I awoke one morning and I knew it was over. The curtains were drawn tight but I sensed the sun was shining outside, the weather was frosty and my fever had burned itself out. My body was as insubstantial as seeds of thistledown carried on the breeze, and I was as weak as a new-born lamb. But that was how I felt: re-born. How good it was to be alive!

I turned my head and Maman leant towards me. She took my hand and put her other hand on my brow and then she smiled. Her face was pallid but her eyes glowed.

"You're back with us, Maria. Thank God. At one point, we thought we had lost you. You have had meningitis, Doctor Molinari says, and you're lucky to have pulled through."

"How long?" I rasped.

"Five days. Vincentello has been very worried about you. He left on Christmas Day as soon as we realised you were very ill but he has sent to ask after you every day."

Vincentello. The memory of my nightmares flooded back as did the thought that he was the man I had to marry. Fatigue sat on my limbs like hoar frost. I thought of Raphaël and the tears welled up.

"You've been rambling for some of the time, calling out," Maman said. "But we couldn't make out what you said."

That was a relief, for I was sure that in my fever I called upon Raphaël. I snuggled down under the covers and closed my eyes.

"That's right. Sleep now. I'll look in on you later." She closed the door behind her and the tears squeezed out from beneath my eyelids, wetting the pillow.

***

I had to stay in bed for a further week until Doctor Molinari considered me well enough to get up. Sophia had heard I was ill and came to ask after me several times. When Maman considered the time was right she showed Sophia up to my room.

"Now, don't stay too long, Sophia," Maman said. "She's still weak and, above all, she mustn't be upset." Sophia nodded and sat on the bed next to me, taking my hand. She smiled at me and I gave her a pale smile back. We had hardly seen each other since our quarrel and I didn't know what to say to her.

"We've all been so worried about you, Maria. Everyone has been asking after you and Monsieur le Curé even said prayers for you in church. Orso has been beside himself."

Orso. I would rather have had him than Vincentello. But neither of them could compare with Raphaël.

I sighed. "I'm very grateful for everyone's concern. I suppose it's not yet common knowledge but my father says I must marry my cousin Vincentello. That's what he was doing here on Christmas Eve – surveying the goods." The corners of my mouth turned downwards.

Sophia frowned and pressed my hand. "I had so hoped that you and Orso might marry. You would have been my sister then. He'll be devastated when he knows."

"Please don't say anything yet. My father will want to announce it formally and he would be furious if it were already known around the village."

Sophia nodded. "And what about Raphaël? He came back to the village yesterday and has a meeting with Papa today before the school year begins about council business."

"He won't know anything about my illness or this business with Vincentello. Will your father tell him I have been ill?"

"I expect so; the village has talked of little else for a week. Maria, your mother told me not to upset you and I don't want to. But you really must put Raphaël out of your mind. After all, your parents have decided that you have to marry Vincentello. You can't go against their wishes."

"Don't remind me," I replied, turning my head on the pillow, the tears stinging my eyes. "Would you do something for me, Sophia?"

"If it's something that is in my power to do, I'll do it gladly."

"Please would you go tomorrow to the urn at Santa Giulia's

shrine? You know the one – where you and I used to put notes for each other. Raphaël and I hide letters to each other there. He's sure to have written one to me and I'm desperate to know how he is. He'll no doubt worry about me when he knows I've been ill and I'm still unable to hold a pen. But would you please tell him when you see him, as you're bound to, that I'm much better. That's all."

"That's all?" Sophia said. "You persist in this misguided fling with Raphaël. Do you know what you're doing, Maria?"

"Please, Sophia. Just this once. I'll never ask you to do anything again."

She sighed. "Very well. But this is the one and only time I'll do this. I will *not* act as a go-between. You know how I feel about the whole business. You would have been much better off with Orso; now you have to marry Vincentello. No good will come of this." She shook her head.

"Thank you, Sophia. This means so much to me."

Maman came to the door. "That's long enough, Sophia. We mustn't tire her out when she's still weak."

"Of course, Madame Orsini. I was just leaving, anyway."

She kissed me on both cheeks and walked towards the door. She paused on the threshold and looked at me with an expression that I couldn't interpret. She followed Maman down the stairs and the heavy front door closed on her.

Chapter 12

Adorable Maria,

Imagine my dismay when I arrived back in Zaronza and found that you had been ill. If only I had known that your life was in danger, I would certainly have come back to Zaronza without delay.

All the time I was with my family I missed you: your violet scent that would enable me to pick you out among a thousand women; the light touch of your fingers on my arm; your mellow voice; your kisses like the wing of a butterfly brushing my lips; but above all your rippling, raven hair that flows like a dark waterfall when you untie it.

I haven't yet mentioned our love to my parents but I think my mother suspects something. She is so perceptive and knows her son well. I longed to confide in her but thought it more prudent to wait until our future is certain.

Please forgive the brevity of this letter. On my return I have had so little leisure since I must prepare my classes for the new term. I long to see you and to know that you are really better, my dearest love.

I was out of bed and sitting, dressed, in the chair in my room near the window when Sophia handed me the note. With greedy hands, I tore open the envelope and devoured the contents. Sophia sat on my bed watching.

"Did you find it behind the urn?" I asked.

"I didn't need to. When I returned home yesterday, Raphaël had already talked to Papa and knew about your illness. He was unable to contain himself." She looked away. "He told me about your love and I said to him that I already knew. He begged me to give you this letter. I agreed this time, but, as you know, I don't want to become a go-between. I have already compromised myself enough in this affair which I don't approve of, and I told Raphaël as much. Don't ask any more of me, Maria."

I looked into her face, which was closed and severe. Nodding, I changed the subject with difficulty and we talked of unimportant things until it was time for her to go. Why Sophia was so much against my relations with Raphaël I couldn't work out. But I saw that if I wanted to keep her friendship I had to remain silent about it. I had no one I could confide in: I was alone again. In a day or so I would be well enough to go out again and then I would have to tell Raphaël about Vincentello before it became common knowledge. He would know what to do.

***

After another week, the doctor said I could go out again but not too far and certainly not to tire myself out. It was almost four weeks since I had last seen Raphaël and I couldn't wait much longer. Maman allowed me to go to see Sophia and stood at the gate looking down the alley as I crossed the square. The fatigue was still heavy on my limbs and I was tired to my bones by early evening. I had eaten barely anything for more than a week during my illness and even now was able to stomach only light broth and rusks. The thought of a large meal still filled me with disgust but Maman was doing her best to feed me up. My cheeks had hollowed out, there were dark rings around my eyes and my dresses hung on me. But as I walked across the square and filled my lungs with fresh air, the life flooded back into me. Only the shadow of my future on the horizon prevented me from being happy.

As for Vincentello, I hadn't seen anything of him since Christmas Eve. Despite Maman's claim that he had often asked after me, he clearly didn't care. I daresay he was waiting to see if I survived or not, so that he could make other marriage plans if necessary. That wasn't the behaviour of an ardent bridegroom-to-be. I dismissed him from my mind and thought of Raphaël instead. When would I be able to see him again?

The opportunity came sooner than I had dared to hope. Papa went away from home on business and Maman had retired to her room with another of her headaches. I worried about her a little. They came more and more often and, since my illness, she too had seemed tired and worn out. She had used herself up nursing me. Now I had to try to help her as much as I could. I wondered if I should ask Sophia to teach me how to sew and cook properly. She would have been more patient than Maman.

I dared not hope that Raphaël would be at our meeting place, even though it was a Wednesday afternoon. I struggled up the hill and was quite out of breath as the shepherd's hut came into view. A slight drizzle was falling but it wasn't cold. As I approached, a shadow stepped out from behind the walls. I shrank back, afraid it wasn't him, but how could I have mistaken his slim silhouette and that ink-black hair?

Raphaël ran towards me, stumbling on a loose stone, and caught me into his arms. We stood pressed close together for a few minutes before he stepped back and held me at arm's length.

"I've missed you so much. My poor darling, what a terrible time you must have been through in your illness. I was desperate when I heard about it but I couldn't do anything. I've been on the point of coming to your house a hundred times to ask for news but the thought of your father and of the harm it might do to you kept me away. Did Sophia give you my letter?"

"Yes, she did, and I was so grateful for it. But she doesn't want to act as a go-between."

"I know. She made that clear to me at the time. I can't blame her and I wouldn't presume on my friendship with her."

I frowned at that, but he didn't seem to notice. He

continued, "I left letters for you at our hiding place in the hope that you might be able to go there, but each time I went I saw that they were still there."

"You can't imagine how much I wanted to go to the shrine and find your letters. But this is almost the first occasion I've been able to go out. Maman watches me very closely, and it's only good luck that has allowed me to get away this afternoon."

He nodded. I had to tell him about Vincentello but the words stuck in my throat. I didn't know how to begin.

"I have something to tell you. Let's go and sit down."

We entered the ruined hut and sat on a large stone underneath the part of the roof that was still in place. This gave at least some shelter from the drizzle.

I took his hand in mine, put my head on his shoulder and told. When I had finished, he remained silent, his regular breathing the only sound. But he pressed my hand so hard it almost hurt.

Raising my head from his shoulder, I looked into his face. His eyebrows were drawn together and there was a deep furrow between his eyes. His face was like granite, his full lips pressed against each other.

He turned to me. "You couldn't have given me worse news. When is this wedding going to take place?"

"I don't know yet. It seems that Papa has arranged everything with Vincentello, but the date of our engagement isn't yet fixed, partly because of my illness I suppose. I imagine this would have been discussed already, if I hadn't suddenly fallen ill. But I can't imagine that Papa will delay announcing it much longer. And no doubt Vincentello can't wait to take possession of his new property."

I buried my face in my hands and the hot tears soaked my palms.

Raphaël stood and struck his fist into his palm. His eyes flashed. I didn't think I had ever seen him look so handsome.

"We have a little time, then, but only a little. What can we do? I must think. I'm sure there must be something, some course we can take to fight off this threat."

He took my hands and kissed my damp palms. "Don't worry, my love. I'll think of something. Will you meet me here again next week? In the meantime, write to me if there's any further news. I'll go to the shrine early every morning to check our hiding place."

I nodded and he pulled me up into his embrace.

"I must go now, Raphaël. Maman has another of her headaches and I'm starting to be worried about her. Papa is away from home, but he'll come back this evening and I must try to help Maman by preparing his supper."

"You're so good," he said. "I don't know your cousin but I'm sure he's not worthy of your little finger."

We clasped each other for a moment and then I set off downhill towards the village. At the bend in the path, I turned around and saw Raphaël pacing about striking at the undergrowth with his stick. I continued and he was lost to sight.

***

It was as I had suspected. My father and Vincentello had arranged everything between them.

The day after my meeting with Raphaël, Papa announced to my mother and me at lunch, "Now that Maria is well again, we shouldn't delay our plans any longer. I have spoken with Vincentello, and he's content for the marriage to be in late March. We're now at the end of January, which gives you two months to prepare. The engagement will take place at the end of February."

I gasped. So soon? Maman didn't say anything but nodded in agreement. I wasn't even to be consulted. It was all agreed without me. Yet again, I felt like a barrel of olives to be weighed, priced and sold to the highest bidder. I said nothing.

What could I have said? My parents knew I was opposed to this marriage but my wishes didn't count for anything. What counted was the family honour, keeping the family possessions together – acting in the family's best interests. That word, "interests," had come to spell misery and bitterness for me. I never wanted to hear it again. Was this how it had to be for women? Couldn't we exercise any free will, any independent judgement? But then a thousand years of Corsican history weighed against me. I was like a straw chased before the wind, powerless to struggle against it.

After lunch, I couldn't escape to my bedroom as I craved, since Maman wanted to talk to me about the arrangements. I tried to feign interest but it was so hard when every fibre of my being wanted to resist. At last, she went off to see to something she had asked Annunciata to do, and I flew upstairs.

Dipping my pen in the inkwell I dashed off a note to Raphaël telling him the proposed dates. It was so hasty that blotches of ink spattered it. I sealed it and hurried downstairs to the hallway. I slipped out of the house, across the square and along the road to the stairway. A black figure was walking down the road ahead of me in the same direction. Madame Paoli. But she was far away enough not to hear my hurried footsteps and she didn't turn around. I felt about in the slot but nothing was there for me and I stuffed my note inside before running up the steps. Panting, I hurried home, counting the days until the following Wednesday.

***

It was a bright and blustery day, more like March than early February. The wind chased small cottony clouds across the sky and the hills on the other side of the bay were as clear as if they had been polished. Small fishing boats bobbed up and down on the waves. The sun warmed my back as I climbed the hill to the shepherd's hut. As ever, Raphaël was there first. He was smiling as he took my hands.

"I think I've found a solution," he said and my heart soared. He drew me into the hut away from the breeze. He had spread out his coat on the ground and we sat down on it, warmed by a patch of sunlight slanting through the broken roof. Raphaël put his arm around my shoulders.

"Now," he began. "When you left me last week, I was almost in despair. I knew I had to find a solution but, although I racked my brains, I couldn't think of anything that would get us out of this situation."

He paused. I nodded, willing him to go on.

"I received your note telling me about the dates," he continued. "My despair deepened since there's so little time. I couldn't sleep as I tossed in my bed trying to think of something. And then it came to me."

He paused again and looked into my eyes. "It's a risk, but one I'm willing to take, if you agree to it."

"What is it?" I asked, my heart pounding.

"I remembered a story my mother told me about an old Corsican custom. By a strange coincidence, it was during the last Christmas holidays when I was staying with my parents – and you were so ill, although I didn't know it – that she told me. A young man and woman who lived in the next village to my parents' fell in love but both families strongly disapproved of the match since they had been bitter enemies for many years. Their hostility stopped short of actual *vendetta*, but there was no question of a marriage between the two families."

"What happened to the lovers?"

"They decided to elope, only for one night, but they made sure everyone realised that was what they had done. They knew that when they returned, everyone would consider that they were effectively married. To preserve the family honour, the two families would have to accept the match. In fact, the young man would be bound to take her as his wife – if he didn't it would be a slur on the girl's honour and that of her family, and would certainly be grounds for her brothers to murder him."

"Is this what you're suggesting we should do?"

"Precisely, my love. We disappear together for one night and, when we return, we are considered man and wife and no one can object."

I thought of Papa. If anyone could find objections, he would.

"But how can we manage this – and when? My parents watch me closely. I have enough difficulty getting away to meet you."

"Don't worry, Maria. I'll arrange everything. I already have a plan. Your engagement party is fixed for the evening of the twenty-eighth of February, isn't it?"

I nodded.

"In that case, we must avoid doing anything to arouse suspicion in the time leading up to that date. The inspector is coming during that week and I have to do a lot of preparation, so we must leave it to the last minute. It would be better not to meet but we can write to each other from time to time. It must appear that you accept the engagement. Try to look resigned, even happy. The night of the twenty-seventh, go up to bed as normal but don't get undressed. I'll come for you in the early hours and you will leave a note for your parents telling them that we have eloped. When we return we'll marry properly before the mayor and, if you want, have a blessing in church as well."

My heart contracted as I thought of Papa's fury when he realised what we had done. I could only hope that he was as familiar with this custom as Raphaël's parents. After all, we were almost in the twentieth century, and while many Corsican traditions remained, French influence was increasing. Moreover, Zaronza was not one of the isolated villages of the Bozio, where these practices persisted. But I kept these thoughts to myself. Raphaël was so enthusiastic about the idea, and, even if it was a risk, we had to try it. It seemed the only course open to us if I was not to be condemned to a loveless marriage with Vincentello.

"How will I know when you come for me? It won't be easy to leave the house without my parents knowing. Papa always sleeps soundly, but Maman is a light sleeper. And the front door grates on the flagstones."

"I'll call beneath your window." He cupped his hands together and blew between his thumbs to produce a surprisingly authentic owl's shriek.

I laughed. "Where did you learn to do that?"

"Oh, during my misspent childhood in the Bozio. My friends and I would go around the village trying to scare the old people into thinking it was the spirits of the dead. I was always the most accomplished at it."

"And now you're a respectable pillar of the community in Zaronza."

He lay back on the coat and crossed his hands behind his head. "Not as respectable as all that. After all, I'm planning to elope with the daughter of one of the village's most illustrious citizens."

He smiled his crooked smile and pulled me down towards him, enfolding me in his arms. He kissed me with even more urgency than usual, covering my mouth, face and neck with his lips, and his hand slid down my side, brushing my breast.

I didn't stop him as it continued downwards. I was drunk with the thought that we would soon be together and no one would be able to come between us.

Much later, as the sun's rays slanted across the horizon and the chill of late afternoon rose, we parted. By then we really were man and wife, in all but name.

Chapter 13

It was hard to keep to Raphaël's plan that we shouldn't meet in the days leading up to my engagement party. We realised that it would be folly to tell anyone about it, but the secret almost burnt my lips when I was with Sophia. But I knew that she had always disapproved of my relations with Raphaël. She would have been even more disapproving if she knew what had happened the last time he and I met on the hillside. So I said nothing and pretended that I was resigned to my fate. She was a little wistful at times, which I took to be disappointment on Orso's behalf. She didn't mention him, except to say that he stayed in Bastia most of the time and came to visit their father less often.

Vincentello came over to see me a few times, but for the most part he was there to see my father and work out their business partnership. Proximity made me feel no warmer towards him. He was so lacking in social graces. How my parents didn't see that, or comment on it, I don't know. He was good-looking, but coarse, and seemed to think that I should rejoice in my good fortune in marrying him.

"The girls in my village are all jealous of you," he informed me.

"Is that so?" I replied, straightening my shoulders and raising my chin.

"Oh yes. But the combination of my lands and your father's possessions will make a powerful business interest. And, of course, I will gain a pretty young wife as well." He bowed, assuming that I would be grateful for the compliment.

I turned away and looked into the fire, straining to suppress the smile that came to my lips. What a fool the man was! But he would look even more foolish once Raphaël and I had carried out our plan.

"Your father certainly won't regret taking me on as his business partner," he continued. "I've got many good ideas that will surely result in greater profit. Your father will do well to follow them."

I didn't think Papa would take kindly to being told how he should run his business, but I kept this information to myself. None of it would happen anyway. I endured a few more minutes of Vincentello's chatter – he didn't seem to notice, or to care, whether I responded or not – and then he announced that he had to leave.

"Until Saturday," he said, pressing my hand to his lips. Saturday was to be the day of our engagement party. I had almost forgotten about it, since it wasn't going to take place. But I nodded and smiled, just as if I were looking forward to it as much as he was.

***

Raphaël and I hadn't written to each other since our last meeting, not wishing to draw attention to ourselves, and I had visited the shrine only once. Two days before we were due to carry out our plan, I decided to go and see if he had left a letter for me. Our elopement seemed unreal, and I wanted to reassure myself that it really would take place. Scrabbling in the slot, I found an envelope. Raphaël's note was very brief but at least it provided the assurance I craved.

My beautiful Maria,

Now you must truly believe that I am yours and yours only. I cannot wait for Friday, when I will prove it to you once and for all and we will be together forever. Take care, my darling Maria, until then.

I hid it in my sleeve as usual and climbed the steps. As I emerged onto the road, Madame Paoli was waddling past. I couldn't avoid her.

"Now, now, Maria," she said, wagging her finger at me. "I don't think you need to pray to Santa Giulia anymore. I told you that you would be married within the year, didn't I?" Her eyes twinkled and she tapped me on the hand.

"Good morning, Madame Paoli. You certainly did, and you're quite right that I no longer need to go to the shrine –" *(although for a quite different reason; after Saturday, Raphaël and I wouldn't have to hide our letters any more)* "– but I wanted to thank the saint for my good fortune. It would be rude not to." I almost choked on the words.

"Quite right. One should always be thankful for good fortune. Now, let me give you some advice about marriage. You should always let your husband think he's getting his own way. Make him believe he's the master and never cross him directly. In that way, you will be mistress of the house and he won't interfere in domestic matters. However, there's no reason why you shouldn't influence his business affairs. Let him think that your ideas are his. Plant the seed in his mind and it will grow."

Having given me her words of wisdom, she nodded and tottered off towards the bakery. I had to press my lips together to subdue the rising bubble of laughter. Poor Monsieur Paoli! There had never been any question of him thinking he was the master, either of the household or of his business affairs. Everyone knew who had always been in charge in that marriage.

I thought of my parents. While my father doubtless left domestic arrangements to Maman, I couldn't imagine him taking any advice from her, direct or indirect, on his business affairs – nor could I see her offering it. I felt Vincentello was unlikely to tolerate any interference from his wife, either. He wasn't very intelligent but he was arrogant and conceited; not a happy combination. I couldn't picture being married to a man like that, and was relieved that, thanks to Raphaël's plan, it wouldn't happen.

Much of the time was taken up with preparations for the engagement. I couldn't take it seriously and hummed under my breath as I helped Maman.

"You've seemed happier recently, Maria," Maman said. "I'm pleased that you have come to see sense. I know that your father is content too. It's in your own best interests to welcome this marriage and to be friendly to Vincentello. I'm sure he will turn out to be an asset to the family and support your father like a son."

A shadow crossed her face but it was soon gone again, and she turned her attention to her cooking.

Since I didn't share Maman's convictions about Vincentello's future, I said nothing.

***

Friday dawned misty and cold. I was awake long before first light, having been unable to sleep much. When I had dozed off, the dream about sliding into the chasm recurred. This was ridiculous! Raphaël would come to take me away from all this. There was nothing to fear. My parents and Vincentello would no doubt be furious when they found out, but they wouldn't be able to do anything. They would have to accept the situation.

The day dragged past, despite my being kept busy helping Maman. I kept going out into the corridor to look at the clock in the hall but the hands crawled around the face. A delicious tingling in my stomach prevented me from eating much, despite Maman's entreaties.

"You really must eat up, Maria. You still haven't regained all the weight you lost during your illness. I would like to see your face fill out again."

"I'm sorry, Maman. It's the excitement."

She smiled.

At last, supper was over. Maman settled by the fire with some sewing. Papa, content that all the necessary arrangements for the engagement were well in hand, went to his study as usual to look over some papers.

"May I go to bed, Maman, if there's nothing you need me for? I'm tired and want to be at my best tomorrow evening."

"Of course, that's a very sensible idea. I think an early night would do us all good."

I kissed Maman and climbed the stairs, shielding my candle against the draught. As agreed with Raphaël, I didn't undress but got into bed and pulled the covers over me. The long vigil then began until Raphaël came to fetch me. My heart was beating so hard that I could almost hear it, but I forced myself to be calm. I would have liked to read a little to pass the time, but if Maman saw the candlelight under my door, she would have surely come in and might have noticed that I had not undressed.

After a while, Maman came upstairs. She paused outside my door and I was afraid she would open it, but after a moment her footsteps moved on. A little later, Papa's heavier tread echoed in the hallway as he climbed the creaking staircase. I hoped I would be able to go down it later on without making so much noise. For a few minutes, a gentle murmur of voices floated down the corridor. It stopped, and the house was silent apart from the clock ticking in the hallway and the movement of the floorboards as they settled.

When I was sure my parents were asleep, I re-lit my candle and stole out of bed to my writing table.

I hesitated about what to write, but then decided that simple honesty was best:

Dearest Maman and Papa,

When you read this I shall be far from here. Raphaël Colombani and I have eloped. We love each other and intend to marry. I am sorry for the trouble I know this will cause you, but I cannot marry Vincentello.

I don't love him and never can. I will always be your devoted daughter but I must marry the man I love.

Your loving,

Maria.

I folded the paper and laid it on my pillow, where Maman would find it in the morning. My father's reaction would be terrible, I was sure. Maybe he would be tempted to disown me, in which case Raphaël and I would have to leave Zaronza. I wondered if our elopement would affect his career, in any case? A chill wave washed over me; we should have thought of this. But I was carried along by my desire to avoid this marriage at all costs and to be with Raphaël. Perhaps Raphaël had thought about it but considered it worth the risk and didn't want me to worry about it. In that case, he was brave and I loved him all the more for it.

The clock in the hall chiming the hour broke into my thoughts. Two o'clock. Raphaël would be here soon. Making as little noise as possible, I gathered a few belongings, which I put into a bag, and fastened my thick shawl around my shoulders. I sat on the bed, my heart thudding, and waited for his call.

The clock chimed three and still I waited. Four o'clock, five. Where was he? He should have been here long ago. I opened the window and peered out, but all was darkness. I went back and sat on the bed, wringing my hands. What had happened? Why hadn't he come? Had he had an accident? The very thought chilled me to the bone. Another idea then crept into my brain. Maybe he had had second thoughts. Perhaps the risk was too great after all. I knew how much his post here at Zaronza meant to him. Was he afraid he might have to give it up? Was it possible that he never really loved me after all, that he *was* the womaniser I once suspected him of being?

These thoughts succeeded each other like clouds scudding across a March sky. I no longer knew what was truth and what wasn't. But, as six o'clock struck, I knew that he wasn't coming, that my hopes were dashed and that there was no escape for me. I continued to sit there as the rosy glow of dawn filtered through the curtains. A heavy weight in my stomach was pressing me down. He had betrayed me and abandoned me to my fate. I was too numb even for tears.

Maman and Papa began to stir and the familiar sounds of the household waking up came to my ears. It was too late. I had to go through with this dreaded engagement. With frozen fingers, I picked up my note to my parents from the pillow, ripped it into tiny pieces, and then put it into my pocket to burn later.

"What *is* the matter with you this morning, Maria?" asked Maman as I struggled to swallow my coffee and bread and jam. "You were so cheerful yesterday but today you seem like a completely different person. You really must try to look happier when our guests arrive this evening."

I nodded, afraid that if I tried to speak the tears would come gushing out. Maman sighed and turned back to her work.

All day, I moved about like an automaton. My limbs were as if weighted down with lead. I couldn't believe what Raphaël had done to me. But I had to stare the truth in the face.

It was time to change. I put on the violet dress that Sophia had altered for me. It was a little large for me since my illness but I didn't mind. It could have been sackcloth and ashes for all I cared. I clasped my pearls around my neck and slid my silver bracelet over my wrist.

Maman put her head around the door. "Maria, please hurry. Our guests will be here soon."

I walked down the staircase as if going to my execution.

I stepped into the salon, where a fire was blazing. Vincentello was already there and smiled at me as I took my place at his side. The first guests arrived. Since this was mainly a family affair, we had invited very few: some village notables, including the mayor and Sophia, an old aunt of Maman's on her mother's side, some distant cousins and Vincentello's sisters. Only one of them came. The other pleaded a previous engagement in l'Île

Rousse. They were not a close family, but I already knew that.

Vincentello and I must have made an odd couple. He was grinning like a monkey while I couldn't force the smallest smile. My father frowned at me but said nothing.

Sophia kissed me on the cheek but moved away as if she didn't want to talk to me. She looked at me strangely, a haunted expression on her face. Orso was invited but hadn't come, preferring to stay in Bastia.

When all the guests had arrived, Papa gestured to Vincentello and he kissed me in front of the assembled company. I would sooner be kissed by Monsieur Agostino, the old Marseille bore. Maman handed me the traditional plate of *fritelli*[2]. I offered it to Vincentello and everyone ate one to seal the engagement. I forced one down; it tasted of sawdust.

Now we were as good as married. It only remained to go before the mayor for the official ceremony and then the church blessing. In some parts of Corsica, the family dispensed with those ceremonies and the couple were already considered man and wife. I would have preferred this to the sham of a ceremony, but Maman and Papa insisted on going through the whole rigmarole. Even so, an engagement was binding and couldn't easily be broken without loss of honour.

Oh, Raphaël, why did you desert me when I needed you most? Where were you?

Vincentello squeezed my arm and I turned my head to face him. At that moment, I knew I would never feel anything but loathing for him.

---

[2] Fritters made of chestnut flour.

PART 2 – DISENCHANTMENT 1900-1916

Chapter 14

May 1900

It was late May, and Vincentello and I had been married for two months. The sun was already hot by midday, but the countryside was still green before the heat of summer scorched the fresh colours into brown and the *maquis* crackled underfoot. The aromatic scent of the hillsides behind the village wafted over the arbour. I was sitting beneath the vine in the shade, sewing baby clothes in my inelegant stitch.

In that time, my life had changed in some ways. In others, it had scarcely altered at all. We lived in my parents' house and occupied my old bedroom. This was at my father's insistence. I might have hoped for a home of my own since I was still subject to my parents' scrutiny and approval. At least Vincentello didn't tell me what to do all the time; I suspected he didn't care enough. In any case, he was anxious to ingratiate himself with Papa. Still, though I regarded having to share my bed with Vincentello as a violation of my privacy and my girlhood bedroom, it was better than living with him in his own family residence, which was smaller than ours. It seemed to suit him, too, since he thought he would save money that way.

"This is a very convenient arrangement, Maria," he said. "I'll be able to rent the house to a suitable family and it will be a very welcome addition to our income."

But he hadn't yet done anything about it, and the house remained empty. And he couldn't sell it, because you never sell property in Corsica but pass it on to the next generation. When I reminded him about the house he always said, "I will do it in good time. Remember, I'm busy working with your father."

Surely it wasn't so difficult to find a tenant for the property? I was sure I could have managed it quite well, but I knew that it would injure Vincentello's pride to suggest that he allow me to see to it. Any suggestion that he wasn't quite up to the mark was regarded as a mortal insult.

I laid my work in my lap and enjoyed the warm breeze breathing over the nape of my neck. Raphaël used to kiss me there. Raphaël. For a moment, my heart expanded as I thought of him. It contracted again as I recalled the crushing blow of the night before my engagement.

I hadn't seen him again since then, and took great pains to avoid the places in the village where I might meet him. Even if he had come to the house I would have refused to see him. I was so angry with him and so hurt. He had raised my hopes only to break them like a glass shattering on flagstones. Once he had taken what he wanted, he had abandoned me and betrayed me. That's how men are, I thought. And I assumed that, in the end, he considered the risk to his career too great. After all, schoolteachers were supposed to be models of respectability and morality. Running away with a woman wouldn't have been a good example to his pupils.

So I had resolved to put him out of my mind and to lock and bar that part of my heart. But sometimes he came creeping back in, and it was very hard. The hardest part was when I discovered I was expecting a child a few weeks after my marriage. I was gripped by sickness and nausea in the morning, and excessive tiredness throughout the day. Doctor Molinari had said, "This is a little too soon after your illness for my liking, Maria. You must look after yourself. Above all, no shocks or strenuous exercise." But I felt quite well – as well as I imagined one ever feels in that condition. The sickness had passed, but I was still drained, and the smell of onions or garlic frying made me gag. That was why Maman had pushed me out onto the terrace to breathe the fresh air.

"I don't want you being sick on the clean floor," she said.

"Annunciata has only just washed it."

Whether the child was Raphaël's or Vincentello's I couldn't tell. What did it matter? One was a deserter, the other a boor. Neither was the ideal choice of father for my child.

I cast my mind back to the wedding. I wondered how many brides had gone to their wedding, as I had done, like an animal going to a sacrifice. Papa had paid for a photographer to take pictures of the wedding party, first outside the town hall and then after the church blessing. The photographs were on display in the salon but I couldn't bear to have one in my bedroom (it was still *my* bedroom even if he shared it with me). Papa and Vincentello were wreathed in smiles. Maman looked serious, but then she always did. I just looked like a sulky, bad-tempered schoolgirl, although I felt as if my life had ended.

After that there was the wedding night. I shuddered to think of it. Vincentello had drunk too much, no doubt celebrating his good fortune. I lay still and thought of the view from the tower, the scent of the *maquis*, the sound of birdsong at dawn, anything to take my mind off his coarse fumbling and groping under my nightdress. He was not so drunk that he was unable to perform, but thankfully he didn't seem to notice that I was no longer a virgin. When he had finished, he rolled onto his side and after a while his heavy breathing told me he was asleep.

There was no tenderness, no words of love, but then I didn't expect anything like that from him. This was all a business transaction for him. For that reason, I was careful to smear the contents of a small phial of pig's blood on the sheets. Nothing would have pleased me more than for him to declare the marriage invalid, but Papa would have turned me out and I would have had nowhere to go. I was a prisoner, for life.

The tears welling up, I took up my sewing again and closed my mind to these thoughts.

***

Vincentello was always prying into my things. He opened the cupboard in my bedroom and rustled my dresses about and rummaged amongst my linen in the drawers.

"I do wish you wouldn't do that, Vincentello. You make everything in a mess and then I have to tidy it all up again. What are you looking for?"

He smiled, but it didn't reach his eyes, which were cold. "Oh, I just want to make sure you have no secrets from your husband."

My heart quickened. What had he heard?

"Of course not. What secrets could I have? I was just an innocent girl when we married."

He said nothing but continued to fumble amongst my clothes.

"Aha!" he said.

I craned over his shoulder, trying to see what he had found. He pulled something out from beneath the folded shawls on the shelf above my gowns. My box! The one I hid Raphaël's letters in! I had thought it would be safe up there, but then I had no idea that even Vincentello would stoop to search amongst my possessions. I held my breath.

"What have we got here?" he said. "Maybe there's money inside. Eh, Maria?" He shook it. The bundle of letters slid around and the pebbles rattled. I had moved the bits of jewellery the box formerly contained to the inlaid casket that my parents had given me on our engagement.

"I can assure you that there's nothing of interest to you. It contains some childhood keepsakes, nothing more."

"And if they are nothing more, why did you hide the box up there?"

"I didn't hide it, Vincentello. I simply put it away so that there would be room for your possessions as well. After all, this is your bedroom too." It sickened me to say that, but I didn't want him know about those letters.

"Where's the key to your childhood treasures, then?"

"I don't know, it's got lost and I can't find it." My hand involuntarily went to my neck where the gilt chain hung, concealed by my collar. I took it off when I undressed at night, in case he asked about it.

He moved towards me, the smile gone from his lips, which were transformed into narrow, straight lines. I shrank back.

Someone knocked at the door.

"Come in," I said, my heart beating like a frightened rabbit.

"I'm sorry to disturb you," Papa said. "Vincentello, Jean Cesari has arrived and we must go over this contract with him before he leaves."

"Yes, of course, Father." Vincentello placed the box on the bed, and hastened to follow Papa downstairs. At the door he paused and looked back at me. Not a flicker of affection crossed his face.

I closed my eyes and took a deep breath. I should have destroyed Raphaël's letters. What were they to me now, anyway? But somehow I couldn't bring myself to do it. Even so, it was too dangerous to keep them in my room, I saw that now.

Waiting until I was sure they were safely installed in Papa's study, I unlocked the box, took out the packet of letters and tiptoed up to the attic. The door stuck on the floorboards and I had to push it hard to open it. It scraped against the floor and the unoiled hinges creaked as the door gave. I waited, the letters pressed to my chest, but no sound rose from downstairs. I groped across the floor, only a small *oeil de boeuf* window lighting my way. In the corner of the attic was a heavy chest, covered in dust, which I knew contained some old velvet curtains.

Before raising the lid, I wondered if I should take another look at the letters, and my hand was halfway to the ribbon tied around them. But no. There wasn't enough time. What if Vincentello were to come upstairs? In any case, it was no good raking over the coals of the past. I lifted the lid, wrapped the letters and the key to the box in the smooth curtain material, and rearranged the curtains around them so that the tell-tale hump disappeared. I draped an old blanket over the chest to hide the marks in the dust.

Vincentello never came up to the attic, and in any case he would have a hard job finding the letters amidst so much jumble. Even so, I promised myself that I would hide them in a safer place at the first opportunity. In the meantime, I hoped he might have forgotten about the box, but, knowing him, that was unlikely. I hurried down to the kitchen.

***

Sure enough, after supper Vincentello came up to my room. The box was still on the bed, where I had thought it prudent to leave it. He picked it up and shook it.

"Well, have you found the key?"

"No. I told you, I've lost it."

Vincentello reached into his pocket for his knife, unfolded it, and inserted the blade into the lock. He jiggled it around for a while until the lock gave with a click, and the lid sprang open. Emptying the contents onto the bed, he rummaged through them, fingering the seashells and pebbles, and unfolding the notes from Sophia.

"Is that all?" he snarled.

"What else did you expect? I told you it only contained childhood keepsakes."

He pursed his lips, flung the notes back on the bed, and left the room. I breathed out, and a wave of relief washed over me. I gathered up the scattered items and Sophia's notes, and replaced them in the box.

The next morning, when Vincentello and Papa went out, I took the box up to the attic, unearthed the letters, put them inside and wrapped the box in the material, taking care to cover any traces again. Now Vincentello had seen what was in the box, I didn't think he would have any further interest in it. But

I would have to find a secure hiding place. I went downstairs and threw the key into the well.

***

Sophia and I hadn't seen each other very much since the wedding. When we had, a distance remained between us. Anyway, it was not considered proper for a married woman to run around the village gossiping, even though I had little else to do. Maman treated me like a china doll and insisted that I rest all the time. If I so much as bent down to pick up a handkerchief she scolded me. There was no question of taking a walk up to the tower. Really, despite my condition, I wasn't made of glass. And it was so dull sitting about all the time.

So I resolved to go and see Sophia anyway. I had a good excuse: I wanted her to help me with the baby's clothes. The simple sewing was not too difficult for me and I was becoming more skilled with practice. But more advanced stitches were still beyond me, and embroidery was just a distant vision.

Maman watched me walk across the square, just as she had done when I was convalescing in January. I approached Sophia's kitchen door, which was ajar as usual in the afternoon heat. I stopped short. Gulps and sniffs issued from the room. Someone was sobbing. I pushed the door a little. Sophia's head was on the table and her shoulders were heaving.

"Why, Sophia, what on earth's the matter?"

I crossed the threshold and put my hand on her arm. She raised a blotchy face disfigured by tears, her eyes red and sore. She sat up and dabbed at her face with a handkerchief that was already soaked. I took mine from my pocket and offered it to her.

I drew up a chair and waited for her to calm down. She hiccupped a few times and took a deep breath.

"I heard this afternoon…" she began.

"What did you hear, Sophia?" I squeezed her hand.

"Papa told me that Raphaël Colombani is going to leave the village. He has been appointed to a post in his own village back in the Bozio. Papa was very surprised since he's done such good things with the school. Raphaël wouldn't give a reason but he was adamant that he had to go. So a new schoolmaster will be appointed and he will start after the summer break."

I closed my eyes. I had thought I no longer felt anything for Raphaël and had resolved never to see him again. But my stomach contracted and the tears stung my eyes.

"I know you loved him, Maria, but now you're a married woman. I always told you there was no future for you with him, anyway."

I bowed my head to hide the tears.

"Yes, you did," I said, biting back all the things I wanted to say.

"He was such a good friend to me," Sophia continued. "He loaned me books, he taught me Italian, he was *interested* in me and thought I was intelligent. He respected my opinions and talked to me about all sorts of topics. What shall I do without him?"

Yes, I thought, what indeed? And what would I do? Raphaël had injured me to the quick and proved that he was faithless, but I did love him. Now I was shackled to a man I could never love.

We sat there, wrapped in our thoughts, as the sound of dogs barking and cocks crowing flowed in through the open door.

Chapter 15

Sophia and I didn't have much to say to each other after her revelation. I sat with her for a while, but my back ached terribly from the hard chair and a small niggling pain was starting up in the pit of my stomach.

Sophia's reaction to Raphaël leaving was stronger than I would have expected. Had there been something between them after all? Raphaël always swore there wasn't, but then he went on to prove he couldn't be trusted after that. So I didn't know whom or what to believe anymore. It was all in the past, anyway, and it was best if Raphaël left the village.

Crossing the square, the pain in my stomach became more intense. I assumed it was the heavy lunch that Maman had insisted I should eat. "After all, you're eating for two now," she'd said. My appetite had still not completely returned after my illness, but I forced myself to finish my plateful.

As I went along the corridor to the kitchen to find Maman, a sudden burst of pain made me double up. Something wet slid down my leg. I touched my ankle and, bringing my fingers up to my face, saw that they were covered in blood. I crumpled onto the floor.

"Maman! Maman!" I screamed.

She dashed into the corridor. "Maria! What is it? Are you in pain?"

"I have a terrible pain here." I gripped my lower abdomen. "And look…" I held up my blood-stained fingers.

Maman went white. "Santa Giulia!" she exclaimed. "You're having a miscarriage. Quickly, if we get you to bed we might be able to stop it in time."

Annunciata, alerted by the noise, appeared on the threshold

of the kitchen.

"Prepare a warming pan and bring extra sheets," Maman ordered. "Heat up some water as well, and then run for Doctor Molinari."

Annunciata hesitated.

"Hurry up!" Maman shouted. "We have no time to lose!"

I had never heard her raise her voice like that. Annunciata jumped and withdrew into the kitchen where she started banging about.

Maman helped me along the corridor and up the stairs. A trail of bloodspots accompanied us. Maman pulled off my dress and wiped off as much blood as she could. I was helpless and racked with sharp pains in my stomach. She eased my nightdress over my head and gently laid me in bed, tucking the bedclothes loosely over me.

"Pull up your knees. There might still be time."

I did as she said, but the pain was almost unbearable and the sheet beneath me was sodden with blood. The sweat broke out on my brow and I panted nonstop. Feverish activity went on around me but I was borne far away on waves of pain. I was aware of warmth on my side as someone slid the warming pan in next to me. I wanted to cry out but no sound came out of my mouth.

After that, I heard a male voice. The sheets were pulled from me and fingers were groping between my legs.

"No!" I screamed, thinking in my fever that it was Vincentello, and tried to push the fingers away, twisting my body away from them and the pain.

Little by little, the pain subsided and I stopped my feverish twisting. Someone held me up and put a glass to my lips. A dreamless sleep then descended on me and I slid into it as if into a pool of water.

I opened my eyes and a male face was bending towards me. I shrank back, thinking it was Vincentello, but my eyes focused and it was the kindly face of Doctor Molinari.

"How do you feel, Maria? Do you have any more pain?"

I shook my head and shifted in the bed. The sheets were dry; they must have changed them while I was asleep. The room was stifling. Someone had lit a fire. Maman was standing at the end of the bed.

Doctor Molinari sat down on the bed and patted my hand. He took a deep breath and looked me in the eyes. I swallowed.

"I'm sorry, Maria," he began, "but I have some bad news."

"I've lost the baby," I whispered. And tears slid from under my eyelids.

He nodded and cast his eyes down.

"Yes. We did everything we could but it was no good. I'm very sorry for you, Maria. I must admit that I was afraid of this, given your illness earlier in the year. It takes a long time to recover from a sickness like that – longer than you think – and you were still not strong. Also, with your family history…" he raised his hand, as if all this were obvious.

"What…?" I said, raising my head from the pillow, but I was still too weak to say the words.

Doctor Molinari turned to look at Maman, who flushed a little.

"I'll let your mother explain. But before that, I'll give you something to make you sleep. I will come back later to see how you are."

He made me swallow something and, again, I fell into welcome, soothing sleep.

***

I stayed in bed for a couple of days until the doctor said I was well enough to sit up. Papa and Vincentello were away from home when I lost the baby. But that was probably just as well. It was difficult to see what they could have done, anyway. Fortunately, I had my bed and my bedroom to myself. Maman had made up a bed in a guest room for Vincentello.

He came in to see me when I was sitting up in bed. "How do you feel?"

"Empty," I replied.

"My son," he said and shook his head.

"It was my son, too. And anyway, who knows? It might not have been a son; it might have been a little girl."

Vincentello looked at me as if the prospect was unthinkable. I refrained from telling him that the baby might not even have been his, although I was tempted to do so just to see his face.

Having nothing further to say, Vincentello left. Was that all he cared about? That he had lost his son? Didn't he feel an ounce of sympathy for me? I didn't ask for affection; after all, I didn't feel any for him. But he could have shown a little more concern, especially if he wanted a son. I winced at the thought of it, but I was his wife and his property so could do little to resist it.

As I considered the future of our marital life, Maman came in. She pulled the bedclothes around me, like she did when I was a little girl, and sat down on the bed beside me. For a few minutes, she was silent and looked into the fire, which was still burning despite the early summer heat.

"Maria, when Doctor Molinari was here two days ago, he mentioned something about our family history. He evidently assumed that you knew, but I have never told you, since it's still so painful to me." She pressed her lips together and folded her hands in her lap. "But now I owe you an explanation. You're grown up and you have been through something I wouldn't wish on any woman."

She paused and breathed in. I remained silent.

"When I married your father, I was much older than you. It was an arranged marriage, which is quite right and proper. I never expected anything else. Your father is a fine man, and our families were clear that it was a good match for both of us. Over the years, we have developed a strong respect and affection for each other."

She had never spoken like this before. I held my breath, not wishing to distract her, and willed her to go on.

"Not long after our marriage, I became pregnant. Your father was so happy that he would have a son – the first of many, we hoped. But it was not to be. I lost that baby, just as you've lost yours, and also the five that came after that. It appeared that I couldn't carry a baby to full term. I prayed to every saint I could think of, especially to Santa Giulia, who is known to favour the prayers of women. But they went unheard."

She blinked as a glint of something appeared in her eyes.

"But what about me, Maman?"

She smiled and put her hand over mine. "You were the last of my pregnancies. And by some miracle you clung on. You have always been determined, Maria, and I think that saw you through. Your father and I were both delighted. But, of course, you were a girl."

That told me everything. I was not the boy they had longed for.

"After you were born, I was unable to conceive again." Her voice shook. I saw the sadness behind her eyes.

I pressed her hand. I didn't know anything about this, of her miscarriages. But now I knew the terrible empty feeling and the bitter disappointment that she must have felt each time it had happened. All that promise ending in nothing but a welter of bloody sheets and an empty womb. Tears of sympathy stung my eyes.

"When you became pregnant, I had such hopes for a grandson, as did your father. But I'm afraid you might have inherited my failure to bear children."

I grew cold, despite the fire. Could this really be true? I felt nothing for my husband, but at least a mob of children would have brightened my days and brought noise and gaiety to this silent house with its echoing corridors. They would have given me something to live for, something to devote my life to.

"I think it's best if you don't say anything to Vincentello. It would be too disappointing for him. And, who knows, I may be wrong. I do hope that I am. Now, you should get some rest. Doctor Molinari says you will be up and about in a few days. You may do some simple chores but nothing too strenuous for a while until you have built up your strength again."

Maman left me to think about what she had just told me. Wrapped up in my own concerns, as I always had been, I had never realised that my parents could have had their own tragedies. Somehow it was difficult to credit one's own parents with feelings and hopes. I had always thought their main role in life was to prevent me from doing what I wanted. Now I saw why things had turned out the way they did. The biggest tragedy was that nobody was happy.

***

Gloom settled over the house like frost. Papa's face showed that he, too, feared I was unable to carry a baby. He said nothing but I imagined he saw the family name descending into obscurity with no one to hand the family possessions on to. The atmosphere was infectious, and sometimes I caught sight of Vincentello looking at me from under knitted brows. It was almost as if he thought I willed this misfortune on myself. I supposed he, too, was afraid that his chances of founding an Orsini dynasty were at risk of being thwarted.

I escaped to the tower to think or to see Sophia as often as I could. Vincentello didn't care as long as I was compliant in bed, which I was, through gritted teeth. Sophia and I sat in her kitchen, often saying little.

The end of the school year came and Raphaël would have left the village. I had not seen him since my marriage and didn't want to. I had never visited the shrine again. If he had written to me I didn't want to know about it. What good would it have done, in any case? What could he have said? He must have heard of my miscarriage through the mayor or someone else.

The whole village would have been aware of it, after all. I wondered if he ever speculated that he was the father, or if he assumed it must have been Vincentello. I would never know, but a small voice that I tried not to acknowledge hoped the baby was Raphaël's.

Chapter 16

1906

Six years had passed since my miscarriage. Despite Vincentello's efforts, I had not been able to conceive again, and I feared that it was my fate to be childless. My husband consoled himself with other 'ladies' at Santa-Lucia. He tried to keep it a secret but some of the village women delighted in hinting at it. It was nothing to me. As long as it kept him away from me, I was happy. We still lived with Maman and Papa; Vincentello's house at Casaccia remained empty. What a waste! But my opinions had no bearing on the matter.

Vincentello was so shiftless. It was not that he was lazy; rather that he was incapable of doing anything right. He had no sense of business and was always trying to get Papa to enter into ridiculous speculations. I knew they had arguments behind closed doors. I could see that Papa was disappointed in him but he couldn't do much about it. After all, he was the one who had been so keen to make him his son-in-law, and now he had to live with the consequences. At least Papa kept a firm hand on the reins.

I was more concerned about Maman, who had aged before her time. Little by little, with the help of Sophia and Annunciata, I had taken over the running of the house and was now a competent cook as well as a passable seamstress. If only I had taken the trouble to learn about these things earlier. Maman sat in the kitchen, her sewing on her lap, looking into the fire. Sometimes I saw her mouth working as if she was talking to someone. When I talked to her she looked at me blankly at first, and then recognition returned to her face, as if she was coming back from a long way away. Her hair was quite grey and she had put on a lot of weight.

Oh, Maman. If only I had known about your lost babies. You had no one to confide in, and I only ever thought of myself and my feelings. What had we come to?

***

One day, I was coming back from the village store and opened the door into the hall. It grated as usual on the flagstones. As I removed my headscarf in the echoing hallway, I was aware of a row coming from the direction of father's study. He and Vincentello were having another quarrel. This was becoming all too common.

My father was raising his voice and I could hear almost everything. "You imbecile! What have you done? Why didn't you consult me before taking this step? You could have ruined us. You might still have done."

Then a lower voice – Vincentello's – but I could only make out odd phrases: "Seemed a good plan at the time…have to move with the times…old-fashioned ways…can't continue."

"Can't continue! Can't continue!" Papa was shouting now. "What are you talking about? How do you think I've managed to run a successful business all these years? Tell me that, you young fool. You know absolutely nothing about business. You're not worthy of the Orsini name. I rue the day I negotiated your marriage contract with my daughter."

He couldn't have rued it more than I did, but this turn of events made me very anxious. Papa seemed unduly angry.

"You have no right to talk to me like that," Vincentello shouted. "What do you know about modern business affairs, anyway? I'm far better in touch than you are and I have good ideas for taking the business forward."

"Good ideas? You wouldn't know a good idea if it rose up and hit you in the face!"

"You're going too far, sir," Vincentello replied. "And as for this perfect match with your daughter, she's incapable of bearing a child, let alone a son. Who should rue it more than me?"

"I'm going too far?" Papa replied. "Listen to me, you young scoundrel. If you insult my daughter, you insult me and the family. *You* go too far. I won't tolerate this. I won't tolerate it, do you hear me?"

Papa was almost screaming. I had never heard him so angry.

For a moment there was silence, and then it sounded as if a heavy piece of furniture had fallen to the floor. The door of Papa's study opened and Vincentello appeared, his face as white as fresh *brocciu* cheese. We confronted each other for a moment.

"Your father. He seems to have had some kind of fit." Vincentello gestured towards the open door. I ran towards it, pushing him aside. Papa was lying on the floor next to his desk, his limbs contorted beneath him. Papers that he had dragged with him were scattered over the floor. His face was red but his lips were blue.

"Papa!" I rushed to him. "Papa, what is it? It's me, Maria. Can you hear me?"

His limbs twitched but he gave no sign of having heard me. Vincentello was standing in the doorway, his shoulders hunched.

"Go for the doctor. Go now, Vincentello!" I screamed.

He hesitated, and then pulled open the front door and set off at a run across the square.

I cradled Papa's head in my lap. His colour was high and he seemed to have stopped breathing. I loosened his collar and necktie. Maman appeared in the doorway, alerted by the noise. She screamed – a noise I had never heard before, like a wild animal in pain – and stumbled across the flagstones to throw herself on her knees beside him.

"Antonio, oh Antonio, Antonio," she crooned and pushed me aside. She smoothed his temples and kissed his face, but

Papa didn't move. She held his head and made soothing noises as if to a small child, stroking his face all the while. I sat back on my heels and waited.

A short time afterwards, Vincentello returned, panting, followed a few seconds later by an even more breathless Doctor Molinari, who was getting stouter by the day. He took Maman by the arms and almost lifted her into a chair. She was gasping like a cornered animal. The doctor opened his bag and took out his stethoscope. Pulling aside my father's shirt, he pressed the instrument to his chest. He felt his pulse. Finally, he drew a small mirror from his bag and held it before my father's nostrils. He looked me in the eyes and gave a small shake of his head. I already knew: Papa was dead.

I bowed my head and started to sob. Maman looked at the doctor with wide eyes.

"He will be all right, doctor, I'm sure. He's just a little tired. He works so hard, you know. A good night's sleep and he will feel much better. Don't you agree? There's very little wrong with him. He's strong. He would never leave me like this." She smiled and looked at Papa as if he were just taking a nap. "You are just sleeping, Antonio, aren't you?" She continued to smile and croon.

Vincentello was still standing in the doorway, his mouth slack, his arms by his sides as if rooted to the spot. Doctor Molinari fixed me with his gaze.

"Your mother needs looking after. Take her to her room and I'll come up shortly and give her something to help her to sleep. In the meantime, your husband and I will make the necessary arrangements."

Vincentello stood there like the imbecile he was.

"Monsieur Orsini?" Doctor Molinari said.

"Yes, yes, of course. Take her out of here, Maria, and leave us to sort all this out."

If only I had had any confidence in his ability to do so. The doctor and I exchanged a long look, and then he helped me to raise Maman to her feet. I put my arm around her waist and helped her out of the room and along the corridor to the staircase. It was like dragging a sack of logs. Every few paces she stopped and asked, "Your father is quite alright, isn't he, Maria? He's just a little tired. I keep telling him to take a rest. Vincentello can do the work with your father in charge."

"Yes, Maman, just a little tired. Now come along. You've had a shock, and a good night's sleep will do you good."

I steered Maman to her room, helped her to undress and pulled her nightdress over her head. All of a sudden our roles were reversed. Six years before, it was she who had nursed me through my meningitis and then through my miscarriage a few months later. Now it was my turn to give back to my mother all the devotion she had spent on me. But I was afraid that she had already passed to a place where we couldn't follow. Now I was alone with Vincentello, who would never be able to replace my father.

***

Papa was not a man who showed his feelings – except when he was angry, of course – but I knew he loved Zaronza, the severe, granite house in which he had grown up and the craggy scenery of Cap Corse. Just as I did. He sometimes mocked Corsican superstition, but, even so, he had a deep attachment to the island's traditions. So I asked Madame Gaffori to improvise a mourning song for him, as she had done for so many others. In a frail, thin voice she stood next to my father's body and sang of his many qualities and his wisdom, of the tragedy of his death and the grief of the village. The haunting tune has stayed with me ever since.

We buried him in the little cemetery on the hillside outside the village, overlooking the bay and the peaks beyond. As if to mirror my mood, a fine drizzle was falling and low clouds swathed the hills. I left in Maman the care of Annunciata. She wasn't well enough to come to the funeral. She didn't seem to know what was happening. Poor thing: I didn't know if she would ever regain her wits.

On returning to the house, I went to check on Maman, who was staring into the fire and rocking back and forth. Vincentello called me to his – once Papa's – study. He was sitting in Papa's chair behind the desk. Although unbidden, I sat down.

Vincentello pressed his fingertips together, steeple-fashion, like Papa used to do.

"Now, Maria, you realise of course that I am now the head of the family."

"Naturally, I'm aware of it," I replied. "How could I fail to be?"

He ignored the ice in my voice. "I think it would be useful for us to review the legal position in which we find ourselves following your father's death."

He cleared his throat and played with Papa's letter opener, an ancient *stylet*[3].

"Your dowry, in other words the land and money you brought with you, and my property are in theory separate by the terms of the marriage contract but in practice brought together by our marriage. Your father left the rest of his property, including this house, to you, but your mother has the right to live here until her death. However, since you're my wife I effectively control the bulk of your property, except for your personal effects. Your father married us to keep the family possessions in the Orsini name together. This was an admirable objective and one that I'm happy to pursue, even if an heir eludes us so far."

I already knew all this. Where was he going? But the words 'so far' struck a chill into my heart. I kept my expression fixed.

He stood looking out of the window onto the terrace, his back to me, tapping his palm with the *stylet*.

---

[3] A type of narrow-bladed dagger, much in use in Corsica.

"I know you have little respect for me, Maria, and even less affection. Ours is a marriage with little mutual comfort. However, I'm prepared to accept it on that basis in view of the considerable advantages I married into. Also," he paused, looking round at me, "I'm prepared to leave you alone most of the time, provided you make yourself agreeable to me every so often so that you bear a child and don't interfere in my running of the business."

"I blame you for Papa's death, Vincentello," I spat out. "If you hadn't angered him, he would still be alive now. And I can never overlook that you're not half the man he was. But I don't seem to have much choice in the matter and I have to accept the situation as it is."

He made an impatient gesture, brushing aside my words.

"Your father had a weak heart. Doctor Molinari knew about it. It was only a matter of time. And he was never prepared to accept new ideas and move the business forward in the way that I wanted. We'll see who turns out to be the better man."

I already knew the answer to that, and I was afraid that Vincentello wasn't up to the task of running the business. But I was relieved that he didn't appear to want to be vindictive. I would have dearly loved to be rid of him, but I knew that women had few rights in this matter. I needed to consult Sophia, who might know of some way or be able to find out.

In the meantime, I nodded and swallow the bitter words that rose in my throat like bile.

"Will that be all?" I asked.

He inclined his head.

"In that case, I must go and see to Maman."

I closed the study door behind me and leaned against the wall, my hand over my eyes.

***

Sophia couldn't give me much comfort. She didn't know

much about the law but consulted some of her father's books while he was out at the town hall.

"I know he's unfaithful to me, Sophia. He has a mistress in Santa-Lucia, I'm sure of it. When he claims to be away on business, I know he's with her. It's nothing to me but isn't this grounds for divorce? I will do anything provided I can get my own property back and live in peace with Maman."

Sophia shook her head and took my hand. "There's little you can do but put up with it, Maria, as so many other women must do. As a woman, you are considered a minor, and Vincentello's quite correct when he says that he controls your property. As for divorce, his adultery is not enough in itself. He would have to bring his mistress home to live in your house, and he's never going to do that. Or you would have to prove that he has ill-used or injured you."

"He's careful not to raise a hand to me or give me cause for complaint." I thought of his coarse love-making, but even that didn't amount to ill-use. And how could I have proved it, even if it did?

"Try to see the bright side, Maria. You are a respected married woman with a secure position. No one will ever marry me. Much as I love Papa, I will always have to keep house for him. I will never know how it is to be married."

"Believe me, Sophia, it's better never to marry at all than to be a prisoner in a loveless marriage, as I am. I get nothing out of being married to Vincentello. Absolutely nothing!"

I banged my fist onto the kitchen table and a pile of dishes jumped and clattered.

"Calm down, Maria. You won't achieve anything by getting yourself in a state like this. Just be grateful for what you have got. There are so many women who are in a worse position than you."

I supposed she was right, but it was difficult to believe it. How I envied her being able to sleep uninterrupted in her own bed every night. Vincentello and I now occupied separate rooms, but that didn't stop him from coming in regularly at night to try to get a child on me. How disagreeable it was! Even though I tried never to think of Raphaël, I couldn't help making the comparison between them.

***

Thinking of Raphaël made me realise that I had never retrieved the box containing his letters from its hiding place in the attic. Now that Vincentello was starting to feel possessive about the place, he might well decide to take an inventory of what was stored in the attic. He would then certainly have found the box, and I wouldn't have been able to explain its presence. I had to find a place to hide it. While I still shrank inside at the thought of how Raphaël behaved to me, his letters were evidence of the only romance I had ever had in my life, and all I was ever likely to have. I couldn't get rid of the letters, even if I knew I might never read them again.

Annunciata had no love for Vincentello. He was always brusque and haughty with her, so I knew she was on my side and wouldn't give me away. Her son was a mason and had done some work on the house some years ago to Papa's requirements.

"Annunciata," I asked as if it were nothing of importance. "I wonder if your son would be able to do some masonry work in the attic for me? I want to block up that large niche at the gable end. I'm afraid it weakens the wall and it might make the roof dangerous. There's no need to bother Vincentello with this. It's a very trivial matter."

She raised her eyebrows at this obvious nonsense but I didn't expand on my decision and she agreed to ask her son about it. He came and surveyed the attic and agreed that this might help to support the roof there. He wasn't about to turn down work.

"I would like it to look old – as if it has been there a long time, so that it blends in with the rest of the wall," I said.

He scratched his head at this odd request but didn't question it and arrived one day, as arranged, when Vincentello was away from home "on business." I had already hidden the box in an old sack and told the son that there was no need to move it. In little more than an hour, he had built an authentic-looking wall. Even I couldn't tell it had not been there for two hundred years.

I defied Vincentello to notice anything. My secret was still safe.

Chapter 17

1910

Days, weeks, months and years succeeded one another. Nothing in Zaronza changed very much. The light over the bay at sunset was the same as ever. The ruined château and the watchtower still presided over the village. The scent of the *maquis* pervaded the hillsides, where I often found myself walking when Maman didn't need my attention. This is what my world had shrunk to. These were the things in which I took pleasure. But then, it was always like that, until that brief period when, like a comet swinging over the horizon, my life had blazed with glory. Sometimes, I wondered what had happened to Raphaël. But the bitter taste of his desertion always came back, and I tried to think of something else.

Some of the older people had died, a few of the younger ones had married – not Sophia – but fewer and fewer babies were born. I was thirty and there was still no sign of a baby. I had to reconcile myself to the fact that it was not going to happen. Vincentello was disappointed too, of course, but for different reasons. He still took his pleasure elsewhere, and it wouldn't have surprised me if he had fathered a bastard or two. I supposed it was my fault that I couldn't conceive, but at least I had been spared the mental and physical agony of any further miscarriages.

Maman never recovered from Papa's death, either in mind or in body, although I guessed that she was declining before that. She was shut up in her own little world and needed care like a young child. She barely spoke except to utter strings of words that meant nothing to anyone except her. Vincentello ignored her, and I'm sure he would have liked to be rid of her, but family honour demanded that she must be cared for within the family home. Thank goodness I had Annunciata to take part of the burden off me sometimes, so that I could walk in the hills and think while she tended to Maman.

Vincentello was more and more restless. Of course, he would never confide in me, but I had the impression that the business wasn't thriving. If I tried to offer help or advice he rejected it straight away. His stupid pride got in the way. If only he had taken me into his confidence, I'm sure I could have helped. After all, family and financial ties yoked us together: why not listen to me from time to time?

"How could anyone make a go of a business on Cap Corse?" he asked one day while I sat sewing in front of the fire. He wasn't expecting a reply.

"It might have slipped your memory," I said, "but Papa did."

"Oh Papa, Papa," he spat out. "He's always on your lips. To hear you talk, anyone would think he were Pascal Paoli, he was so talented and gifted! Let me tell you this: the business he bequeathed me was built on sand. He had no idea what he was doing."

"It took you long enough to find out," I said.

He glared at me. "And if that weren't enough, the economic situation is terrible, we never get any rain to speak of, and the land here is so poor that you can't make anything grow. No wonder people have been leaving Cap Corse in droves for years. Phylloxera has destroyed most of the vines, and there's not much else in the way of natural resources. This is a desert, a wasteland!"

I dropped my sewing in my lap. "You blame everything and everyone but yourself, Vincentello. Doesn't it occur to you that some of the things you have done were ill-advised? Why don't you ever want to take anyone else's advice? Monsieur Franceschi would have been pleased to help, but you were rude and surly to him."

"Oh, he's another one who doesn't know what he's talking about. It's all, *'That's how we did it in my day.'* Well, it's not *his* day any longer. It's time for us younger ones to take over." He nodded to emphasise his point.

I sighed. "But you would do better to keep on the side of the mayor. He's an influential man with many business contacts of his own. Why do you have to push everyone away?"

"What do you know of business? You're only a woman. Why don't you just keep to your sewing and cooking and wiping your mother's dripping nose since she's incapable of doing it for herself?"

I glared at Vincentello. My voice shaking with anger, I said, "My mother can't help herself. She needs my care and attention."

"Bof," Vincentello said and looked away. "I'll tell you where the place to be is: Puerto Rico. That's where there's money to be made." He wagged his finger at me. "Cap Corse is finished. There's nothing here worth having."

I didn't even know where this Puerto Rico place was. I knew he was burning for me to ask, but I said nothing and bent my head to my sewing again. After a moment he stamped out of the room, banging the door as he went.

For the next few weeks, Vincentello talked of nothing but Puerto Rico. It appeared that it was an island off the Americas, a little similar to Corsica. Unlike Corsica, though, it had fertile areas where sugar cane, coffee and tobacco grew in abundance. For the past fifty years or so, Corsicans had been emigrating to Puerto Rico and there was now quite a colony of them.

"A distant cousin of Papa's, from Morsiglia, went there about twenty-five years ago," Sophia said. "Now he owns a thriving farm and has had a splendid house built. He tried to get my father to go out there to join him, but Papa didn't want to leave Corsica. I was happy with his decision because I suppose I would have had to go with him, and I would much rather stay here, even if I am an old maid."

I was happy too, since I would have lost my only friend.

It now seemed that almost everyone in Cap Corse knew, or was related to, someone who had gone to Puerto Rico. In my girlhood, I was only vaguely aware of people leaving Zaronza, and I had no idea where they were going or why. Nobody close to our family had left, which I supposed explained the lack of discussion about it in our house – added to the fact that Papa didn't often think it worthwhile to update Maman and me even on local, let alone international, affairs.

One day, Vincentello came in for lunch rubbing his hands, a broad grin stretching across his face. He wasn't often in such a good mood. Unlike Papa, who would always wait until he had finished his cheese before announcing anything of importance, Vincentello could never hold himself back when he had something to say.

I had adopted Maman's habit of serving him while standing up. This was preferable to eating with him at the table. He didn't seem to notice. No doubt he thought it was his due as head of the family.

"Now, Maria, I have some news that is going to transform our lives."

He was always making announcements like this, which didn't often come to anything, and the usual creeping worm of doubt was already at work in my head. I waited for him to go on.

"For some time," he continued, "I've been despairing of running a business here in Corsica. So many things are against it, despite my best efforts. There's no money to be made here, I'm quite sure of that. I'm now thirty-five and don't intend to waste my best years in a rural backwater like Zaronza."

He looked at me. I gave nothing away, my face set in stone. I thought I knew what was coming.

"For the past few months, I have been corresponding with an old friend from Casaccia, Antoine Filipini. He left Corsica for Puerto Rico seven years ago. After all, he had four brothers and they were hard-pressed to make a go of it on the small properties their father had left them. When he went he had very little. Now he's the owner of a coffee plantation, has a new mansion and smokes the best Havana cigars. He says it's an El Dorado."

Trust Vincentello to think of the cigars. He had recently taken up the habit of cigar-smoking. The fumes gave me a headache and lodged themselves in the folds of every garment and curtain in the house.

"Now, here's the good news. His business is so big that Antoine is looking for someone to run the plantation for him with a view to becoming a partner if all goes well. He's offered me that position and I have accepted. He has agreed to give me time to wind down the business here and make the necessary arrangements. We will sail in three months' time."

He sat back, puffing on his after-lunch cigar, looking at me as if he had offered me a treasure chest full of diamonds and rubies. I stared back, my mouth slack. I couldn't breathe, but it wasn't just the smoke from his cigar that deprived me of air.

At last I stammered, "D–do you mean, leave Zaronza, leave Corsica?"

He smiled. "That would appear to be the logical conclusion."

"But what are you thinking of? How can you abandon everything Papa built up, the business he established? It's not possible."

"It's more than possible, Maria. It's a *fait accompli*. This is a wonderful opportunity – don't you see? And I'm generously offering you the chance to share in it."

"But I don't want to. I can't imagine leaving Zaronza, let alone Corsica. What about this house, what about our lands and possessions?"

"Oh, the house. Well, we can rent that out and lease the lands to some farmer. No doubt we will come back from time to time to see to things."

I didn't share his optimism about finding tenants. But I had another, even greater concern.

"And what about Maman?" I asked. "She can't possibly make the journey to Puerto Rico. She's not strong enough to travel. And even if the journey didn't kill her, she's too frail to make a new life in a new place. She needs to be cared for in familiar surroundings."

He contemplated the glowing tip of his cigar. "Well, maybe she would be better off staying in Corsica. Annunciata could look after her here."

My mouth dropped open. "I can't believe what I just heard," I said. "Do you really think I would be cold-hearted enough to leave my own mother, who is frail and ill, to go off with you on some wild jaunt that's likely to end in disaster?"

"This is no wild jaunt and it won't end in disaster." (He appeared to have ignored the first part of my objections.) "I told you, prosperity is guaranteed. You only have to look at the evidence. So many people have made a success out there. Why should we be different?"

"*We* are different because *you* are incapable of making a go of anything," I flung the pent-up words at him. "You have no commercial sense, you have almost destroyed the thriving business that Papa left, and yet you persist in pursuing your madcap schemes. Oh, this position with your friend sounds all well and good, but I predict that within five minutes you'll have fallen out with him."

"When I want your opinion," he spat, "I'll ask for it. This legendary business of your father's was a castle in the air. I have done what I can with it but I can't do any more. Too many things are against me here. The opportunity Filipini offers comes only once in a lifetime, and I don't intend to let it pass by. I've made up my mind, Maria. We are going to Puerto Rico and we are going in three months' time."

"No," I said, lingering over the words. "*You* are going to Puerto Rico. Don't expect me to come with you. I *cannot* leave Maman and I *will not* leave Corsica."

My heart pounding, I ran down the corridor and wrenched open the front door. Blinded by tears, I stumbled up the well-worn path to the tower and flung myself onto the flat stone. I would not go with him; I *could* not go. How could I possibly leave Maman? The only people who loved me were here in Zaronza. I wouldn't leave them to go to a place I didn't know with a man I didn't love. He couldn't ask that of me. We would be far better apart. Maybe he would come around to see that.

The calming scent of the *maquis* and the warmth of the spring sun brought me back to my senses. It was a ridiculous plan. I was even more surprised that he wanted to saddle himself with me, since I was sure he had no more affection for me than I did for him. But, as I sat there, an idea came to me and started to develop.

***

After supper, which we ate in a dense silence, I said to Vincentello, "I would like to talk to you. Please may we go to your study?"

He sat down behind Papa's desk and prepared the inevitable cigar. "Well? Have you come to your senses?"

"My senses have never deserted me. If you mean have I changed my mind, the answer is no."

He opened his mouth to speak. I held up my hand.

"Wait. I have a proposition to make. This marriage hasn't been a happy one for either of us. We openly agree about that. But we have property in common which we can't simply leave to decline in neglect. Even if we come back from time to time, which I doubt, we can't trust tenants to look after our property in the way we would ourselves."

"So, what is your proposition?"

"As you know, I don't want to leave Maman and we can't take her with us in her condition. It would be her death. If you're still determined to take up your friend's offer, I propose that I stay to look after our business interests here and oversee our property. If you think about it, you'll see that it's advantageous to us both. You will have your freedom while I will ensure that the family possessions remain intact."

"*You?!*" he blurted out. "Why, it's unheard of. Women are incapable of running anything. They need a man's guidance to keep them on the straight and narrow. You don't know what you're saying, Maria."

I took a deep breath, holding down the torrent of words I really wanted to speak.

"I think you'll find there are examples in Corsica of women who manage their own property quite successfully. After all, a woman must run the home and the household budget, and see to the children's upbringing and education. She has to take many decisions in a day so that everything continues to run smoothly. You men may not see it, but much effort and ability go into these things. I don't see that managing our lands and interests is a great deal different."

Vincentello took a puff of his cigar and considered me through the smoke rings.

"Think about it, Vincentello. Your freedom."

"Very well," he said. "The idea is absurd, but I'll give it some thought. I'll let you know my decision tomorrow."

I had to wait until lunchtime to hear Vincentello's verdict.

"Well, Maria," he said. "I have thought about your proposal."

He paused. I held my breath.

"And I've decided that it makes some sense for me to go out to Puerto Rico on my own – at least to start with. If things turn out well, as I'm sure they will, I don't exclude your joining me later on."

I wanted to dance on the table and sing until I was hoarse, but I just nodded and remained silent.

"In the meantime, you can stay here in Zaronza and

administer our property. I shall make the necessary arrangements to allow you to do this."

"Thank you, Vincentello. I don't think either of us will regret this decision."

A bubble of happiness welling up inside, I went to see Sophia to tell her of my good fortune. She didn't appear quite as joyful as me, but then Sophia was like that.

"I'm glad that you're going to stay in Zaronza. And Papa will be, too. He's very fond of you. But it's a rather irregular situation, isn't it? You will be neither married nor unmarried, simply living apart almost on opposite sides of the world. What about the long-term future; have you thought of that?"

"Oh, Sophia, for me it's enough that he's going away and that he has agreed I can stay here in Zaronza – at least for now. I was so afraid for a while that he would force me to go with him and leave Maman behind. I couldn't have endured that. Although we're still married, I don't care what he does in Puerto Rico as long as I'm left alone."

"And what will people in Zaronza think?"

"I don't care what they think," I replied. "It's common knowledge, anyway, that Vincentello is not a devoted husband. And people would have thought far worse of me if I had gone with him and left poor Maman behind here. You know how attached we Corsicans are to our families."

***

And so, a couple of months later, I accompanied Vincentello to Bastia, where he would sail for Marseille and then Puerto Rico. The bulk of his luggage had gone on before, and Monsieur Franceschi had lent us his pony and trap. I felt that seeing him off was the least I could do, since he had allowed me to stay on Corsica. A small part of me also wanted to make sure he left, that it was true and not a dream.

We trotted in silence up the steep, winding road, crossing the

Col de Teghime, from where you can see both sides of Cap Corse. Sometimes the weather is quite different on each side of the pass, but on that day it was beautiful. Small clouds sat as if anchored above the mountains of the cape, and the landscape in the distance shimmered in the haze. As the road descended towards the town from the pass, we could already see Bastia below us with the shining sea beyond.

How I love my native Corsica! I can't imagine living anywhere else. And yet, this journey could have been so different if Vincentello hadn't agreed to my proposal. I would have been taking this road for possibly the last time in my life. I closed my eyes and breathed deeply, drinking in the scent of the *maquis*. No. I would have died rather than leave this behind.

But what if Vincentello had been Raphaël? Would I have gone with him?

I couldn't answer that question.

We arrived at the port. Vincentello's ship sailed that afternoon. I was going to stay overnight with distant cousins in Bastia, who would accompany me back to Zaronza the following morning. Annunciata was staying in our house to look after Maman in my absence.

"Well, Maria," Vincentello said. "We must part here. I'll write to you when I arrive in Puerto Rico, but since I shall be very busy, don't expect me to write very often."

I didn't care if he never wrote at all, but I kept this to myself. I hoped he was not going to try to kiss me. Instead he held out his hand and we shook, like strangers. Ten years of marriage were reduced to this.

"Goodbye," he said.

"*Bon voyage*," I replied.

He turned and strode up the gangplank, carpet bag in hand. He didn't turn around and was soon lost in the throng of passengers on deck.

Something told me I would never see him again.

Chapter 18

Vincentello was as good as his word and wrote to me from Puerto Rico. His friend had settled near a place called Yauco, where the land was at its most fertile. He was full of enthusiasm for his prospects in this Promised Land. Everything was perfect: Filipini and his family were charming, the work was agreeable, even the climate was more to his taste than the Corsican variety. He was welcome to it.

I was revelling in my new-found freedom. Although Vincentello's departure caused something of a stir in the closed society of Zaronza, nobody was all that surprised. I sometimes wondered what had happened to his mistress in Santa-Lucia. I presumed he must have paid her off – unless of course she went to Puerto Rico in my place. If so, she was welcome to it, too. She would soon find out that living with Vincentello would be an entirely different matter from seeing him for a few hours each week.

The business took up a good deal of my time. I had taken over Papa's study – I could never think of it as Vincentello's – and spent many evenings sitting at his desk poring over the accounts that Vincentello had kept so badly. What a mess they were in! It looked as if a spider had fallen into the inkpot and then crawled all over the ledgers. No wonder Papa was disappointed in him.

Monsieur Franceschi was a great help to me. Whilst I was sure he didn't entirely approve of a woman running a business, he was careful to keep his opinions to himself. He could see that I was quick to learn and well-organised. I was suddenly reminded of Raphaël's comment that I had a practical bent, and a knot formed in my stomach.

Within a few months, the business was back on course. Although I couldn't say that it was thriving, at least it was no longer causing me such concern. I had leased out part of our lands to a farmer from Patrimonio, who was looking to establish new vineyards with a phylloxera-resistant strain of vines. And I had managed to let Vincentello's house at Casaccia to the new schoolmaster there and his family.

"You know, Maria," Monsieur Franceschi said one day, as I served him a glass of *vin de myrtille,* "I'm sorry that you and Orso never got together. I should have been delighted to see a match between you, but your father had other ideas and wanted to keep the family possessions in the Orsini name. I can understand that, of course; it's no criticism of your father. It's a pity Orso has never married. And it's a pity you aren't free. But, of course, you're still married to Vincentello."

On reflection, Orso would have been a more congenial husband. At least he loved me, according to Sophia, which was more than Vincentello had ever done. But I didn't love Orso. And, at the time, Raphaël had dazzled me. I couldn't see anything or anyone else beyond him.

"We can never know how things will work out, Monsieur Franceschi," I replied. "What seems like a good idea at the time turns out with hindsight to have been a mistake. But one thing I've learned in my life is that it serves no purpose to look back. Regrets are all very well but you can't live on them."

"What a wise little thing you are turning out to be," he said, patting my hand. "I have always been fond of you, Maria, but when you were a young girl I thought you were too flighty and headstrong – and that was despite your parents' strict upbringing." He sighed and sipped his wine. "I should have liked to see you and Orso married, though." He shook his head.

My biggest concern was Maman. She had deteriorated even more in the past few months and now kept to her bed. She no longer recognised anyone, but at least she was docile and complied with whatever Annunciata and I had to do. Thank goodness for Annunciata. I don't know what I would have done without her. She looked after Maman if I needed to go to Bastia. But she was aging, too. Maman was like a new-born baby and required a great deal of care and attention. She often wet the bed but it was no use being impatient with her. It wasn't her fault. We just had to strip the sheets, wipe her down and start again.

Doctor Molinari called round quite often to see her. She didn't recognise him, either, but seemed pleased to see people. The doctor didn't really know what was wrong with her; he couldn't give her illness a precise name but said she suffered from premature aging. She was only sixty-four. Other old people in the village lived much longer than that and had all their wits about them. It was just bad luck.

***

One day I was doing my accounts in Papa's study. On such a dank, misty autumn day I was obliged to light a lamp. Vincentello had left for Puerto Rico about eighteen months before, and his letters were sporadic. But when he did write it was with undimmed enthusiasm for this El Dorado, although he was vague about the details of his life.

The heavy knocker thudding against the door broke my concentration. I waited a moment to see if Annunciata would go to open it, but she didn't, so I assumed she must be upstairs with Maman. When I opened the front door, a tall stranger was standing on the threshold, looking about him.

"Good morning. I wonder if Madame Orsini is at home."

"I am the younger Madame Orsini, if it's me you want to see. Madame Orsini Senior is unwell and can't see visitors."

He took off his hat, revealing greying temples.

"I'm so sorry; I didn't know. And I apologise for disturbing you. I have recently arrived from Puerto Rico on a visit to my family in Santa-Lucia and I have news of your husband."

"Please, come in."

I stood aside to let him enter, then took his coat and hat and hung them on the stand in the hall. Should I show him into the salon or the study? The study, I decided. He might as well see that I was serious about running the business if he was going to report back to Vincentello. Gesturing him to the chair in front of the desk I took my place behind it.

"Excuse me," he said. "I should introduce myself. My name is Ignacio Mariani."

I bowed slightly and he continued, "I'm originally from Santa-Lucia but emigrated to Puerto Rico some years ago. I'm combining a business visit to the mainland with the opportunity to see my family. I work as a coffee merchant, and Antoine Filipini is a good friend and business associate."

"Ah yes. My husband went out to Puerto Rico to work for him."

He pursed his lips and looked down at his hands.

"The reason for my visit is rather delicate, Madame Orsini."

My heart stopped. "Please go on."

"I'm afraid that Monsieur Filipini no longer employs your husband, and hasn't done so for several months."

"But what's happened? He hasn't mentioned anything about this in his letters."

But then, they were infrequent enough.

"It appears that there was trouble over some missing money. Monsieur Filipini discovered that your husband was removing funds from the business to place in his own failed speculations. Since he's an old school friend of your husband, he decided not to press any charges. Even so, he sought repayment and, of course, he had to let your husband go. Orsini has been borrowing money from various sources to pay back Monsieur Filipini, and now has a number of sizeable debts."

Oh, Vincentello, you fool! Why did you constantly have to run after these ill-advised schemes?

"I see. And what is your role in this affair, Monsieur

Mariani?"

"Your husband's IOUs are now in my hands, and I am his principal creditor."

"Why have you come to see me about this?"

"It's quite clear to me that Orsini will not be able to honour these debts, so I have come to you for payment."

"How do you know that he will be unable to pay them? And what do you expect me to do about it?"

"The Corsican community in Puerto Rico is close-knit, Madame Orsini. Everyone knows about this affair, and no one is likely to offer your husband further employment. Nor does he have ready capital to invest in a business of his own."

I was surprised that Vincentello hadn't applied to me for funds himself. Was it that he had some sense of shame and failure? Or did he know that Mariani would come to see me anyway? Knowing Vincentello, the latter seemed more likely.

"How, in that case, does my husband manage to live?"

Mariani spread out his fingers and looked down at them again. On his right hand he wore a large gold signet ring, which he twisted as he spoke. "I'm afraid this is also somewhat delicate."

"Please continue, Monsieur Mariani. There's very little you can tell me about my husband that would surprise me."

He coughed. "He's living with a woman – I hardly dare call her a lady – who supports him with the earnings from her… profession."

He didn't need to explain to me what that profession was. Sighing, I stood up and walked to the window overlooking the terrace. The purple bougainvillea was still in bloom, but it wouldn't last much longer.

"How much do his debts amount to?"

"Some fifty thousand francs."

I couldn't help gasping. "I don't know what you expect me to do, Monsieur Mariani. By the terms of our marriage contract, I am not liable for Vincentello's debts. My father made sure that it specified the separation of our debts." I blessed Papa's foresight.

"I have in my possession a letter from your husband requesting you to sell his portion of your common property that is separate from your dowry. He needs your consent for this but believes that you won't reasonably withhold it."

"May I see the letter?"

He reached into an inner pocket, pulled out a sealed envelope and handed it to me. I broke the seal. It was in Vincentello's handwriting and the contents were as Mariani had described. This was too bad! I had worked hard to make something of this property, but then only to see part of it go into the pockets of Vincentello's creditors. I could have refused, I supposed, but if I did would it end there? At least he couldn't touch my dowry or the property that Papa left me. And if I did this he would have no further hold over me – except that we were still married in name.

I turned to Mariani.

"As you might expect, I need to take advice on this matter. And, even if I give my consent, it will take some time to achieve this."

"I had indeed expected both possibilities, Madame. However, I shall be staying in Corsica for a further two weeks. You can contact me here." He scribbled an address on the back of his business card.

"Good day, Madame Orsini."

I shut the door without answering and went back into the study, my steps dragging. I was so tired. When Vincentello left I thought I had got rid of him at last, even though we were still married. But it seemed that his actions in a faraway place still had the power to affect me here. I slumped in Papa's chair and picked up his *stylet*. If Vincentello had been there I would have been tempted to stick it in him. Instead, I tapped it on the desk and lost myself in my thoughts.

After much consultation and to-ing and fro-ing with the

unbending Mariani, it was agreed that he would be the beneficiary of the sale of Vincentello's assets. Monsieur Franceschi put everything in train, and at least that was taken out of my hands. But I could have murdered Vincentello for being such a fool. Since that satisfaction was denied me, I wrote to him instead, making it quite clear that he had no claim on my property and that I would refuse to bail him out again. I also told him that I didn't wish to hear from him any more and that our marriage was effectively over, in deed if not in word. He never sent a reply.

***

Going into Maman's room one morning, I noticed an unaccustomed stillness. I pulled the curtains open and turned to look at her. She seemed to be asleep, but when I touched her hand it was cold. She looked so peaceful. I sat on the bed for a while, just gazing at her. Poor Maman. Her life had not been very happy and she never recovered from the shock of Papa's death. I smoothed her hair back from her temples and leant over to kiss her forehead. Although I was sad, it was a relief. She didn't get much out of life in her last few years and needed a lot of care and attention.

We buried her with Papa in the family grave. They were together again in the cemetery overlooking the village and the sea.

Chapter 19

August 1914

My life was played out against a sombre backdrop. During the spring and summer of 1914, Europe slid towards war and everyone seemed powerless to prevent it. Vincentello had once described Zaronza as a rural backwater, and yet even we were not immune to the changes that were sweeping through the world. The stifling and sultry summer weather matched the prevailing mood. Everyone held their breath, waiting for the inevitable.

An Archduke was assassinated in an obscure place called Sarajevo, the spark that set off the powder keg. The newspapers were full of talk of mobilisation and curbing Germany's territorial aggression, but the nationalists and the peacemakers couldn't agree. At the end of July, the French Socialist leader Jean Jaurès, who strove to prevent war and to make the great powers negotiate, was assassinated in Paris, weakening the cause of peace. The political climate was now dominated by those who wanted to hit back at Germany for taking Alsace-Lorraine in 1870.

Sophia and I sat in her kitchen and read her father's newspaper, spread out on the table. The news made for solemn reading.

"I'm so worried for Orso," said Sophia. "If war is declared he'll be called up to fight. And I know he would volunteer, anyway. Only the other day he said, 'It's time we taught those iron-heads a lesson. I hope I get the chance to do it.' Papa will be distraught if anything happens to him. We both will be."

"But everyone says that if there is a war it will be short. Our army is much better-equipped and drilled than it was in 1870, or so they say. And no one wants to see all-out war, surely?"

"You can see for yourself," Sophia replied, gesturing towards the newspaper. "The peacemakers have lost. All people can think of now is getting revenge on Germany for our humiliation in 1870. It's no longer a question of *if* we go to war, but of *when*."

I thought of all the able-bodied young men in the village: fathers, sons, husbands. I was glad that I had no one close to me who would be caught up in this overwhelming machine called war. I didn't much care what happened to Vincentello. I didn't even know if he would be called up to fight for his country from Puerto Rico.

Raphaël's face flitted across my thoughts. Where was he? Was he still in his village in the Bozio? I had heard nothing of him since he left Zaronza, and I hadn't tried to find out. Neither did I think of him if I could help it, but sometimes I couldn't stop the memories filtering into my brain, like sand in an hourglass. How old would he have been then? Thirty-nine, I calculated. Did they call up men of that age? And did they call up schoolteachers? Raphaël would have hated the idea of war, but would he have volunteered out of a sense of duty? I didn't have the answers, and I saw no point in troubling Sophia with these questions. She, too, was deep in thought, no doubt worrying about what might happen to Orso if war broke out.

The church bell started ringing; not the solemn call to prayer or the hourly chimes but with a wild, hysterical note. Sophia and I looked at each other. The alarm call.

"Is there a brush fire?" I asked. We had so many of them on the hillsides that year. The parched *maquis* was dry as tinder. A single spark was enough to set off a blaze that was soon travelling as fast as a horse can gallop, fanned by the breeze off the sea. The whole village was mobilised then to beat out the flames with brooms and lug cans of water in an attempt to stem the licking flames.

We hastened down the steep alley towards the square. I held Sophia's arm as she stumbled along. We couldn't see any sign of smoke on the hillsides, but people from all over the village were converging on the square. Sophia's father hurried up to us from the direction of the town hall. He was red in the face and puffing.

"War," he said. "It's war." He leant over and placed his hands on his thighs, catching his breath.

"I had a telegram not ten minutes ago. The order has gone out for general mobilisation. The reservists will be called up in the next few days."

Sophia put her hands to her mouth. "Orso!" she gasped.

Monsieur Franceschi just nodded and took her hand. He had wanted to buy Orso out by paying another man to take his place, but Orso wouldn't agree.

The news spread like a plague around the village and reactions varied. The women looked worried, but some of them also looked proud beneath it. The men ranged from silent to swaggering, but nearly all of them believed that the war would be all over by Christmas. That's what the newspapers were saying, after all. Despite the sweltering August heat, I felt cold all over. I prayed that they were right.

***

The units of the 173rd Infantry Regiment were ordered to Ajaccio and they sailed from there for Marseille. They camped there for a few days before embarking on the long train journey up to north-east France. Orso had gone, too, and Sophia and her father looked like ghosts. Monsieur Franceschi was torn between pride in his son and fear that he would fall in battle. Nothing I could say would console them but I tried to do so with my presence, keeping them company and taking their minds off the war by talking of other things. But the war was never far beneath the surface, and whatever we said, its undertones darkened our conversation.

The village was silent and empty without the ringing voices of men. The women stayed in their houses or worked their small plots on the hillside in place of their husbands. Few vehicles passed on the road. Dogs lay and scratched themselves in the dust, while bare-legged children ran about unsupervised on the beach far below the village. Similar scenes must have been taking place in villages all over Corsica. Thousands of men had answered the call to arms. Annunciata's son, the mason, had gone too, although he had a wife and two children.

It wasn't long before we heard news of the first battle in which Corsican soldiers fought, at Dieuze. Reports were confused, and we weren't sure which side had won or lost, or if our troops had retreated or advanced. The newspapers were full of the strange names of the villages in that part of France – Dombasle-sur-Meurthe, Lunéville, Flainval, Mortagne. I tried to imagine the landscape and the villages there, but I had never left Corsica and knew only the rocky scenery of our own island. Surely they weren't fighting in that sort of terrain?

August gave way to September, and the heat and dust continued unabated. News arrived of a new battle, the Battle of the Marne, which was apparently a victory for the Allies and stopped the German advance in its tracks. As before, reports were confusing and garbled, but they were enough to tell us that this was a bloody and ferocious battle in which unimaginable numbers of men fought. It also brought the first casualty for Zaronza.

I was crossing the square one fine day in mid-September when I saw Monsieur Franceschi walking from the town hall. He was wearing his official sash and bearing a piece of paper, his face closed and sombre. He walked towards Janetta Aligheri's house. Her husband had enlisted right from the start, even though they had several children. The hairs on the back of my neck stood up and my arms were covered in gooseflesh.

Even before her piercing screams ripped the air, I knew what news the mayor had brought. She chased him from the house, flinging anything she could find at him. A saucepan sailed past his head.

"It's not true! It's not true!" she screamed, before collapsing onto her knees, wailing hysterically and covering her head with her apron.

Her two neighbours rushed to her aid and she fell into their arms. They lifted her up and walked her between them back into her house. Monsieur Franceschi walked past me back towards the town hall and shrugged. His eyes were filled with tears. A knot in the base of my stomach told me that this would not be the only time he would have to perform this sad duty.

***

And so it continued into 1915, this war that everyone said would be over by Christmas. My business visits to Santa-Lucia and Bastia were now infrequent, since the war had restricted everything; though at least the rents for the lands were still coming in. But the sight of young women everywhere clad in black was becoming all too common. I, too, was still in black for Maman. She had told me that there would be plenty of time in my life to wear it, and she was right. I wore my black not only for her but also for Corsica.

Zaronza was only a small village, but it took its share of casualties as this war to end wars continued, eating up men like some gigantic, greedy monster. No one was spared its voracious appetite. Time and again wives, mothers, sisters, children, parents were left bereft, and I wondered more and more if life would ever be the same again here. Madame Gaffori had long since died, and no one had taken her place as a *voceratrice*[4]. Nobody in the village had her gift, but even if they had, there was never a body to mourn.

---

[4] Performer of improvised mourning songs.

Sophia and her father were no strangers to the effects of the carnage. Orso was not killed, but he lost his right arm in an artillery barrage on the Marne. He was lucky not to have died from gangrene. He spent weeks in a hospital behind the lines and then arrived back in the village one damp March day, brought by the carter from Bastia. No one knew he was coming: he didn't want anyone to meet him off the boat at the port.

I was returning from the village shop, my purchases in a wicker basket, when Orso got down from the cart and reached up with his one good arm for his baggage. The other sleeve of his jacket was tucked into his right pocket – flat and empty, a mockery of his once-robust form. I stopped in the middle of the street, my heart somewhere around my knees, praying that he wouldn't see me. But, as if aware of my presence, he turned his head and looked me full in the face. Etched on his features were hatred, shame, pride, resentment – a thousand emotions. Then the moment passed and he jerked his bag down onto the road, staggering a little, off-balance with his single arm.

I took a step forward and held out my hand, but realised too late what I was doing. The greeting died on my lips and my arm dropped back to my side. I knew he wouldn't want my friendship and least of all my pity. He squared his shoulders and, rigid with pride, set off in the direction of his father's house.

***

As the war went on, Orso was not the only one to return maimed to Zaronza. They arrived singly, no bands or bunting heralding their return; creeping back to their homes like dogs to their kennels. They had left their youth on the battlefields, and what good had it done anyone? Sometimes I encountered a former soldier as I went about my shopping in Zaronza, sitting on a bench, resting his false arm or leg, looking into the distance, and fixing on sights, hearing sounds that we, thank God, would never see or hear. Their empty sleeves or trouser legs were pinned up. Their faces were blank with suffering but they looked with contempt upon those of us who had no knowledge of what they had experienced. To what Hell had these poor souls descended? Would they ever return from it? Their wives and families did their best to help them, but they had passed far beyond our understanding and they never talked of it.

Monsieur Franceschi had to perform his painful duty several more times as the flower of Corsican youth was mown down on the barren fields of northern France. And each time, he met with the same response from a mother or a widow mad with grief. I felt sorry for Sophia's father, but who else did these women have to blame for their troubles? He was, after all, the local symbol of the French Republic, which had condemned their men to their deaths.

Where would all this end? What good would anyone derive from it? The newspapers became less forthcoming about the news, and we could only guess at what was really happening up there on the Front, so far away. Thousands upon thousands of Corsican men were in the thick of the fighting, but, even to my inexperienced eyes, all this achieved was to bicker over a few hundred metres of land, which passed from side to side as fortunes waxed and waned. Did it really take millions of men to resolve a territorial dispute?

***

Annunciata continued to help me in the house, although I didn't really need her. After all, only I occupied this stern, granite building with its echoing corridors and clock ticking in the hall. Papa and Maman were both long gone.

I neither knew nor cared what Vincentello was doing. How different it might have been. I had never loved Vincentello, but maybe we could have achieved a semblance of a life together if only I could have had children. The house was crying out for life and laughter to lighten the gloom. How they would have enjoyed playing at kings and queens up at the old château! How they would have loved to be the brave Corsican captain fending off the French by subterfuge in the watchtower! But it was no use dwelling on the past. So many women were far worse off than me.

Chapter 20

October 1916

A letter arrived bearing a *notaire*'s stamp from Yauco. I recognised this as the place Vincentello had settled in Puerto Rico. My God! What had he done now? No more demands for payment of his debts, surely? I had made that quite clear. I took Papa's *stylet* and slit open the envelope, pulling out a single sheet of paper.

Madame,

I write to inform you of the demise of your husband, Vincentello Pascal Antonio Orsini, on the seventh day of September, 1916, at Yauco, Puerto Rico. Under the terms of his will he has left sundry movable goods to Mademoiselle Flora Novici, resident of Yauco. My investigations indicate that he left no property in Corsica, the same having been disposed of a number of years previously and the capital thereof having been consumed prior to his demise. Under the terms of your marriage contract, the sole use of your possessions, landed or otherwise, reverts to you in perpetuity, there being no other prior claim.

I remain at your disposal, Madame, for any additional information you might require.

So there it was. A *notaire*'s letter drew a line under my marriage to Vincentello in a few strokes of the pen. He didn't even say how he had died, although I assumed he had never left Puerto Rico. As for this Mademoiselle Novici, I supposed she was the lady of easy virtue on whose earnings he had been living.

I went up the hill to the watchtower and sat on the flat stone in the mellow early October sun. It was on a day just like this that Raphaël had declared his feelings for me. That was seventeen years before, but it seemed like a lifetime. How much had happened in those years. At that time, I could think only of romance and of having a handsome lover. Did I truly love Raphaël? It seemed like it then. Did he love me? He said he did, but, if so, how could he abandon me as he did? I had gone over it afterwards a thousand times in my mind but couldn't find the answer. After a while, I had given up trying. But Vincentello's death reopened the old wounds and reawakened my curiosity.

I didn't want to rejoice at the news about Vincentello. After all, it was a terrible waste. He was only forty-one – in his prime. But he never managed to make anything of himself, despite all the opportunities put in his way. Other Corsicans had managed to thrive in Puerto Rico, but his lack of judgement and downright dishonesty prevented him from taking advantage of his chances. From his point of view, it would have been better if he had stayed in Corsica instead of going off halfway around the world to a land he knew nothing about. From mine, of course, it would have been a disaster if he had stayed.

So I looked back on two wasted lives with regret. But, more than anything else, this news told me that I was free. Free.

Standing up, I shook my skirt and brushed myself down. I had to tell Sophia. And I supposed that for form's sake I must put on my mourning again, although I had little cause to grieve.

As usual, Sophia was in her kitchen humming as she scrubbed the oak table. She had always been such a good housewife. What a pity that she never married. She would have liked children, and her father would have wanted grandchildren. It didn't look as if Orso would ever marry either. It seemed that our two families were destined to die out with our generation.

I tapped on the open door and she turned round, giving me

her fleeting smile. Kissing her on both cheeks I handed her the *notaire*'s letter and sat down. She read it, looked at the back of the sheet in case it went on overleaf and then read it again. She placed the letter on the table and looked into the distance, not at me.

A few moments passed, the only sound a pan bubbling gently on the stove. Sophia looked at me.

"So, now you're free."

"Yes. But I don't get any pleasure from Vincentello's death." I told her my thoughts about his wasted life.

She nodded, but I couldn't read the look in her eyes.

"And there's nothing to stop you marrying again."

"I think that's unlikely. I would have to meet someone who wanted to marry me – and I would want to feel affection for them. I can't see the chances of that, especially with this war going on."

"What about Orso?"

I sighed. "Sophia, I have great respect for Orso and I know he's been through terrible suffering, like so many others. But I don't love him and never will. I would simply be exchanging one loveless marriage for another."

"But what about children? You aren't too old at thirty-seven. Do you want your family to die out altogether? Papa would be so pleased if you and Orso were to marry."

"The name will die out anyway if I marry. And I can't marry to please other people. I did that once before, and look at the result – two unhappy people who ended up living apart. In any case, Orso is so bitter and resentful that I don't feel our life together would be very satisfying for either of us. No, Sophia, I don't think I shall ever marry again."

Sophia bit her lip. "I think you're making a mistake."

"I remember when you said that to me before, all those years ago. I made a bigger mistake allowing myself to be forced into marrying Vincentello. He didn't love me and I didn't love him, either. If I had been allowed to marry where I loved, things would have turned out differently."

"If that plan to elope with Raphaël had worked out, you mean."

"You knew about that?"

Sophia blushed and bit her lip even harder.

"How did you find out? I didn't tell you, so Raphaël must have done. But he and I agreed that no one should know about it: it was safer that way. And then he abandoned me that night, so I had to comply with what Papa wanted."

"Raphaël didn't abandon you, Maria."

My head snapped up. "What do you mean? What do you know about it?"

Sophia twisted her hands in her lap. She opened her mouth and breathed in as if she was about to speak but then closed her lips again.

"Is there something you know about it that you haven't told me? Please, Sophia, I need to know the truth after all these years."

She looked down at her hands and then up at me again. Tears were welling in her eyes and she blinked them back.

"I don't know how to start," she whispered.

I placed my hand over hers. "Tell me."

She withdrew her hands from mine and laid them on the table. She fixed the far wall with her gaze.

"I have wanted to tell you. Believe me, Maria. So many times I have been on the point of it and then I was too cowardly when it came to it. While you were still married to Vincentello there seemed little point, but now I can't keep this secret any longer."

She looked at me, her eyes pleading. I nodded to reassure her and tried to stay calm, although my heart was almost bursting out of my chest.

She swallowed.

"My life changed the day Raphaël came to Zaronza. He was so kind and understanding. And he knew so much and taught me so many things. He loaned me books and talked to me about them as if I were his equal. He taught me Italian, he talked to me about history, about the world, about so many things. He was so generous with his time. He was a true friend." She paused. "But then, to me he began to mean more than just a friend. I fell in love with him, Maria, and to this day I still love him."

Sophia buried her face in her hands and the tears flowed unchecked. Flashes of memory came back to me: the time I saw them shoulder to shoulder at the kitchen table; Sophia's insistence that I was making a terrible mistake loving Raphaël; our fierce argument; the time I came upon her sobbing because he was leaving Zaronza. Now it all started to fall into place. How stupid I was not to have seen it. How blinded I was by my own feelings and my own problems.

"Go on."

Sophia dried her eyes.

"When you confided in me about your relations with Raphaël, I thought my life had come to an end. I had expected that he would start to feel the same about me – that proximity would turn his liking into love. Your secret dashed all my hopes. That's why I said you were making a terrible mistake by seeing him. I did genuinely think that you weren't well-suited, but the main reason was that I wanted him for myself."

"We can't choose where we love, Sophia. And if you loved him too, I can't blame you for that."

"Yes, but I did more than try to dissuade you from seeing him. I did something terrible in a moment of weakness and I have never ceased to regret it."

My heart lurched. I couldn't believe that Sophia could do anything awful. She was too honest, too morally upright, too sensible for that.

"What did you do, Sophia?" I asked in a small voice.

"Raphaël came to see me the day before your engagement party. He was very agitated. He had already told me about your relationship, that time when you were so ill one Christmas and he was so distressed. He said that he needed to get a message to you urgently, but that he dared not go directly to your house for fear of compromising you with your parents.

"He had received a message himself that day telling him that his mother was seriously ill and had asked for him to come to her. She was not expected to live for more than a few days. He needed to leave immediately."

"And what happened to this message for me?" My pulse was thudding.

"He gave me a note and asked me to deliver it directly into your hands. He said that, as your best friend, it wouldn't arouse any suspicions if I came to see you the day before your engagement. The note explained why he had to leave and told you to postpone the engagement party by feigning illness. If that proved impossible, you were to make your way to the safe house he had prepared with provisions in Casaccia and wait for him there. Maria, I…" her voice faltered.

My gaze met hers but she looked away.

"I burnt the note, Maria, in the fireplace there." She gestured towards the hearth. "I waited until it was no more than black ashes and then I crushed them to powder with the poker."

The blood drained from my face and a cold, clammy hand gripped my gut.

"Why, Sophia? Why?"

"Because I didn't want you to have him. I thought that if you were irrevocably married he would realise he was mistaken in loving you and would turn to me. I loved him so much that I was prepared to do anything to make him love me. But, of course, he never did. He loved you, Maria. Only you." Her voice shook and she looked down.

"My God, Sophia. Do you realise what you did?"

I looked down, my mouth dry, trying to take it in. Not wanting to believe it. My fingers twisted together.

"But when Raphaël came back to Zaronza, surely he must

have known that I had never received his note."

Sophia hesitated, her hands clasped together in front of her, her knuckles white. She shook her head.

"I swore to him that I gave it into your own hands. He had no reason not to believe me. Instead, he came to believe that you had had second thoughts about becoming the wife of a poor schoolmaster. He was terribly bitter. That's why he left Zaronza and went back to the Bozio."

I covered my face with my hands. Oh God, I thought, tell me this isn't true. But I had to face up to it. In the end he had doubted me, just as I had doubted him because I thought he was afraid of risking his career. What a terrible mess. The anger started to bubble up in my throat.

"And where is he now? What's he doing? I suppose you've kept that from me, as well."

"I have no idea," Sophia replied. "Really. When he left he wanted to forget everyone and everything connected with Zaronza. He said he was disillusioned, and that keeping in contact with me would just remind him of you."

"Do you know what you've done?" I spat out the words. "You have ruined my life and very likely Raphaël's too. What you did made me think he didn't love me and persuaded him that I didn't love him either. How could you do it, Sophia? How could you?"

The hot tears spurted and I couldn't breathe.

"Don't you think I have blighted my own life as well? Not a day goes past without my regretting what I did. I thought that you would be reconciled to Vincentello and that I could win Raphaël's love. But it didn't work out like that. And every day you hated Vincentello a little more. Then I realised what I had done. Oh, Maria, why couldn't you have married Orso? Perhaps I could have married Raphaël and we would all have been happy."

I couldn't speak. I had no words, only a tumult of confused thoughts and memories.

"Maria, I hardly dare ask you to forgive me, since I can't forgive myself."

She pressed her hands to her chest and the tears streamed down her cheeks.

I stood and went to the door, my legs shaking like leaves. On the threshold, I paused and turned to look back at her.

"No, Sophia. Don't ask me. I don't know if I can ever forgive you for this."

PART 3 – RECONCILIATION 1917-1919

Chapter 21

March 1917

I put my arm around his shoulders and lifted him a little, raising the glass to his lips with my other hand. He took a few sips and then nodded to show he had drunk enough.

"Thank you, Madame," he whispered, and I laid him back on the pillow. I tucked the bedclothes around him again. His eyelids closed and he slipped back into sleep. His face was as bleached as the pillow.

"Nurse," another voice called from the opposite side of the ward.

"Yes, I'm coming."

This time a bedpan needed emptying. He looked at me and grimaced and I smiled to reassure him.

"Is there anything else you need?" I asked.

He shook his head and I went to dispose of the bedpan's contents.

This had been the pattern of my days for the past few months, responding to the needs of these broken men and trying to give a little emotional as well as physical comfort. They had all been through things that we dared not imagine.

Corsica had been turned into a hospital island, a place where the war wounded came to recuperate – and in some cases to die. The convent just outside Zaronza had become a base hospital, and each week, received its contingent of the wounded, who had been gassed, machine-gunned, mortared and torn apart by shells, patched up in the dressing stations, and then operated on in the hospitals behind the lines. Those considered well enough to travel were sent on. After a train journey of several days and a sea crossing they arrived here. Some were in a poor state, their dressings unattended to and infection setting in. This was the result of lack of personnel to clean and re-bandage their wounds after their operation, and a journey during which they received little care.

Some were sick with dysentery, piles, trench foot and other illnesses. These men required more nursing care than the wounded. A few with tuberculosis also arrived, although they should have been consigned to isolation hospitals near the Front. These men were put in a separate ward in the basement.

You always knew the ones who were going to die. They had a haunted look about their eyes, as if they could already see beyond this life to something we couldn't yet make out.

***

After Sophia's terrible confession, I spent days and nights thinking through what had happened. What she had done was so outrageous that I couldn't even consider forgiving her – at least not for some time. It had never been my habit to look back too much. But now I couldn't help wondering how my life would have been if Raphaël hadn't been called away that day. I didn't believe in fate. I wasn't at all sure if I believed in God anymore: He made it difficult for us to believe in Him. Even so, maybe the fates had never wanted me and Raphaël to be together, to be happy.

The only comfort I had to cling onto was that Raphaël had loved me. How let down he must have felt, then, when he thought that I had abandoned him. How ironic that each of us thought the other was false. At least I had now found out the truth, but, since he had refused to have anything to do with Zaronza afterwards, he must still have thought I was fickle – that is, if he ever thought of me at all. I wondered where he was. I would have liked to try to find him to explain, but, while the endless war continued and I had work to do, there was little chance of that.

After posing myself so many questions and thinking it all over from every angle, I was exhausted. But this made me determined to do something useful rather than brooding on the past. Owing to the war the business was languishing, but my expenses were small, the house belonged to me, and I had enough money to live on and no debts. And I had no dependents to care for or worry about.

When I had heard about the convent I asked for an interview with the Mother Superior, who had taken on the role of director of the hospital. A tall, aristocratic woman with a natural air of authority, she regarded me with stern, grey eyes.

"Do you realise what you are asking, Madame Orsini? A woman from a sheltered upbringing such as yours is hardly well-equipped to minister to the needs of sick soldiers. And you haven't had any nursing training."

"I would like to try, Ma Mère." I replied. "You're quite right that I have led a sheltered life. I have hardly ever left Zaronza and certainly never Corsica. But what I have experienced in my life has made me used to hardship. Also, I nursed my bedridden mother for several years. She couldn't do anything for herself anymore and I had to deal with everything that this involved. And I have handled my own business interests since my late husband left Corsica for Puerto Rico, so I'm well-organised and resourceful."

Her slate eyes swept over me, judging me. "Hmm. We do need as much help as we can get. The nursing sisters are fully occupied treating the wounded, and we need women who can provide auxiliary support. Few of the village women are suitable. In any case, they have to take the place of their menfolk as well as managing a home and a family and don't have the time. I am inclined to give you a month's trial. But I must warn you: it will be hard work and there will be no room for squeamishness or weakness."

"I won't let you down, Ma Mère."

"And another thing," she added. "Some of these men are psychologically as well as physically damaged. They are liable to cling and seek emotional attachment. You are an attractive woman. Will you be able to remain detached from this? Can you prevent yourself from crossing the boundary between compassion and affection?"

"There again, Ma Mère, life has taught me to keep a barrier around my personal feelings. I think it's unlikely that I would allow anything like that to happen."

She considered me for a few moments. "Very well. You can start tomorrow. Please see Sister Constanza about the details."

She dismissed me with a nod and turned her attention to the sheaf of papers before her.

***

I found I had an aptitude for this kind of work. While I couldn't yet provide skilled nursing care, I could attend to basic tasks and take the burden off the shoulders of the nursing sisters. I could also do simple dressings and administer medicines under supervision. If someone had told me twenty years before that I would be doing this, I would have thought they were mad. I was only interested in romantic stories then, gallant heroes and oppressed maidens. Now, for the first time in my life, I was doing something useful and, although the work was often menial, it gave me great satisfaction.

Even so, despite what I said to the Mother Superior, I found myself becoming emotionally – but not romantically – involved with some of the men. You couldn't help it. They were so grateful for any kindness, any attention, given what they had been through. It was always a wrench when I arrived in the morning to see an empty bed; to learn that the soldier who was ailing yesterday, and whose hand I held while he raved and sweated and twisted, had died in the night. But another soon took his place. And they were bitter.

"You can't imagine how we Corsicans are treated by the French," one said. "If an advance goes wrong, or if we have to retreat, we always get the blame for it. Even some of the doctors behind the lines were harsh towards us. They even accused us of wounding ourselves so we could get invalided out. Can you believe it! And yet we're spilling our blood and guts for France, in a war that hasn't got much to do with us here in Corsica."

He went on to say that, although they did their best at the field hospitals, they were often short-staffed and lacking the right equipment.

"Some who have died might well have lived."

Able-bodied men had flowed out of Corsica, almost fifty thousand of them. Of those that had returned, many were pale shadows of their former selves. And there was another influx of men: the prisoners of war whom the authorities had sent to Corsica since it's not easy to escape from an island. They were housed wherever a secure place could be found and then put to work on the land to make up for the lack of our own menfolk. These were the lucky ones, although they might not have thought so.

***

I continued to read the newspaper, although you never knew if what they printed was the truth or even half of the truth. An article one day talked about the selfless devotion of doctors and nurses in the field hospitals behind the lines. It said they were always looking for volunteers, men and women, to swell their numbers and allow them to concentrate on treating the sick and wounded.

What some of the soldiers had said about the field hospitals made me think. In the convent it was all so well-organised. Yes, I had a role, but I wondered if I could make myself more useful elsewhere. My talent for organisation and my experience with the sick and wounded would surely be of value. The seed of this idea started to sprout but I had no idea how to take it further.

The chief nurse called us together one day in early May and informed us of a circular that the *Service de Santé*[5] had sent around. The Minister of War was setting up a military nursing corps, parallel to the one the Red Cross organised. From what she described, I would be eligible for the trainee grade.

My heart leapt. This would give me the opportunity I had been thinking about.

Part of me threw objections in the way. It would be such a big step. I had never left Corsica, never set foot on the continent. What about the house? What about Annunciata? How would I get there? What was it like to work in a field hospital? Could I deal with the sight of raw flesh and broken limbs, fresh from the battlefield?

A mass of jumbled thoughts and unanswered questions troubled me. All I knew was that the belief was growing that I could be of more use up there than here in Corsica. Like a nagging toothache, it persisted.

I went to see Mother Superior for advice. She stood with her back to me, looking out of the window at the sea, her hands folded in her sleeves.

"You must follow what your convictions tell you to do, Maria, though I would be sorry to lose you, since we find you so useful here. I must admit that, when you first came to see me, I was sceptical. I didn't expect you to last more than a week."

She turned to me, a rare smile lighting up her face.

"I'm very glad to say that I was wrong. You have an aptitude for this work that has served us well. But if you really want to go, I won't stand in your way and you go with my blessing. God will guide your steps. I shall be pleased to authorise your candidacy but you need to hurry: the deadline for applications

---

[5] The *Service de Santé* was part of the *Ministère de Guerre* and organised medical services for wounded and sick servicemen.

isn't far off."

"Thank you, Ma Mère. I'm very grateful for your support. I understand it may take some time for them to make a decision, so I won't leave you just yet."

"I shall pray for you, Maria."

She nodded; the interview was finished.

***

And so they sent off my application. The number of supporting documents the Ministry needed was endless: my birth certificate, judicial record and a certificate of physical aptitude, in addition to my nursing record and the testimonials of Mother Superior, the chief nurse and Doctor Guérin. The days passed and I heard nothing more. I assumed they had turned down my application. Of course, I was disappointed, but tried not to show it and continued to give my attention to our patients.

I had given up hope when, in the early days of July, Doctor Guérin called me to his office. He waved a letter at me.

"Well, Madame Orsini, I have news at last. This letter contains notification that your application is accepted. You have to present yourself at the Ministry of War in Paris, where you will be informed of your posting."

Clasping my hands together, I couldn't prevent a smile from spreading.

"I can't say I rejoice at the news," he continued. "But God knows they need more hands up there, and I'm sure you will acquit yourself well. Good luck."

My head buzzing, my legs faltered as I left his office and I had to support myself against the wall in the corridor. I pressed my forehead against the cool plaster.

Paris! I had never left Corsica, let alone been to a big city. Was I capable of this? The immensity of what I was doing stretched before me like a boundless desert.

Chapter 22

A few days later, having said my goodbyes at the convent and to my few acquaintances, I left the house at Zaronza, not knowing when I would return. My trunk had gone on before me and I had only a small case with essentials for the journey.

"Now, don't worry about the house while you are away," said Annunciata, who thought the whole scheme was folly. "Everything will be safe and I'll make sure it's clean and aired."

I promised to write when I had time. She hugged me and I turned away so she didn't see the tears springing to my eyes. As I crossed the square, I made out Sophia standing in the shadowy passage leading to her house. But I looked away. It was still too soon.

The sun was blisteringly hot and I was glad of the hat Annunciata made me wear. Arriving in Bastia, I made my way to the port and found the vessel on which my passage was booked. Having a little time to spare, I strolled around the alleyways of the old town, dominated by the Genoese citadel. I tried to remember every cobblestone, every doorway, just as I had filled my nostrils with the scent of the *maquis* in the trap on the way to Bastia. For who knew when I would be back?

I had very little idea of what to expect up there in northern France. For a moment my heart sank and I was tempted to stay behind, to return to the comfort and safety of my house at Zaronza, to renounce this venture. But that would have been to let down too many people, not least myself. And I was now a member of the military, so it would have counted as desertion. Shaking these thoughts out of my head, I took a last look at the twin bell towers of the church of Saint-Jean-Baptiste and then walked towards the boat.

The atmosphere was tense on board. German U-boats had been patrolling in the Mediterranean, and the crossing was hazardous. I hadn't taken a cabin, wanting to be near the deck if anything should happen. This was the right decision, since a violent thunderstorm broke out in mid-passage and the sea tossed the ship back and forth. Although I wasn't sick, a headache bound my temples in an iron grip. I sank into a seat, sleeping on and off but never for long.

The crossing was without further incident and dawn was breaking as the port of Marseille came in sight. The sea was calm again after the storm and I elbowed my way through the throng of passengers to the prow as the city swelled before us. I was amazed at the size of the place; it stretched in all directions. Recognising some of the landmarks Raphaël had told me about, I realised with a jolt that I was following in his footsteps. The familiar pang pinched my heart, but soon the boat docked and I had too much to do to give in to it.

Thank goodness for Annunciata and her endless family connections. Her daughter-in-law's uncle, Monsieur Fratelli, was a wholesaler in Marseille and he had agreed to lodge me for a night before I took the train to Paris. The deckhands pitched my trunk onto the crowded quayside and I re-joined it. I had never seen so many people at once. The noise and bustle were indescribable. It was like a dance, of which everyone but me knew the steps. Around me, voices I didn't understand, as well as the soupy accent of Marseille, buzzed like a swarm of bees. People with dark faces wearing strange clothes jostled each other. The sun beat down on the quay, and unaccustomed scents of spices and humanity hung heavy in the air.

The uncle was supposed to meet me there, but no one came forward so I sat on my box and waited. The flood of people parted around the trunk and I received a few resentful glances. Twenty minutes later a portly man wearing a bowler hat hurried puffing onto the quay.

"Madame Orsini? I'm so sorry to have kept you waiting.

Business."

He shrugged and snapped his fingers at a burly man behind him, who hefted my trunk onto his shoulder and carried it off to a waiting horse-drawn cab, leaving me and the uncle to follow. The cab took us to a narrow street on the hillside overlooking the Vieux Port, where Monsieur Fratelli had his house.

Madame Fratelli greeted me with coffee and breakfast, while Monsieur had to go back to his office. Although I was tired, I welcomed her suggestion to show me some of the sights of Marseille once I had rested a little. I was grateful for her company, for I didn't want to venture on my own in that place and it was so huge that I would surely have got lost.

Madame Fratelli had prepared a *bouillabaisse* for supper. She was almost apologetic.

"I thought it might make a change from Corsican food."

She was right; it was delicious. We went to bed early, for which I was grateful since my head was buzzing with everything I had seen. In the morning Monsieur Fratelli accompanied me and my trunk, which I was already regarding as a burden, to the station, an enormous building with a monumental staircase. He waved aside my thanks.

"We are Corsicans, aren't we? War or no war, things would have come to a sorry state if we couldn't show each other a little hospitality."

He helped me with the formalities of the trunk and the ticket, and then excused himself as he had business to see to. He scribbled on a piece of paper the address of a hotel near the Gare de Lyon run by a Corsican couple.

"Their prices are correct," he said. "And it's a respectable and clean establishment. I stay there myself when I go to Paris. Tell them I sent you."

Doffing his hat, he disappeared into the crowd, in a hurry as ever, and left me to wait for my train.

***

The train was crowded and I was lucky to get a seat. As it was, I was squashed into the corner by the window, with little chance of moving even if I wanted to. I resigned myself to looking out of the window at the changing landscape. At first, it reminded me a little of Corsica, although it was not so mountainous. But the vegetation was similar, as was the clarity of the light, which polished the scenery. As we continued northwards, the sky changed and the bright azure turned to a paler blue, wreathed with wisps of cloud. The landscape was softer and greener, too, and the towns were nothing like our Corsican villages. It looked like a foreign country.

After hours of travelling, I had to change at Lyon for the Paris train. My body ached from sitting in one position for so long, and I was glad of the chance to stretch my limbs, but I had to make sure they transferred my trunk from one train to another. I had difficulty making the surly porters understand me; it was hard to believe we were speaking the same language. At last, it was done and I boarded the second train which, if anything, was even more full than the first. There was no chance of a seat and I had to sit on my case in the corridor. The train was stifling, and smuts floated in through the open windows, coating everything in black smears. Madame Fratelli's basket of copious provisions was a godsend. It saved me from queuing at crowded station buffets for food that was no doubt indifferent.

The train travelled on through the night until, early in the morning, we drew into the Gare de Lyon, having crawled through smog-bound suburbs. My back felt as if a regiment had marched across it, and my feet were swollen. My dress was crumpled and smudged with black, and my hair was falling around my face. What a sight I must have been.

I stumbled off the train, straightened my hat and went to look for my trunk. It had been dumped on the platform. I looked around, not knowing what to do. A well-dressed, middle-aged woman came up to me.

"You look lost," she said. "Can I help you at all?"

"Do you know how I can get to this place, Madame?" I showed her the address Monsieur Fratelli had given me.

"It's not far from here. Let me call a porter and then we can share a cab since it's on my way."

She summoned a uniformed man who took charge of my trunk. The woman held my arm and directed me towards the exit where a line of motorised cabs waited. I was too exhausted to speak, except to tell her that I was on my way to nurse at the Front. Five minutes later, we drew up outside a dark stone building with elaborate wrought-iron balconies beneath the upper windows.

"This is your hotel," she said.

I opened my purse to pay my share of the fare but she placed her hand on it.

"I won't hear of it. My son is at the Front. You are doing an invaluable job. Who knows? One day he might need you – or someone like you."

I got out, the cab driver deposited my trunk and case at the entrance, and the cab lurched off along the street. I hadn't even asked her name. For the second time in as many days, I had experienced the kindness of strangers.

The Corsican couple, Monsieur and Madame Poletti, were as welcoming as Monsieur Fratelli had predicted. They put my trunk into a storeroom until I needed it again, and showed me to a small but clean room at the back of the hotel. Without undressing, I collapsed onto the bed and sleep soon overtook me.

Hours later I awoke and the declining light showed it was already evening. I washed my face in the basin with cold water and changed my dress. My rumbling stomach told me I hadn't eaten all day. The hoteliers directed me to a small neighbourhood restaurant where I ate *choucroute* for the first time. I had had more new experiences in a few days in France than in almost the whole of my life in Corsica.

***

The following day, I set out early for the Boulevard Saint-Germain, where I had an interview at the Ministry of War. It was a fine day and I had plenty of time, so I decided to walk, having first assured myself of the way. The heat was not the intense dry heat of Corsica; rather, it was sticky and dusty. The buildings, although grand and elegant, towered over me and I felt closed in. Even the plane trees lining the boulevards seemed grubby and weary. I longed for the open skies and mountains and clear air of Corsica.

Many of the shops were shut, with notices in the windows saying that it was because of the war. The streets were full of vehicles, and people swarmed about like so many ants. Soldiers in uniform strolled along the pavements, every one with a woman hanging on his arm – you would never see behaviour like that in Corsica. Despite their female companions, the men looked sideways at me as I passed. I pretended not to notice. You couldn't escape the casualties of war. Men on crutches or missing an arm or part of a leg were everywhere.

At the Ministry, they showed me to an anteroom where I had to wait for a long time before a clerk ushered me into a stuffy office. The major who received me was rushed and impatient, his desk covered with teetering towers of papers and files.

"You will report to the military hospital at Bar-le-Duc in four days' time," he informed me.

I had no idea where this place was, but I had more important concerns.

"Will I be nursing Corsican soldiers there?"

He looked at me over his *pince-nez*. "You will be nursing *French* soldiers, Madame. All Corsican soldiers are French by definition."

I dared not question him further. After a few further formalities he dismissed me and I was free until I had to take the train, this time from the Gare de l'Est, to Bar-le-Duc. Did I really have to come all the way to Paris to receive news of my posting? Surely a letter or a telegram would have been sufficient. But I realised that the military machine didn't work like that; you did as you were ordered. I would have to get used to it.

Now I was there, I decided to make the most of my few days' leave. Paris was so huge that it was hard to know where to start, so I wandered along the Boulevard Saint-Germain and crossed the river. I arrived at a broad square where fountains played next to a formal garden. The streets in this part of Paris were wide and airy, lined with stylish shops that I would never dare enter. We had nothing like them, even in Bastia. My Corsican lack of sophistication was evident. Having lunched in a small café – something I had never done alone – I continued my voyage of discovery, ending up at a large white church on top of a hill, which I was told was Sacré-Coeur.

After walking around for hours, I realised that dusk was falling and I ought to return to the hotel. I had lost my bearings, since all the streets looked alike, but if I headed back to the river I thought I would manage. As I stood on the pavement pondering which way to go, two soldiers burst out of a café and one staggered into me. He raised his cap.

"*Milles pardons, Mademoiselle.*" His breath was fetid with alcohol.

I raised my eyebrows.

He started to speak in a language I didn't understand: it wasn't French. He leered at me and put his arm around my waist while his friend looked on, sniggering. I twisted away.

He loomed towards me, his mouth puckered as if to kiss me, but I sidestepped him and ran away from them. Their jeering laughter pursued me. At the end of the street I looked back and they were supporting each other, doubled up with mirth. For a man to behave like that towards a respectable woman in Corsica would have been unthinkable. France really was a foreign country.

My heart pounding, I set off a brisk pace until I reached the river and then retraced my route of that morning. By the time I found the hotel again it was almost dark.

"There you are, Madame Orsini," Monsieur Poletti said. "We were getting quite worried about you."

"I'm afraid I lost my way and it took me a while to find this street again. I suppose it will be too late to get a meal at a restaurant?"

He nodded his regret. "But don't worry; my wife will bring you up some soup and charcuterie to your room."

I accepted his offer gratefully and regained my bedroom.

The time passed all too fast. I was just finding my way around and getting used to Parisian ways when I had to leave for the Front. I was impatient to get there, but I was still anxious about what I might find. So many new experiences in such a short time. I had visited Napoleon's tomb, entered a cinema for the first time, wandered around the galleries of the Louvre and explored the spacious boulevards until my feet throbbed. How Sophia would have loved this!

My heart plunged. What a maze life is capable of dragging you into. I still couldn't believe what she had done.

Chapter 23

The journey to Bar-le-Duc from the Gare de l'Est was even worse than that from Marseille to Paris. It took nearly twelve hours; I had understood it should take four or five. The train stopped at every halt, sometimes for minutes at a time. The carriage was airless, even with all the windows open. We kept stopping and shunting into sidings to let troop trains pass or to repair the faulty engine.

Each time, people hung out of the windows, asking "What's going on?", but they were resigned to the delays. They shrugged. "Well, that's the war for you."

Night was falling when the train limped into Bar-le-Duc. Tight-lipped soldiers returning to the Front after leave in Paris shouldered their kitbags and ambled towards the exit. No one was there to meet me but I didn't expect it. And the train was so late that they would have given up by then. Despite it being late July, a fine, chilly drizzle was falling. I shivered in my light clothes.

Two soldiers took pity on me and bundled me into the back of a military lorry along with my trunk and case. The lorry was going to pass close to the hospital and they agreed to take me all the way there. The other soldiers shuffled along to make room for me. One offered me a cigarette but I smiled and shook my head. They sat in silence, each wrapped up in his thoughts. A few took furtive glances at me but looked away when I returned their gaze.

After a frustrating wait at the hospital, when no one seemed to know who I was or what to do with me, a nurse in a blinding-white starched uniform approached and led me to a dormitory. I had to report to one of the surgical wards in the morning. Seven other beds lined the walls. I had hoped for a room of my own, but I was so tired that I pushed my case under the bed, undressed quickly and sank into sleep.

***

People might tell you that war is full of excitement and activity, but it's not true. Bursts of action and fighting were followed by periods when nothing happened: neither advance nor retreat, neither victory nor defeat. Stalemate. We were some distance behind the lines, but the whistle and low crump of shelling and staccato bursts of machine guns in the distance carried as far as our hospital. How the men in the trenches could stand it, I didn't know. It explained the blank-eyed stares of the wounded back in Corsica. For them, the war was over, but it still lived on in their minds, perhaps forever.

News trickled around the hospital of mutinies that had taken place in late May on the Chemin des Dames: men who refused to go over the top any more, believing the attacks they were ordered to make achieved nothing. The authorities moved fast to suppress these rumours, for fear of rebellion spreading like a spark along a trail of gunpowder. They talked of making an example out of cowards and deserters, of courts martial, of firing squads. But how many men were executed we never knew.

The hospital was in a former barracks. They had set up additional huts in the drill square that served as operating theatres and wards. To start with, I worked in a surgical ward as a trainee, helping to care for the men who had been operated on. I learned to re-bandage their wounds and to recognise the signs of infection from their colour and smell. Some were suffering from illnesses and other conditions, such as trench foot or piles, and needed additional care. Thanks to the introduction of vaccinations, there were fewer cases of tetanus now. And inoculation against typhoid had almost wiped out the disease.

We had very little time for thinking. Our days were taken up with repetitive but necessary tasks: rolling bandages, emptying bedpans, stripping or making beds, running errands, a thousand different things. We never had enough clean water and couldn't be sure that the water provided had been boiled long and hard enough. So we used a great deal of oxygenated water to clean the wounds and sprinkle on the fresh bandages. One of my jobs was to take the buckets to get water and then take them back to empty them. At first the weight almost tore my arms from their sockets, but I became used to it.

Some of the doctors could be difficult. They insisted on inspecting wounds that you had re-bandaged only half an hour before and then you had to do it all over again. This all took time and meant that we were often behind. It was no use complaining; that would just end in a critical comment on your record.

I had difficulties with a few of the other nurses, too. They seemed to resent us newcomers. One in particular, Agnès Rivière, had made it clear from the outset that she didn't like me.

"You come here and think you know it all – think you can tell us how things should be organised. Well, let me tell you, I worked at Val-de-Grâce[6] for ten years before the war. I saw everything, did everything. You can never replace us."

I had simply made an innocuous comment about tidying up a corner of the ward where someone had placed used dressings and hypodermic needles.

"I wouldn't even consider it, Agnès," I replied. "I signed up, like the others, because I want to do something useful and I believe I can here. But I don't want to replace you. How could I, as a trainee? Don't you think there's room for all of us?"

She sniffed and moved away.

---

[6] Military hospital in Paris.

Later, I found out that she had other causes for grievance. She was very attentive to one of her patients, a young man with an amputated foot. He didn't seem to notice or to respond to her. But when I came in sight his eyes lit up, and her gaze followed his until it alighted on me. She pressed her lips together and turned back to continue giving him an injection. After that, she always singled me out for the most menial or unpleasant tasks, but I didn't complain. The young man was discharged, and she went about with a long face for a while – until a handsome corporal was brought in with a broken leg and pelvis.

She also had 'her' patients and allowed no one else to tend to them. Even giving one of them a drink of water in her momentary absence was enough to kindle her anger. But she was not the only one who behaved like that. It surprised and saddened me that such jealousy and rivalry could exist among nurses.

I got on well enough with most of the other nurses and auxiliaries. Françoise Marty, a young woman of twenty-five, who shared my dormitory, reminded me a little of Sophia. She was slight and small but with darker hair and features. She came from a farm in the south west, near Cahors, and had four brothers, all of whom were at the Front. By some fortunate chance none of them had been wounded, but Françoise had a haggard look and I knew she was constantly anxious about them.

In a brief moment of calm, we sat on a box in the sun with our backs to the wall of one of the huts. She smoked a cigarette.

"What made you volunteer, Françoise?" I asked.

She sighed. "I was engaged to my sweetheart, Claude, from the next village. He was badly wounded by shrapnel at the Battle of Verdun. They had to amputate his leg below the knee. I was waiting for him at the station in Cahors when they sent him home. Claude got out of the train, with a lot of difficulty, stumbling on his false leg. I ran towards him but he looked through me as if he hadn't seen me and limped past. I ran after him but he shouted at me to leave him alone. Everyone was looking at us."

Her voice shook and I put my hand on her arm.

"He refused to see me and said our engagement was over. My father was very angry and went to see him, but when he came back he wouldn't tell me what Claude had said to him. All he said was, 'You'll have to find yourself another young man, Françoise, if there are any left after this.'"

"I couldn't bear to stay there with everyone knowing it was finished. My parents wanted me to help on the farm, but I thought I could be more useful here. My brothers were all at the Front – and thank God they have been lucky so far. I wanted to do something too."

I nodded. This was a common refrain.

She smiled. "I'm not looking for another fiancé, if that's what you think."

"I didn't think that," I said. "Perhaps your Claude just needs some time. It's a difficult thing for a young man in his prime to be reduced to relying on others. Maybe he was afraid that you would pity him, and if he's proud, he won't be able to put up with that. When this war is over he might think differently."

"Thank you," she said. "It does help to talk with someone about it. I daren't hope that Claude will change his mind. But what about your story? I don't want to pry, but haven't you ever been married?" She glanced at my ring-less left hand.

I gave her an edited version of my love for Raphaël and my marriage to Vincentello.

"I would never have guessed," she said. "We all have our problems, it seems." She continued to puff on her cigarette. We sat for a while without speaking – without needing to – before we had to take up our duties again.

Sometimes, I found myself wondering about Raphaël. Was he still in Corsica? That seemed unlikely. But then where was he? Could he be fighting on these very lines behind which our hospital stood? The 173rd Infantry Regiment was fighting at Verdun and was involved in the terrible battle last year. Sometimes we treated wounded Corsican soldiers, but none of them seemed to know of him when I asked. Could Raphaël be brought in wounded one day? I grew cold at the thought that he might suffer, that they might mark him out for death. In that case, it would be better to die outright.

***

When I had been there a few weeks, around the middle of August, more nurses and doctors joined us. The stream of motor lorries on the road that passed the hospital had greatly increased and an air of expectancy hovered over us. All day armaments trucks and supplies wagons rumbled past on what they called the "Sacred Road" to Verdun, raising clouds of dust. It was an open secret that an offensive against the German lines was planned. Everyone had been talking about it. A series of raids on the enemy trenches took place before the main attack, and the cannons bombarded the German positions for several days to "soften them up." The rumbling of the constant and furious bombardment sounded like distant thunder.

The first wounded from the raids started to come through from the evacuation hospitals nearer the Front. The operating blocks were working around the clock, and some of the more experienced nurses from our ward were sent to the pre-operative service to cope with the influx.

"Some of them are in a terrible state," said Jeanine, who shared our dormitory. "Being shaken around in an ambulance to get here doesn't help. The casualty clearing stations bind them up as best they can, but their wounds are full of mud, straw, horse muck and all kinds of debris. It's very difficult to get them properly clean and some have already got infections. At least they've all had a tetanus vaccination." She shook her head. No one had known, when the war started, that it would be like this.

The operated soldiers flowed onto the wards and we had our work cut out dealing with them. Most had been wounded by shrapnel, but they also had wounds caused by bullets and grenades. The attack itself started on 20th August and the stream became a torrent. We heard that the offensive was an early success, but the price in terms of lives and wounded was high.

The morning after the attack started, news began to come through of the bombardment by German planes of Hospital XII at Vadelaincourt, closer to the front line. Some of the wounded who were due to be operated on there were sent to us instead, and some who had been wounded in the attack on the hospital started to arrive, too.

"How could they possibly drop bombs onto a hospital?" I asked. "It's inhuman. Has the world gone mad?"

"They say there's a munitions dump nearby," Françoise replied. "Maybe they were aiming at that?"

But when the bombs continued to fall on Vadelaincourt, night after night, we saw that this was no mistake. An ambulance driver who brought in a wounded doctor and nurses from Hospital XII confirmed our fears. His hand shook as he sucked on a cigarette.

"Would you believe the bastards were following me and trying to machine gun the ambulance? It's got a bloody great red cross on the top. No one's telling me they were making a mistake."

Later in September, a nurse from Vadelaincourt, Madeleine Lanthier, joined us on the ward. The bombs had damaged Hospital XII so badly that it had closed, and the wounded were transferred elsewhere.

"The first night, I had gone to bed early when they came," she said. "They dropped incendiary bombs on some of the huts and they went up like kindling. The men inside were already badly wounded and some of them couldn't get out – we could hear them screaming. We could see the flames inside. It was like

Hell. We tried to put out the fires with water, but they were burning too fiercely and showers of sparks were landing on us. The next day the bed frames in those huts were just twisted lumps of iron."

Her eyes wide as she relived the horror, she continued, "They kept coming back. You heard the sound of their engines, so different from our French planes. Then they would cut the engines as they dropped the bombs and you held your breath wondering where they would fall. The nurses' billet was so badly damaged that I couldn't open the door into my room at first. When I did shove it open, there was a mass of rubble on my bed and all my belongings had been torn apart. Some of my colleagues were in that hut at the time. Most of them were killed." She looked away, her eyes brimming.

Madeleine narrowly escaped death on several occasions, once diving beneath a bed in a ward just in time as a window blew in and shattered.

"But how did you live with the constant fear?" I asked.

"Oh, you begin to get used to it. Everyone was convinced they were going to die so you just got on with your work. Anyway, I felt I owed it to our poor wounded. I couldn't just give up after all they had been through. Somehow you shut down a part of yourself."

But that part re-emerged at night when Madeleine screamed and writhed in her sleep. After a while, they gave her a room to herself. She was sent back to an administrative job in Paris after that.

Her hands shook too much.

Chapter 24

The steady flow of casualties from shrapnel, gas, shells and bullets became a flood during and after the offensive. The ambulances were not enough. They brought the men in from the dressing stations and evacuation hospitals in whatever transport they had been able to find or commandeer – troop lorries or munitions trucks.

We had taken over some of the workload from Hospital XII at Vadelaincourt, so they set aside part of my ward for triage[7]. The doctors walked amongst the injured soldiers and made a cursory examination of their injuries, doling out life or death as they went. Sometimes the nurses had to take on this task too, because there were too many wounded.

"Head wound – urgent."

"Amputation, left leg below the knee."

"Abdominal wound – inoperable." The nurses gave them morphia and we tried to comfort them as best we could during their last hours. But it was difficult. Those who were going to live needed us, too.

Most of the condemned knew they were going to die and had accepted it. They lay white-faced, their eyes cavernous with the sight of death. A few fought against their fate with bitter words. They had nothing else left to fight with.

***

They brought in a corporal one day, a thickset man in his thirties, with a broad black moustache. He had been wounded

---

[7] The process of assessing the gravity of wounds and illnesses.

in the upper body and shrapnel was lodged in his chest.

"I'll operate on him straight away," Doctor Moran said. "He might have a chance if I can get all the shrapnel out."

He operated for several hours but was unable to remove all the shards of metal. Doctor Moran shook his head. When the soldier came round from the ether, he was convinced that everything was all right and that he would live. We didn't have the heart to tell him otherwise.

He gripped my arm with surprising strength as I gave him some water.

"I'm going to live, aren't I? I'm going to go home again."

"There's every chance," I said, cursing myself for the lie but unable to tell him the truth. He smiled and lay back on the pillow.

Blood poisoning soon set in, and Doctor Moran gave him no more than a few days. Now he was in pain and we gave him morphia but it couldn't calm his torments. He twisted and turned to escape the agony. He fell into a fever and started to rave and I mopped his brow. He gripped my hand again.

"Thérèse," he said. "My love. I'm so glad that we're together again. Where are the boys? Now we can all be happy." He smiled until a twist of pain turned it into a grimace.

His commanding officer came to see him and said he had been mentioned in despatches and would receive a medal. But the dying man didn't even hear. He didn't know who the officer was or what was happening. The officer sighed and moved on to the next one. I watched him as he went around the ward, saluting each wounded soldier. Most of them were subdued.

A piece of metal on a ribbon and a pension for their widows – was this really all they got for leaving their lives in the mud?

On the last day, the dying man was lucid again. Doctor Moran whispered to me that the end was near.

The corporal turned his head to me. "It doesn't hurt anymore. I'm getting better, aren't I?" he said. "That's right, isn't it?"

I said nothing but squeezed his hand. His face sank inwards and his eyes grew large. Now, like the rest of them, he was looking on the death he could no longer fend off. I asked the priest to go to him and he placed a screen around the bed. From the other end of the ward, I heard the murmuring of the last rites, the soldier's acceptance at last that he was dying.

A little later, I went to him. His eyes were closed and I thought he was asleep, so I started to turn away. Without opening his eyes, he said, "She makes the best *daube* you've ever eaten. I so wanted to taste it again." A tear slid out from beneath his eyelid.

He didn't last out the night. Another telegram, another widow mad with grief, another clutch of fatherless children.

And they did cling, just as Mother Superior back in Corsica said they would. A young Corsican subaltern, at least ten years younger than me, had lost his right hand to a shell during the August offensive. They amputated his arm below the elbow. He was a teacher, it turned out, in Ajaccio, where he still had parents and sisters. He was no longer in danger of gangrene or infections and sat up in bed reading whatever he could get hold of. Sometimes he and I talked of Corsica. It seemed like another world. I asked him if by chance he knew a Raphaël Colombani, whom I described as a friend, but he shook his head.

"He must have been in a different battalion."

"Would you help me write a letter to my parents?" he asked one day. "I've been practising writing with my left hand so that I can write on the blackboard again, but it's still illegible. They will have told them of my injuries but I would like them to hear directly from me. I don't want them to worry."

I agreed and went to fetch a pen and writing paper. He dictated me his letter, which covered two pages, and I gave it to him to read.

"You have beautiful handwriting, Madame." Everybody used to say that. At school, it was the only thing I excelled at.

"Or may I call you Maria?"

"You may."

We tried to be friendly but distant; to give them comfort but not to become involved. But we were the first women they had seen for months. Sometimes the air was thick with sexual tension. And we were seeing them at their most vulnerable, naked and fearful. Some of the others did let down their guard, and relationships flourished in the hothouse environment of war.

He smiled and grasped my hand with his good one. "You are beautiful, Maria, just like your handwriting. In fact, everything about you is lovely."

I smiled back but withdrew my hand. "You mustn't speak like that. I'm much older than you and have been married. I'm quite content not to be married or have a sweetheart again. In any case, you'll soon be leaving to go to a base hospital and recuperate. There will be other men who need our care."

"And don't you think I need care – and love? It's because of this, isn't it?" he raised his stump. "You don't want a mutilated lover." And he turned his face to the wall.

It was no use arguing with him. He wouldn't have understood – he wouldn't even have tried to. I felt friendship for him, but nothing more. If I had loved him, his maimed arm wouldn't have been a barrier. But some of the men were so bitter. We could heal their bodies but not their minds. Some said they had been patched up only so they could go back to the fighting again; that the doctors saved only those who had a chance of being able-bodied again and fed back into the machine of war.

We nurses were on our feet all day. Sometimes it was very hard. It wasn't only the sight of the wounds and the terrible mutilations. It was also the stench of gangrene and pus, the sounds of men groaning and raving and the odour of death that you could almost taste. Exhausted after my shifts, I tumbled into bed and plunged into a dreamless sleep.

Whenever I found time, I wrote to Annunciata. But I rarely

received a reply, and when I did it was one small sheet covered with her formless writing, as if an inky beetle had trailed over the page. Things were much the same at Zaronza, it seemed. I would have loved to have someone else to exchange letters with but, of course, it was impossible to write to Sophia. Perhaps I could have written to Monsieur Franceschi, but somehow I couldn't summon up the nerve.

***

As autumn wore on, the cold took us in its grip. I was not used to the damp, penetrating chill of northern France. Following a heavy cold, I developed a persistent cough that lasted for several weeks. I longed for the sunshine and pure Corsican air.

Christmas provided a little light relief. The offensive was over in October and, since we had regained territory from the Germans, the sector had become much calmer. We decorated a Christmas tree in the ward, and handed out chocolates and cigarettes donated by the public to our patients. Some of the nurses set up a crèche in the chapel and the walking wounded attended Midnight Mass. I joined them for form's sake, not out of any great conviction, although the responses were ingrained on my memory and I said them automatically. How did they keep their faith after all they had been through? How could a loving God have allowed such suffering?

After Christmas, I was granted a few days' leave, the first in more than five months. Sometimes on a Sunday or whenever I had a free afternoon, I wandered around Bar-le-Duc, but it was always full of soldiers and was not a relaxing place to be. When they came back behind the lines to rest they stripped the shops of any delicacies and took over the cafés, carousing and singing too loudly. Apart from that, I had little chance of outings or leisure. I was tired and needed to get away from that place.

I considered going back to Corsica, but the journey was too

long. I would barely have arrived before having to leave again. And I wasn't sure that I would have the courage to return to Bar-le-Duc after seeing Corsican seas and skies and mountains and my beloved Zaronza and Annunciata again. I didn't think I could tear myself away from them. I could understand why some of the men deserted at the end of their leave; it must have been even more difficult for those with wives and families. How did they summon the strength to come back?

In any case, my promise to myself that I would see this through couldn't be broken. And so I decided to go to Paris again and stay at the Corsicans' hotel. When I left in July they had said there would always be a bed there for me. At least in Paris I would be able to distract myself with the sights, even if it was January.

I took the train in the opposite direction from Bar-le-Duc. It was full of soldiers going on leave, and the atmosphere was much more cheerful than during my previous journey. They sang and joked and played cards, even though space was restricted. One or two attempted to flirt with me but I had taken to wearing my wedding ring again to deal with just this prospect. When I removed my gloves, they soon stopped and left me alone. No doubt some of them were married themselves, but I couldn't find it in my heart to blame them or to begrudge them their forced gaiety.

Monsieur and Madame Poletti greeted me like a long-lost daughter and spoiled me during my stay. They gave me the same spotless, comfortable room at the back of the hotel. "This is *your* room," Monsieur Poletti said, beaming. Although I tried to insist on paying the full rate, they waved away my objections and let me have the room for a trifling sum.

They wanted to know all about how it was at the Front, but I was evasive. I wasn't there for that; I was here to forget, to gather my strength for the next onslaught. They soon realised that the war was not something I wanted to discuss, and we talked about Corsica instead. They also came from Cap Corse, but from Erbalunga on the other side of the cape, north of Bastia.

"One day we'll go back permanently," Madame Poletti said. "We still have a house in Erbalunga and I miss it so much there. But few people can make a living from fishing or growing olives these days. I've never really got used to Paris." She sighed.

"How long have you been here?" I asked.

"Oh, nearly forty years," Monsieur Poletti replied. "We try to go back to Erbalunga once a year, in the summer. But it's always hard to leave again."

I understood just what he meant.

My few days in Paris were the tonic I needed. Armed with recommendations from the Polettis, I resumed my tourist wanderings, ate better than I had done for months, and regained my lost energy.

As I walked across the Pont Alexandre III one day, a man in uniform with ink-black hair was strolling along ahead of me. He had Raphaël's height and build. My heart stopped and my knees threatened to buckle beneath me.

"Raphaël! Raphaël!" I cried out and quickened my pace. Stumbling forward, I grasped him by the arm and turned him to face me. He raised his eyebrows and I saw my mistake.

"I'm so sorry; I thought you were someone else. Please excuse me."

He smiled, touched his cap and walked on.

My cheeks red hot, I clutched the parapet of the bridge and supported myself against it. How could I be so stupid? What were the chances of meeting Raphaël like that, assuming even that he spent his leave in Paris? What must that man have thought of me? There were enough women of bad reputation in Paris already; I didn't want to be classed among them.

But I knew that once this war was over, I had to do what I could to find Raphaël again.

Chapter 25

1918

Refreshed by my leave in Paris, I returned to Bar-le-Duc in early February. The weather was dreadful. Freezing rain like melted snow fell from a slate-grey sky, and a biting north-east wind made it seem even colder. Black, bare trees raised skeletal branches, and the landscape was drained of colour. Even the grass looked grey. I would never get used to the climate here. But then I thought how it must have been for our poor soldiers in the trenches. At least I had a warm bed. And, being so far behind the lines, we were in much less danger than they were.

Things continued much as before, but I felt less tired and more hopeful than before I went to Paris. At last, I was awarded my nursing diploma, which was a great satisfaction to me. There were those who didn't share this opinion.

"They hand out diplomas like confetti these days," Agnès said. "I suppose you can only expect standards to slip in wartime."

I ignored her, knowing that she was just trying to make me answer back and draw me into an argument. The chief nurse and the doctor in charge had both given me good mentions on my record, and I knew from the men's attitude that they thought my care was good. Sometimes they were in great pain and having their dressings unwound, their wounds cleaned and the bandages rebound was agonising. But having dealt with my mother for so many years, I had learned the knack of gentleness.

"That's much more comfortable," one soldier with a leg wound said. "It hardly hurts at all when you do it, Madame."

Many of these poor boys were young enough to be my sons, scarcely more than schoolboys. And that's how I thought of them, for beneath the bravado they were scared and vulnerable. What a shock for them the reality of the war must have been: far away from their families, having to show bravery in front of sometimes terrible odds, having to put up with poor conditions and bad food, coping with the daily and constant fear of death and seeing their friends torn to bits. And yet how robust the human spirit must be to endure all this and still survive.

After we had regained the territory lost to the Germans in 1916, this sector was less active. But in March the Germans attacked again, further north in Picardy. They tried to drive a wedge between the armies and push our soldiers back. The vibration of engines on the road outside our hospital was constant as they moved troops northwards to try to contain the attack. The news was confused but not reassuring.

Doctor Morisseau, the chief doctor, called a meeting.

"The hospitals in the north are struggling to keep up with the workload," he said. "The *Service de Santé* has asked if we can supply qualified volunteers to go to Amiens, where they are in great need of extra hands. I need hardly tell you that it will be dangerous, and that you may find yourselves very close to the front line."

Without hesitation, I raised my hand along with a score of others. It might be dangerous, but at least I would be doing something useful. And now I had my diploma, and more than eighteen months' nursing experience. They sent our names to the Ministry and we received our orders to transfer.

Françoise bade me a tearful farewell. As an auxiliary without a diploma she had to stay at Bar-le-Duc.

"I wish I could come with you," she said. "I'll miss you."

"I'll write to you when things are settled and I know exactly where I will be stationed," I said, pressing her hand. "I can't promise to write very often – I expect we will be rushed off our feet up there. But I do promise that I will stay in touch." We had already exchanged addresses in Corsica and Cahors some time ago.

She dabbed her red-rimmed eyes with her balled-up handkerchief. My own eyes smarting, I said goodbye to my other friends who were remaining behind. They would still be needed here.

***

Another endless journey took me and my well-travelled trunk up to Amiens. The scars of war were far more obvious there than in Bar-le-Duc. Ruined buildings and factories raised jagged walls and twisted girders to the sky and the roads were full of rubble.

My dormitory building was about fifteen minutes' walk from the military hospital, and the thump of shells and zinging of bullets accompanied my journey to and fro each day. Sometimes German aeroplanes came over and dropped bombs on the city not far from the hospital. My heart raced as I walked there as fast as I could, dashing for the nearest doorway every time I heard the whine of a missile nearby. One day I stumbled over some fallen masonry, tearing my stockings and gashing my knee. Surely they wouldn't bombard the hospital? But then look what they had done to Vadelaincourt.

All the roads converging on Amiens from the north and east were crammed with civilian refugees escaping the German advance. Lorries full of reinforcements, munitions and provisions forced their way in the other direction. Some refugees made for the station but it wasn't easy to get a place on a train. Others flooded out on the roads towards Paris. In their panic to escape, they had brought with them the most unsuitable things. One elderly woman clutched a cartwheel of a cheese to her chest. A middle-aged couple pushed a handcart along filled with gilt-framed pictures. Most carried ill-tied bundles that scattered their contents on the road as they went.

Their features tight and drawn, they glanced over their shoulders from time to time. Was it regret for what they had left behind, or fear of the advancing Germans; or both?

It was easy to get to know people in wartime. In a short time, I became friendly with an older nurse in her late fifties, Odette Combel, who was on the same ward. Despite our immediate rapport we were still not on first name terms, perhaps because of the age difference. Although she was a Parisian by birth, she had nursed in Bordeaux before volunteering to nurse closer to the Front. She had been in Amiens for several months already.

"They offered me Calais or Amiens," she said. "I chose Amiens because they suggested for a woman of my age it would be easier and away from the front line." She snorted. "Little did any of us know!"

She was hard-working and fierce in her care and defence of the wounded. She spoke her mind, and I didn't know how she got away with some of the things she said to the doctors. I assumed they respected her age and experience. She reminded me a little of Annunciata. She had the same bluntness, the same rough warmth. Like me, she deplored the paperwork and tedious process involved in getting supplies and medicines. The sister in charge of supplies required a chit with the signatures of the senior nurse and the hospital administrator. For medicines, we had to have a doctor's signature as well.

Getting a doctor's attention was often difficult. Like us, they had plenty to do. But not all of them were equally devoted to their patients.

One day I come across Odette in tears and stamping about in the courtyard.

"What is it, Madame Combel? What's happened?"

She waved her arms. "Oh, that Doctor Bruel! We need more morphia but he's having his lunch and told me to wait until he's finished. It wouldn't take long but the wretched man is more interested in his *pot-au-feu*."

Doctor Bruel arrived at last, puffing on a cigar, and signed the chit. I didn't like the man. He was something of a dandy and was much given to eyeing the younger, prettier nurses. Rumour had it that it went well beyond that sometimes, and that some of the nurses succumbed for fear of getting a bad report on their records. Madame Combel and I were lucky that he spared us his attentions: her because of her age, me because of my wedding ring. I was glad I had held onto it. All the same, I kept out of his way as much as possible.

"It's dreadful a man like that abusing his position in that way," Madame Combel said. "He should be ashamed of himself."

But even she couldn't confront him with it.

***

The rumbling and shell bursts came closer each day. The building shook with every impact and lumps of plaster fall to the floor, shedding dust everywhere. I had been working in the hospital for only a few days when the order went out to evacuate all the hospitals in Amiens and move the wounded further away from the Front. They ordered us military nurses to go with them, but the nursing nuns had to stay until they received permission from their Order. We prepared our wounded for the journey, although some of them were really too weak to travel, and packed as much equipment as we could, everything from kitchen utensils to ether. We stacked the packing cases in the courtyard, ready for transport to the train.

Someone had agreed to look after Odette's trunk, since there wouldn't be room for her take it with her. Even so, she fretted about it. I could not have cared less about mine and left it behind at my lodgings. I was tired of dragging it about with me and crammed what I could into my case and a knapsack.

"My box! I don't like leaving it here," she said. "There are so many useful things in it. And my shoes and dresses."

"Maybe you can come back for it later," I replied.

"With the Boche coming closer every day that seems unlikely," she retorted. "I don't want *them* getting hold of my things."

This was a common outlook. No one said so, but everyone was expecting the Germans to take Amiens. When we went to the sister in charge of provisions to claim our rations for the journey, she pressed more on us than we were entitled to.

"Take it," she said. "We don't want to leave anything behind for the Boche."

So I crammed yet more into my already overloaded bags. We left for the station, picking our way amongst the rubble and debris, with our ears tuned constantly for the wail of shells. We skirted craters in the streets and tripped on paving stones sticking up like uneven teeth. We passed houses with doors and windows blown in and one whose whole front had collapsed, revealing a fireplace and curtains blowing in the breeze. A picture hung askew against the rear wall. I wondered if the people were inside when it happened or if they had managed to get away.

No one had told us yet where we were going. But we made our way to the hospital train, which was made up of goods wagons, and took our makeshift seats with the other staff from the hospital. We waited for some time before the train juddered out of the station, only to stop again after a few hundred metres and reverse back to the platform. This happened several times until we wondered if we were ever going to leave. In the end they told us that the train would leave in two hours' time.

"I'm fed up with this," one of the others said. "I'm getting out to stretch my legs."

"Don't go too far," the chief nurse said. "The train might start without you."

She smiled and disappeared down onto the platform. After about twenty minutes, she returned, her face aglow.

"Look what I found," she said, brandishing a bottle of

champagne and a box of chocolates in front of the astonished faces in the wagon.

"Where did they come from?"

"There's a bombed-out shop just outside the station. Some of the stuff is damaged but there's still plenty there. Don't want to leave it for the Boche to have a party, do we? Come on."

So Odette and I and some of the others jumped down onto the platform and followed her to a building with a hole in the roof. The timbers were sticking up through it. We went inside the shop and the acrid smell of spirits caught the back of my throat. It was full of broken glass from the shop front that crunched underfoot. Puddles of liquor reflected the light but some of the packages were intact. I felt uneasy about taking things, and hesitated at first. But then I reasoned, like everyone else, that we might as well profit from them, rather than leaving them to the Germans.

Odette's find sweetened the bitterness of retreating from Amiens. We returned to the train, laden with bottles and packets. I had pocketed sachets of scented soap from a shop next door. I was longing for a proper bath, when I could soap and scrub myself all over, but I had no idea how long I would have to wait for it.

At last, the train pulled out and this time we left the city, although it crawled along like a snail. The journey was like something from a nightmare. Streams of refugees lined the roads alongside the track, parents pulling small children by the hand, the elderly stumbling along as best they could. The train stopped and started without warning. On several occasions, German aeroplanes wheeled downwards like birds of prey and fired on us, and we threw ourselves to the floor of the wagon, our hands over our heads. Did they know this was a hospital train? How could they do this?

In the early evening, the train stopped at Beauvais and we were told to get off. We were marched to a former barracks some distance from the station, where we crammed into a dormitory. We were too tired and discouraged to talk.

After four or five moves in as many days, our unit was detailed to a former boarding school, which had become a temporary military hospital. Everything had been done in such a hurry that at first we had to wash at a pump in the courtyard in full view of everyone else. So much for my bath! Wounded soldiers were arriving in droves since the Amiens hospitals had closed and the convoys of ambulances continued day and night. There was so little room that the wounded were placed on their stretchers in the corridors, waiting to be attended to. Their groans were imprinted on my memory for life.

Odette and I were in the pre-operative unit and looked after the wounded once the clerks had taken their details. The work was exhausting for we had to act fast and not keep the surgeons waiting. That was difficult because some of the wounds were oozing green pus or giving off the stench of infection. We washed them in oxygenated water, which was in short supply. There were never enough nurses or equipment to cope with the influx. Many of the wounded didn't receive enough care after their operation and their wounds became infected. Because of this, scores died of gas gangrene in the first weeks.

"I don't understand them," I said to Odette. "They should bring in more nurses from the hospitals in the interior. I can't think why they don't."

She agreed and shrugged.

***

This situation continued for several weeks before the flow of wounded tailed off. The Germans came very close to Amiens, but they never managed to take it and our soldiers pushed them back. We weren't aware of it then, but this was the turning point of the war. Throughout the summer and early autumn we continued to struggle against lack of equipment, military organisation and the regular risk of enemy bombardment. At night, we had to work with tiny candles in glasses to avoid showing light that might guide the enemy planes to the hospital.

After dark, Doctor Péraud prowled around outside and if he saw a chink of light coming from the building shouted, "Put out that light, dammit!"

The Germans had put in place a huge cannon to try to reduce Paris to rubble. We worked with its regular booming in the background. We operated on the most seriously wounded, while sending the others by train to be operated on at hospitals in the interior. Poor souls. How many of them died because they should have been treated earlier? The Germans watched out for the hospital trains and bombarded them. I couldn't believe it; it was an evil and inhuman act.

The end came not long after. At eleven o'clock on the eleventh day of the eleventh month, we became aware of a new sound. Silence.

Chapter 26

April 1919

As if the scourges of that war weren't enough, a new one arose: an epidemic of what they started to call Spanish influenza. By a horrible irony, it sought out the young rather than the old and they died very fast. We started to see cases in the late summer but another wave began around the time of the Armistice. The *Service de Santé* isolated returning soldiers with the symptoms, but with so much movement of troops and people the disease spread quickly.

Because of her age, they considered Odette to be less at risk from the disease and asked her to join a team nursing the influenza sufferers. I stayed at the military hospital in Beauvais and continued to tend the wounded for a few months after the end of the war. The fighting might have been finished, but its overspill continued. I remained for five months before receiving my discharge and taking the train again, via Paris, for Marseille. Train journeys had marked out my time in France. At least this one was going in the right direction.

And so, after an endless and wearying journey, I found myself back in Zaronza after almost two years. Annunciata, faithful old Annunciata, had kept the house clean for me, although it smelled musty when I opened the front door.

"They rang the church bell when the Armistice was announced," she told me. "But no one had the heart to celebrate."

Those who had welcomed the chance to give Germany a bloody nose were now just relieved that the horror was all over. Those who had predicted it would last only a few months had been proved terribly wrong.

Once the initial relief had died down, it was time to count the cost of this terrible war. The prisoners of war were sent back to their families in Germany and Austria, and the true extent of the carnage became clear. No one knew how many Corsicans had died at the Front. Some said it was twenty thousand; others said even more than that. The emptiness of the villages and the fields and the lack of menfolk were a brutal reminder. Few had emerged unscathed and even fewer unchanged.

The convent had continued its work for a few months, but by the time I returned to Zaronza even that had emptied. The men returned to their villages or their homes on the continent. So I had nothing to do there and had to decide how to spend the rest of my life.

For the past two years or more, since Sophia admitted to me what she had done, I had lived in a kind of limbo. My work had filled my days, but I had often found myself thinking about Raphaël and wanting to set things straight with him. I couldn't bear that he must have thought badly of me all those years. He must have considered me shallow, faithless and attached only to money and social position.

I hadn't spoken or written to Sophia in all that time. I hadn't even seen her very often, since my work kept me so busy at the convent and then I left for the Western Front. Whenever I had seen her I looked through her as though she didn't exist and she cast down her eyes. I wasn't able to forgive her then. But on my return, after all I had been through and all I had seen, our quarrel seemed so petty. So many people had had their lives broken and had far more to complain about than we did.

So I couldn't spend the rest of my life ignoring Sophia and nurturing resentment. It was against my nature and I wanted to start again with her. But before that, there was something I had to do: find Raphaël, wherever he was, and whatever he was doing.

***

First I went to Bastia, to the headquarters of the 173rd Infantry Regiment. If he had joined up they might know of his whereabouts. The adjutant who received me was friendly enough but didn't hold out much hope.

"I don't think we can help you, Madame Orsini. Are you a relative of this Raphaël Colombani?"

"Not a relative, no. But I was a close friend at one time."

He tugged at his moustache. "I have had our records searched and can't find any mention of his name. It's possible in that case that he joined another regiment on the mainland, although that would have been unusual. You must understand that I'm unable to make further enquiries for you. We have to give priority to relatives. I am sorry."

He showed me to the door and saluted.

I strolled along to the port and looked across the water towards Genoa. I hadn't expected this setback but I wouldn't give up. My next step had to be to visit his village in the Bozio and try to find him, or news of him, there. I had never been into the interior of Corsica, and a tingling in my spine gripped me. The island was my homeland and its roots were deep inside me. When I was at the Front I had missed it so much that it was like something stuck in my throat that I was unable to swallow. And yet I knew so little of Corsica. I had travelled more than a thousand kilometres to volunteer on the Western Front, but I had rarely been more than twenty inland.

***

I told Annunciata that I was planning to visit an old friend in the interior.

"I'm not sure how long I shall be gone, but it will be no more than a few days. You're not to worry about me while I'm away."

"On your own? Why, Mademoiselle Maria," – she had always called me that, even after I was married – "what if you get set upon by bandits? They might rob you, or even worse."

I smiled. "Annunciata, after what I've lived through, I'm not afraid of my native Corsicans. And anyway, what bandits? So few men have returned from the war that hardly anyone lives in the hills now, and those who are there have to work the land or are unable to because they're maimed. I'm sure I will be quite safe."

She shook her head and bustled off, grumbling to herself. After a moment, she returned bearing the *stylet* from Papa's desk.

"Here," she said. "If you persist in this foolish adventure you might as well be able to protect yourself."

I laughed. "If someone really wanted to do me any harm, I doubt if this would be enough to deter them. But if it makes you happier I'll take it."

The image of Vincentello tapping the blade against his palm flashed through my mind, followed by the memory of my own desire to stab him with it when I heard how he had been so foolish in Puerto Rico. That was in another life, another world.

Annunciata insisted on packing me a picnic basket with enough provisions for a large family.

"You never know when you might be able to find something to eat. And you don't know what filthy stuff they might serve up at a *bistrot*. Anyway, it's not fitting for a woman to go into one of those places. It's simply not done. The men wouldn't like it. They would think you were a…" She waved her hand, leaving me to guess the word. Having experienced so much freedom in Paris, where no one turned a hair at a woman dining on her own, it was strange to be back in Corsica. I wondered if I would find it hard to get used to. What would Papa and Maman have said if they could have seen where I had been and what I had done? I had seen men naked, I had washed and dressed their intimate parts, I had heard them swear and curse. I had been to the gates of Hell and back. That was not the destiny for which they brought me up. The world had changed.

Pursuing me with last-minute instructions, Annunciata watched me onto the bus that stopped at the corner of the square, and waved a corner of her apron as it took off in a cloud of fumes. We trundled along the winding roads, over the Col de Teghime, the same route I had taken with Vincentello the day he left Corsica for ever. Bastia spread out before us as we descended the hillside. The bus stopped at the Place Saint-Nicolas and I walked from there to the train station, laden down with a case and Annunciata's picnic.

I had to wait an hour or so for the little Micheline train to arrive. A throng of passengers got off and I took my place, my baggage stowed carefully under my seat. I was glad of the picnic, although I found it hard to eat much. The train started and rattled along through the suburbs of Bastia and the flat lands alongside the Étang de Biguglia before turning westwards to start its journey up into the mountains.

The train often stopped at the little halts along the way, in addition to the unscheduled stops for cows and goats on the line. It was a beautiful early May day and the mountains reared up on all sides. I pressed my face to the glass and drank it all in. After a couple of hours, we arrived at Corte, where I had to leave the train. Dusk was already falling as I toiled up the hill from the station to the centre of the town.

The citadel dominated the town high on a rocky pinnacle, against its backdrop of jagged mountains. So this was where Pascal Paoli had made his headquarters, the capital of Corsica's short-lived republic, which Raphaël told me so much about. Annunciata had arranged for me to stay with a distant cousin of hers, Jean Colonna, whose family had an apartment in the Cours Paoli. The town was dusty and a little down at heel. It was difficult to imagine that such a cultivated man as Paoli had chosen to rule the island from this place. And yet it stood for the very essence of Corsica.

I was weary after my journey and the trudge up from the station. But Monsieur Colonna and his family greeted me with warmth and extended the traditional Corsican hospitality, which included a huge meal.

"I'm so grateful to you for your hospitality and your kindness tonight." I said.

"I hope you'll excuse me if I'm curious, Madame Orsini. But it's unusual for a lady to travel alone. May I ask what your business is in the Bozio?" Monsieur Colonna asked.

I smiled; he was unaware of just how much travelling I had done alone in the past two years.

"Of course. I'm going to find an old friend who comes from the village of Altizani. We lost touch many years ago and I would like to resume our friendship."

"And what is this lady's name? Perhaps we might know of the family."

The colour rose in my cheeks. "It's not a lady. My friend was the former schoolmaster at Zaronza, many years ago. His name is Raphaël Colombani."

"Forgive me for being so inquisitive. Of course, many families have the name Colombani and I don't know of anyone of that name in Altizani. But then, I rarely go as far as that. And how do you plan to get there? It's right up in the hills and the route isn't easy."

"I was hoping I might find a carter or a farmer who could take me there."

Monsieur Colonna thought for a moment. "I think I might know someone who could help you. I'll make enquiries first thing tomorrow."

The meal over, Madame Colonna ushered me to my room and I was grateful for the chance to go to bed. But I found it hard to get to sleep, despite my fatigue.

When I did fall into a fitful sleep it was filled with shapeless, haunting dreams. I was sliding over the precipice again, my hand slipping out of Raphaël's, while Vincentello smiled his mirthless smile in the background.

***

When I awoke the next morning, the sun was streaming through a gap in the curtains. I hastened to dress and made my way to the dining room, where the delicious smell of coffee made my mouth water.

Monsieur Colonna had been as good as his word. "An acquaintance of mine, who runs a delivery service between here and Aleria, will be glad to take you all the way to Altizani in his van."

"Oh, but it must be out of his way," I protested. "And surely he'll want payment."

"You don't need to worry about that." He twinkled. "The man owes me a favour or two."

I had to meet him at the Place Paoli, a little way up the street. I waited beside the statue of Pascal Paoli, resplendent in his wig and eighteenth-century costume. He was a handsome man, it seemed, not unlike Raphaël to look at. My heart quickened at the thought of Raphaël. Maybe I would see him today – for the first time in nearly twenty years! I wonder if he had changed very much, if he had lost his youthful slenderness, if his ink-black hair was now peppered with grey, if his smooth face bore the lines of care. I dared not think of the possibility that he might have been disfigured, like so many others.

The van arrived and the driver hefted my luggage and the picnic basket into the back and then helped me into the passenger seat beside him. It was quite a long drive to Altizani and he had to make several stops on the way. But a little before noon, we drove into the square there, having climbed far up into the hills. The carter lifted my bags down and tapped his cap before driving off in a haze of fumes.

The place seemed deserted. Of course, it was almost lunchtime and no doubt this village had suffered just as much as the others from the war that drained its lifeblood. But smoke rising from chimneys around the square showed that there were people around.

I stood in the square for a moment, wondering what to do next. A dog trotted across it at a purposeful pace and disappeared down an alleyway. An old woman dressed in shapeless, faded black – the uniform of all old women in Corsica, and many young ones now – emerged from the church. She stopped and eyed me up and down. They didn't get many outsiders here.

Leaving my bags, I approached her. "Excuse me, Madame, I wonder if you can help me. I'm looking for the house where Raphaël Colombani lives. Perhaps you could direct me there."

She crossed herself and touched the cross around her neck. The flesh under her weather-beaten skin turned pale.

"You don't know, then, Madame."

I shook my head. "Know what?"

"So many men from this village fell while fighting for France over there. I'm afraid that he was one of them. He left a widow and three children. I'm sorry, Madame."

My legs gave way under me and black patches appeared across my vision, merging into one, enveloping shadow.

Chapter 27

A face swam into my vision and became sharper, more defined, as my eyes cleared. I was lying in a small, dark room with a fire crackling in the hearth.

"Drink this, Madame. It will make you feel better."

A hand brought a glass of clear liquid to my lips. I sipped, coughed, and sipped again. Corsican *eau de vie* made of myrtle berries. Warmth spread through my veins and the life returned to my limbs.

"Where am I? What happened?"

"You're in my house. Old Josef helped me to carry you in here. You fainted."

It all flooded back. Raphaël. Oh, no. How could this be? It couldn't be true; there must have been some mistake. It wasn't him, it was another Colombani. But, as I tried to convince myself, I knew underneath that it was true. That I never had the chance to establish the truth between us. That the hope had trickled out of my life.

I struggled to sit up, a terrible emptiness in the pit of my stomach. The old woman looked at me, her eyes bright as a dormouse, her cheeks sunken like a fallen apple.

"I'm so sorry to cause you all this trouble, Madame," I said.

She shook her head. "You had a shock. I should have tried to break the news more gently."

"You mentioned a widow and children. Do they live in Altizani still?"

"Oh yes, the poor woman. She has almost nobody now, except her children. Her brothers were killed at the Front and her father hanged himself out of grief. There's been such tragedy here. She struggles to make ends meet. She will get a widow's pension but I don't suppose it will add up to much. We do our best to help her but she's proud, too, and doesn't want charity. She takes in washing, although there's precious little of that, and she cooks and cleans where she can."

So, he had forgotten me, after all. He married and had children. I pictured him bouncing them on his knee by the fire while his devoted wife looked on. A band tightened across my chest. That could have been me! It should have been me. And it would have been me, if it hadn't been for Vincentello – and, of course, Sophia.

"I would like to meet her," I said. "I knew Raphaël many years ago when he was the schoolmaster at Zaronza on Cap Corse."

I looked into her eyes. Something about her invited confession.

"There's no point in keeping secrets any longer. I might as well tell you that we had planned to marry, but my parents would not have accepted the match and I had to marry someone else. My husband also died – but not in the war; far away from France or Corsica. There was unfinished business between me and Raphaël. That's why I'm here. But it must remain unfinished." Tears stung the back of my eyes but I brushed them away.

The old woman nodded. "I'll take you there," she said. "But first, you must eat something to restore you. I was about to have my lunch, anyway, when we met in the square."

She was right. In my excitement at the possibility of seeing Raphaël again, I hadn't eaten since early that morning, despite my picnic basket. I was weak from hunger, although I didn't know if I could force anything down past the lump in my throat. I swung my legs to the floor and crossed the room to the table. I was still a little shaky but the danger of fainting had passed. She served me a bowl of thick Corsican soup and ate her own standing up. She grimaced in apology.

"I got used to eating standing up while serving my late

husband," she explained. "Now I can't sit at the table to eat."

"My mother was the same," I replied. "And I adopted the habit when my husband was alive."

We finished our meal in silence.

"Now I'll show you Letizia's house," she said.

"Thank you for looking after me, Madame. I'm most grateful."

"I only wish you hadn't heard the news from my lips. But it's perhaps better that you knew about it before you meet her."

She walked with me to the corner of the square and pointed down the road to a small, neat house set slightly back from the rest. She turned away and walked back to her own house without a backward glance. My heart pounding, I tapped at the door, which was slightly ajar.

"Who is it?" a voice called.

I cleared my throat. "I'm sorry to disturb you. It's an old friend of your husband, from Zaronza."

The door opened and a small woman with thick, dark hair stood there. She was younger than me. A small child, who couldn't have been more than three years old, clung to her skirts. He peered at me from behind them and then he buried his face in his mother's dress again.

The woman looked me up and down. "I didn't know he still had any friends in Zaronza."

"This was a very long time ago," I said. "Almost twenty years. I have only just heard of Raph…of your husband's death. I'm so sorry. It was a shock to me."

Her mouth twisted. "You had better come in. I'm sorry the house isn't tidier but I wasn't expecting visitors."

I looked around. It seemed clean and tidy enough to me. A bright fire was burning in the grate. She gestured to a chair and I sat down, removing my headscarf. She said nothing but sat down herself and waited for me to begin. Her little boy still clung to her and I smiled at him. He grinned back and then buried his head in his mother's lap. He had ink-black hair and twinkling chestnut eyes.

To break the silence, I said, "I understand you have three children, Madame."

"Yes. This is Antonio. The other two, Raphaël and Maria, are at school."

My eyes widened. Although Maria was a common name, was she named after me?

"It can't be easy to bring up three children on your own."

"We manage," she said.

"You must be wondering why I'm here."

She considered me. "You are Maria, aren't you?"

"Yes. My name is Maria Orsini and I knew Raphaël when he was the schoolmaster at Zaronza."

She sighed. "I have always known about you. Raphaël made no secret that there had been a great love in his life but that fate was against it. I resented you for it." She looked away. "Oh, he was a good husband and he was fond of me. We had a good life together. But he never loved me as he had loved you."

My heart was too full for me to speak.

"What did you come for, anyway? Raphaël has been dead for two and a half years."

"I only found out about it today. Your little one" (I pointed at the little boy) "can only have been a baby when it happened."

She nodded.

"This is very difficult for both of us, Madame Colombani," I began. "But I don't mean you and your family any harm. I hardly knew what I would find when I arrived here today. But I came because it was something I had to do."

She looked at me, not giving me any help. I couldn't blame her. After all, I was a rival, even if Raphaël and I had had no contact for years before they married.

Breathing deeply, I looked her in the eyes. "Yes, I loved him, Madame, just as I can see that you did. We parted because of a misunderstanding. I had to marry someone else for family reasons, and Raphaël left the village a few months later. I never saw him again, nor had any contact with him. I didn't know anything about his life after he left Zaronza. The full extent of the...misunderstanding...only came to light a couple of years ago, and it was to repair it that I came to see him. But it would seem I'm far too late."

Something like sympathy flickered across her eyes but disappeared again.

"What stopped you from coming before, if you found out about it two years ago?"

"The war," I replied.

I told her about my desire to do something to help and about my work at the convent. I described my journey to Bar-le-Duc and my experiences on the Western Front there and at Beauvais. Her interest quickened: it was up there, after all, that her husband had died. I tried to keep the more unpleasant details of death and injury to myself. I didn't yet know how Raphaël had died.

I finished and for a while we fell silent. Antonio played on the hearthrug with some cotton reels and murmured to himself in his own language. He had forgotten his earlier shyness.

"If it's not too painful for you, please tell me about what happened to Raphaël."

"Yes," she sighed. "I owe it to you. There isn't a day that goes by without my thinking about him. I last saw my husband in May 1916, when he came home on leave. That was a rare event, and Raphaël said that they seemed to give Corsicans fewer passes than they did to mainland French."

I had also heard this from other Corsicans.

"Antonio was only a few months old. Raphaël wasn't here for the birth and hadn't heard about it until a few weeks afterwards, since letters took so long to travel. When he came home on leave that last time, he was terribly changed. First, his uniform was covered in lice and he had a beard of several weeks. We had to boil his clothes with lye soap and scrub him with it, too. Once he had cut his beard he looked better, but he was very thin, and there were dark hollows around his eyes. Worst of all, he seemed changed inside himself. Before that, he was a great talker."

I smiled. "I know."

"But this time he barely said a word. He would go for long walks on his own and come home exhausted. Then he would just sit looking into the fire. At night, he had dreadful nightmares and would grip me in his sleep until it hurt. I realised that things must have been terrible up there, but I never asked him about it, and he never told me.

"The night before the end of his leave, he said, 'Letizia, today I almost walked off into the hills rather than go back there. I could hide out for years without anyone finding me, like the *vendetta* bandits of old. But when I thought about it I realised that I couldn't betray my fellow soldiers. I have to go back; it's a point of honour.' I pleaded with him to take the *maquis*. I said I would help him. But he refused. 'The authorities would put you under terrible pressure,' he said. 'Your life would be very difficult and I don't want that. But even more than that, I can't let down the thousands of other Corsicans who are laying down their lives up there. This war is an insane waste of life but I can't abandon them. I must go back.'

"I knew then that I couldn't persuade him. Once Raphaël had decided on a course of action, he rarely went back on his decision. So, one morning in May, with the mountains in the distance in the haze and the birds singing, he put his uniform back on, kissed me and the children and walked out of that door, never to return."

The tears striped her cheeks. The fire had burned down, and I rose to place another log on it.

"He wrote as often as he could, but they were always being moved from place to place, and sometimes even the writing materials were hard to come by. One day, in mid-September, a telegram arrived." She shuddered. "I knew what was in it before I had even opened it. I don't remember very much about that day, except that I screamed until I fainted. Strong hands were around me but I kicked and struggled. I think I went a little mad for a while.

"The village women helped with the children, and bit by bit I came to my senses again. In late September, a letter arrived from his commanding officer, with a medal in it and a few lines about how he had died. It was during the Battle of Verdun. His unit had to advance to take the German position but they fought back fiercely. Raphaël was hit directly by something called a mortar and died instantly. He would not have felt anything, his commanding officer said."

The tears were coursing down my cheeks, too, but at least he hadn't suffered. He didn't have to endure the bumping anguish of a stretcher, the long journey behind the lines from the evacuation hospital, the agony of an amputation under insufficient anaesthetic, the lingering death from gangrene or shrapnel poisoning, like so many of them. I thanked God for that.

Before this war, I had always thought that battles were short affairs. The opposing sides lined up, fought each other and then one was declared the winner. This Battle of Verdun went on for months and took its terrible toll in lives. And it was just one of many in that war.

"Did the letter say what date Raphaël died?" I asked.

"Yes, it was the seventh of September, 1916."

I started. That was the day Vincentello died in Puerto Rico. Both of the men in my life were snuffed out that day.

"That date will always be written on my heart," she said.

And on mine, I thought. And on mine.

Chapter 28

We talked on. The fire burned low and the sun's rays slanting through the window lengthened. Childish voices outside, raised in argument, broke into our soft murmuring. The door burst open and two children tumbled in, the girl pushed by the boy.

"Now, behave yourselves," their mother said. "You can see we have a visitor. Be polite and go and say hello. This is Madame Orsini from a village called Zaronza, where your father was the schoolmaster before he came back here."

The children came and presented themselves to be kissed. The girl, Maria, resembled her mother, with her delicate features and slight stature. But she had Raphaël's eyes. The boy, on the other hand, looked even more like his father than his little brother did. The resemblance was so striking that I caught my breath. This was just how Raphaël must have looked at the same age.

"Good afternoon, Madame," they said.

"You must be Maria," I said. "How old are you?"

"Eight, Madame."

"And you, Raphaël?" I almost choked on the name.

"Ten, Madame."

"In that case you will be taking your *Certificat d'Études* in a couple of years' time, won't you?"

"Yes, I will. Most of my friends want to leave school afterwards but I want to stay on and study. I would like to be a school teacher like Papa."

"So would I," the girl cried, not to be outdone.

"That's enough, both of you. You know there's no question of it. And you mustn't be a nuisance to Madame Orsini with your chatter. Go and cut yourselves some bread. There's some fig jam in the *buffet* as well."

"But, Maman..."

"I said, that is enough. Go along now."

The children obeyed and prepared themselves a snack. Antonio ran to join them and they took their bread outside.

"Forgive me for being inquisitive, Madame Colombani. I don't want to pry into your affairs, but you seem to be opposed to your children staying on at school."

"Oh, I'm not opposed in principle, Madame. But they must both go out to work as soon as possible. I wouldn't have the means to support them at school. They would have to study for many years and then go on to the *école normale*. I don't see how it would be possible. In any case, we have some land that Grandpa Colombani left that needs working and tending. Raphaël will have to do that, while Maria gets work until she marries."

"But there are scholarships they could apply for, surely, if they are clever enough?"

"Yes, of course, but they're few and far between and there's no guarantee that either of them would pass the examination. I wouldn't wish them to get so far, only to have their hopes dashed."

I didn't argue with her, but an idea was taking root. For the moment, I nodded and remained silent, and then I realised that evening was drawing on and I had no means of getting back to Corte, still less as far as Zaronza. I hadn't thought about what I would do when I got to Altizani. I couldn't think beyond seeing Raphaël again.

"I've already stayed too long, Madame Colombani. Please forgive me. I've kept you from your work and your household chores. I must find somewhere to stay in the village since it's too late to leave tonight." I thought of the old woman who was so kind to me when she realised the effect of her news on me. Perhaps she would give me a corner to sleep in for the night and something to eat? I would be able to pay her.

"You're welcome to stay here with us tonight." I started to protest but Letizia raised her hand. "At first I wasn't glad that you had come. But now I am. You have helped me to lay the ghost of Maria, who always hung over my marriage, to rest. Talking about Raphaël to someone else who loved him did me good, too. You may have Maria's bed and she can sleep with me. She'll regard that as a treat."

"In that case, I accept, but only on one condition."

She raised her eyebrows.

"That you allow me to help you prepare the supper."

She smiled and I helped her lay the table. And then I prepared an *omelette au brocciu* and rinsed the salad while she stirred the soup. Antonio ran in, his mouth smeared with fig jam and I wiped his face with a cloth and sat him on a chair next to me with a cushion under him. His shyness had evaporated. The other two joined us and childish laughter punctuated the meal until the children's heads started to nod.

Letizia picked Antonio up and gave her hand to Maria. Raphaël followed behind, his feet dragging with fatigue. How good it is to be young, I thought. Children play like puppies without a care and then fall into an untroubled sleep. I cleared the table, washed up and tidied away while Letizia put the children to bed. I riddled the ashes in the grate.

Letizia showed me to my room and I dragged off my clothes and slipped between the sheets of Maria's narrow bed. It had been such a long and emotional day and I was exhausted. I slid into a deep sleep and dreamed of ink-black hair, dancing chestnut eyes and a dazzling smile.

***

The sun was already high when I awoke. I threw on my clothes and joined Letizia in her kitchen-cum-living room. She set a bowl of coffee and a slice of buttered bread before me. The two older children had long since gone to school. Antonio was sitting on the threshold watching the street outside like a little old man, his arms clasped around his knees.

"I'm sorry to have slept so long," I said. "I don't want to be any trouble to you."

Letizia smiled. "It's no trouble. I let you sleep on. You must have been in great need of it."

I sipped my coffee and the idea that had come to me the previous evening started to take shape.

"Letizia," I began. "May I call you that?"

She nodded.

"Letizia, I've been thinking about what you said yesterday, and I have a proposal to make."

She paused in her work.

"I think it would be a great shame if your children weren't allowed to pursue their ambitions. If they stay here in Altizani there's very little for them to look forward to, beyond the kind of life their grandparents led. And I think they're too intelligent for that."

Her face took on a guarded look. I continued.

"I have a little money – not a fortune, but more than I need for my own use. And I have a large, echoing house at Zaronza. My maid Annunciata isn't getting any younger and can no longer take on some of the chores she used to do." I took a deep breath. "My proposal is that you come to live with me at Zaronza and keep house for me. In return, your children will get a good education and a good start in life."

Her face closed up.

"I don't want anyone's charity. I've managed since Raphaël died and will go on doing so."

"At the expense of your children's future? And I'm not offering you charity. On the contrary, you would be doing *me* a favour. I have never had children and am most unlikely to marry again. I can't imagine anything worse than growing old alone in that great barn of a house, much as I love it there. It needs children to make it live again."

"But what about their friends? And the land that Grandpa Colombani left? What would I do about that – I won't sell it."

"They can come back sometimes and visit their friends. And they will surely make new ones. As for the land, I quite understand that you wouldn't want to sell it: it is their birthright, after all. But perhaps you could find someone locally who could lease it and make more of it than you can at the moment."

She wrung her hands. "I don't know. I have few relatives here now, but I have to think of the children. This is their village, where they were born and have been brought up. And it was Raphaël's birthplace. I wouldn't want to betray his memory."

"Who's suggesting that you would betray it? Don't you think you will carry his memory within you for the rest of your life? Where you are doesn't matter; it's *what* you are that does."

She reflected for a moment.

"I can't give you an answer straight away. I must think about it for a few days."

"Of course. Take all the time you need to come to a decision. I won't press you for a reply."

I would have liked to say more to persuade her, but had a sense that this would be a mistake. Instead, I had to arrange to get back to Zaronza. I didn't want Annunciata to think I had been kidnapped or murdered by brigands.

Letizia walked with me to the square, Antonio between us, hanging onto our hands. A villager had agreed to take me in his cart to Vizzona, where I could catch the train to Ponte Leccia and then to Bastia.

"I will write to you in a few days," Letizia said.

I pressed her hand and climbed up beside the man.

As we trundled off down the hill, I turned around. She was standing watching us. Antonio waved and I raised my arm in reply. We rounded a corner and they were lost to view.

***

During the afternoon of the following day I alighted from the spluttering bus at Zaronza. I had to spend the previous night in Bastia. Annunciata appeared as if by magic and fussed over me. I decided not to say anything about my proposal to Letizia until I had received her answer.

Once I had refreshed myself and looked through the few letters that had arrived in my absence, I decided to go up to the watchtower to think. It was unseasonably hot for early May – and much warmer at Zaronza than up in the hills at Altizani. The sun was touching the bay with gold as its rays lengthened. I never tired of that sight.

I stretched my back against the stone and pondered the events of the past few days. The news of Raphaël's death was shattering, and now I would never have the chance to mend things with him in person. But, if only Letizia would accept my proposal, I could do something to keep his memory alive. I wasn't being entirely unselfish. This would be the family I had never had. I longed to hear the house ringing with children's laughter, to see the children grow up and fulfil their early promise, to have something useful to do again.

My thoughts flickered to Sophia. I had thought about her a great deal, too, during my journey home from Altizani. What she did was very wrong, but I couldn't let it hang between us for the rest of our lives. I was sure she had punished herself enough for it. She loved Raphaël, too. I smiled. In some ways, he *was* a womaniser without realising it, since he had made all three of us – and who else besides? – love him.

The chill of evening drew on and I descended the stony path, but instead of unlatching the garden gate, I walked on towards the square. I climbed the alleyway to Sophia's house and hesitated in the little passageway. I pushed open the kitchen door and there she was, bending over the fire, stirring something; so small, so frail. My heart turned over.

"Sophia," I whispered.

She whipped round and we met in the middle of her kitchen, clasping each other, tears cascading down our cheeks. We stayed like that for a long time before sitting down opposite each other, holding hands.

We talked long into the evening, and the years peeled away.

***

A few days later, a letter arrived, postmarked Altizani. Unable to breathe, I picked up Papa's *stylet*, slit open the envelope and removed a single sheet.

Dear Maria,

I have thought carefully about your proposal and the answer is yes. I must think of my children's lives and I am now convinced that this is the best course for their future. I hope you will allow me a few weeks to sort things out in Altizani and the children must finish the school term before they move.

I have talked this over with Raphaël and Maria. At first, they were unhappy at the idea of leaving their friends. But when they saw that this move would give them the chance to become what they dream of being, they were happier about it. We must give them time to adapt to a new place and new friends but they are now excited about the move. It will be a new start for us all.

Bien cordialement,

Letizia

A bubble of joy welled up as I dashed off a reply. Only one cloud hung over the horizon: Annunciata. How would she react? Would she think her place was being usurped? Holding the letter I walked down the corridor to the kitchen. She was on her knees washing the flagstones. She struggled to rise and I went over to help her up.

"I think I'm getting a little old for this," she wheezed.

"I think you are, too," I replied. Her face fell. "But I believe I have the answer." I waved Letizia's letter and told her the news.

She broke into a gap-toothed smile and clasped her hands.

"Why, Mademoiselle Maria, this is wonderful news. This house needs children to bring it alive. Oh, I'm so pleased. Now, we'll need to do some baking for their arrival. I'll make some *fiadone* and *canistrelli*. Children always love those."

I laughed. "But they aren't coming for several weeks. It's much too early to start baking."

"Very well," she frowned. "But we'll need to prepare their bedrooms and check over the linen. Oh, there's so much to do."

"Well, I'll help you. And, of course, you'll still be in charge. You can be a kind of grandmother to the children."

She beamed and we hugged each other.

Chapter 29

Zaronza, May 1924

I was never able to understand how Vincentello could leave Corsica for good – how anyone could. For me, even two years away was far too long.

A light breeze was blowing off the sea today but I could still smell the *maquis* on the hillsides behind the village. Its scent has always been there in the background: not exactly sweet, more aromatic. When I walk on the hills, which is no longer as often as I would like, and tread the wild thyme underfoot and brush the cistus and rosemary with my hand, the perfume rises up and prickles my nostrils. It's strongest after rain.

I often come up here in the evening, just to think. I have always loved watching the sunset without anyone to disturb me. When I was young it was Maman wanting me to help or Papa scolding me or lecturing me about something. Now, there are other calls on my time. I never tire of seeing the sun dipping towards the horizon and touching the sea with gold. The colours turn from crimson to purple when the sun slips behind the hills on the other side of the bay. It's time then to go down the hill and home.

The ruined château and the watchtower stand like guardians over the village. Whatever the weather, they are always there, always the same. Whether a warm breeze or a howling gale is coming from the sea, they are constant. I like coming up here even in blustery weather, but I have to grip tightly to the rail the *commune* has put up to stop people plunging onto the rocks below.

But this evening was perfect, like that evening so many years ago when Sophia told me Raphaël was coming to the village. The sunset brought the memories flooding back. My life changed then, although I didn't know it at the time. It's still vivid in my mind: it could have happened yesterday. So much has happened in twenty-five years. It's like another life.

Young Raphaël is now fifteen and growing so like his father. He and Young Maria – we call her that to avoid confusion with me; they call me Tante Maria – are both very intelligent. Raphaël passed his *Certificat d'Études* with flying colours. In fact, he was second in the whole of the region. He still holds onto his idea of becoming a schoolmaster, and I think he will make a very good one. He has his father's gift for story-telling and his ability to inspire.

Maria has moved on from idea of becoming a teacher and is starting to be interested in medicine. She's always asking me how it was to be a nurse during the war. In fact, I think she would like to become a doctor. Very few female doctors exist, still, but if anyone can make a success of it, she will. She's quietly determined and has a way about her that would make her good with patients. Sophia adores her – they are rather similar in some ways – and hopes she will carry the torch of the women's rights that she has always encouraged. She will have many barriers to overcome. Women took on men's work during the war and proved themselves just as capable of it. But afterwards, everything went back to how it had been before.

Young Antonio is the charmer of the family. He's always playing practical jokes and getting himself into scrapes. I can't imagine where he gets that from. But you can't remain angry with him for long. He fixes you with his chestnut eyes and twinkles and it's all I can do to avoid gathering him up and smothering him with kisses.

Letizia and I often sit by the fire in the kitchen and talk. Sometimes we speak of Raphaël. More often we talk about the children and their future and how they light up our lives. I wonder if we might soon hear wedding bells. When she first arrived, Letizia was very shy and retiring, still wearing her widow's weeds. Recently, she has started to dress in more colourful and elegant clothes. And I wonder if this isn't because Orso comes calling quite often. I'm sure he's not here to see me – I discouraged that long ago – and I'm happy to remain unmarried. But, judging by the care he takes with his own appearance and the colour that rises in Letizia's face when he appears, I think we might have a romance on our hands. I couldn't be more pleased.

I've never removed Raphaël's letters from their hiding place. They are my secret and I want them to remain so. Maybe one day someone will find them. But why live in the past when we have the present and the future before us?

***

Zaronza, September 2010

The shadows were lengthening and the mountains basked in an ochre haze by the time Rachel turned over the final page and placed it on top of the rest. A light breeze ruffled the leaves of the fig tree and the air was filled with the heady scent of ripe fruit and the *maquis*. She smoothed out the papers, shuffled them tidy and replaced them in the box. Drawing her knees up, she encircled them with her arms and gazed into the distance.

A succession of thoughts pursued each other. This unusual story had shed light on some of the mysteries but had left other questions unanswered. Raphaël and Letizia Colombani were her great-grandparents, then; the father and mother of Grandmother Maria. Rachel had already guessed, from the way his letters had stopped dead, that Raphaël and Maria Orsini were not destined to be happy together. As Maria described it, the shepherd's hut on the hillside where Rachel was sitting must have been the one where they met in secret. The same place she had sought to be alone to read Maria's memoir. What a catalogue of misunderstandings and broken dreams! Maria never had children of her own, but nonetheless lived through Raphaël's children. What happened to her in the end? Why did she write down her story? That must have been unusual for a Corsican woman, many of whom, Rachel expected, could barely read and write at that time.

Rachel thought of the two extraordinary women that the story revealed: Maria Orsini and Grandmother Maria Colombani, who appeared only at the end as a young girl. Even so, she was already showing the strength of character that would carry her far away from Corsica to follow her vocation. That must have been rare, too. Both women, in their own way, were products of their age but ahead of it as well. Maria's friend Sophia, too, had ideas that were well beyond her time. Rachel had never known any of them, and her heart lurched at the loss.

Her first reaction was to find the answers to the questions Maria's story had raised. But it was already too late to go back to Santa-Lucia. She looked at her watch: seven o'clock. The faint ringing of the bell in the village drifted up the hillside. The café owner said her grandmother went to bed at eight. And she had looked so tired when Rachel left her that morning. She couldn't go and disturb the old lady again now. Gathering up the carrier bag, she straightened her skirt and set off down the hill, pausing only to dispose of the remains of her picnic in a rubbish bin at the top of the alleyway. Maria's manuscript, still in the carrier bag, she left in the car under the seat. She would read it all again later, but, for the moment, she just wanted to mull it over.

Arriving back at the guest house, Rachel followed the passage to the back terrace, where Pascal and Angelina were sitting with a couple of the other guests.

"Come and join us," Pascal said.

"Would you like a glass of *vin de myrtille*?" Angelina asked.

"Well, just a small one. I thought this evening I might drive to that little restaurant in the next village."

Pascal nodded.

"Well, what did you think of our saint?"

Rachel frowned. What saint? Oh yes, the cathedral.

"Very interesting," she replied, crossing her fingers under the table that he wouldn't ask her any more. She wasn't ready to talk about what she had really been doing all day, and certainly not in front of the other guests.

"Yes, a bit grisly, but worth the visit. One of the prettiest churches on the island, in my opinion."

One of the other guests disagreed with Pascal, citing another Pisan church that she found more appealing. Soon, a good-natured argument was in full flow. Rachel took advantage of the distraction to excuse herself and seek her bedroom before going out to eat.

***

"You're up early. Where are you going today?" Angelina asked.

After a fitful sleep, Rachel had woken early and went down to breakfast as soon as she felt it was appropriate. The sky was overcast and ragged clouds hung over the mountains, obscuring their summits.

"I thought I would just drive beyond Santa-Lucia and see where I end up," Rachel replied, waving her Corsica guide book. That was vague enough not to commit her to anything.

She swallowed her breakfast fast and went downhill to find the car, which was now sandwiched between a 4x4 and a van. Easing it out of the tight space with extreme difficulty, Rachel pointed the car towards Santa-Lucia again. I haven't even been in the other direction yet, she thought, and there's the rest of Cap Corse to visit.

She parked in the marina again at Santa-Lucia and made her way through the now familiar backstreets to Madame Santoni's house. During her sleepless moments she had made a mental list of questions to ask her. But she knew that the old lady had to explain things in her own time and in her own way. She wouldn't be hurried or led, so Rachel would have to be patient. Even so, she quickened her step and serpents writhed in her stomach.

This time, a younger, slimmer version of the café owner in Zaronza opened the door.

"Yes? Can I help you?"

"My name is Rachel Swift and I've come to see Madame Santoni. Is she in? Or is she still doing her shopping?"

"She's not well. Taken ill yesterday. She will insist on doing everything for herself and she's probably overdone it."

A chasm opened in Rachel's stomach and she took a deep breath.

A faint voice came from inside.

"Who is it, Antonia?"

"A foreign lady," Antonia called over her shoulder.

"I know who it is; let her in."

"Are you sure, Granny? You're not up to receiving visitors."

"Let her in."

Antonia stood aside for Rachel to enter and gestured to the sitting room. As they crossed the room, she muttered, "Not more than ten minutes. She's worn out and you're not to tire her out."

"I'm not deaf," Madame Santoni said from the bedroom. "You're getting as bossy as your cousin. And shut the door."

"I'll be back in ten minutes," Antonia said, wagging her finger.

Rachel sat on the chair next to the high bedstead. The old lady had altered in the space of a day. The pallor beneath her wrinkled skin had increased and her face had sunk inwards. Only her button eyes were as bright as ever. Her twisted fingers grasped the bedclothes like hooks. Rachel took one of her hands. It was cold, though the room was warm.

"I'm so sorry. I hope I didn't tire you out yesterday. You were obviously shocked when you first opened the door and thought I was Maria."

Madame Santoni shook her head. "I'm old, that's all. But I'll be fine again tomorrow. Now, did you read it?"

Rachel nodded.

"Good. I expect you want to hear the rest. But don't interrupt. You can ask any questions you like when I've finished. First, give me a drink of water."

After taking a few sips, the old lady waved the glass away and settled back on the pillows with a sigh.

She spoke in a feeble voice and Rachel had to lean forward to catch what she said.

"I already told you that your grandmother left the island when she was fifteen. Her elder brother had just gone off to Ajaccio to train as a teacher, and she didn't see why she couldn't do what she wanted as well. But her mother, Letizia, didn't agree. She and that chap she married – Orso something-or-other, the old mayor's son – thought it was good enough for her to become a teacher and stay in Corsica. But Maria was adamant about studying to be a doctor, and the only place she could do that was on the mainland. Tante Maria stood up for her, and even paid for her to go, which caused a bit of friction in the family. It turned your grandmother against Corsica, too. She said it was a primitive place that needed dragging into the modern world. As far as I know, she never came back.

"As for Maria Orsini, she patched things up with Letizia, who by then was living with her youngest son in the old mayor's house along with Orso and his sister. They went on like that for a few years until Orso upped and died of a heart attack. They say his experiences in the war probably caused it. By that time, I'd left the village myself and I only heard second-hand about them from time to time. Maria's friend, Orso's sister – what *was* her name?"

"Sophia?"

"Yes, that's it. Sophia. She was never strong and got carried off by pneumonia or some such not long after her brother. Letizia moved back in with Tante Maria and they stayed in that big old house until the war came and the island got overrun by Italian and German soldiers."

Madame Santoni coughed. "Give me some more water, please."

She gulped the water and coughed again.

"Perhaps I should leave and let you rest. I can always come back tomorrow," Rachel said, although she was burning to know the remainder of Maria's story.

"No. I'm alright. There's not much more. The war came and Maria was then in her sixties. She always resented the Germans because of what they did in the Great War and because Raphaël was killed during it. According to my friend Giulia, who was still in the village – she died a long time ago – Maria would disappear for days at a time and then suddenly reappear without saying where she'd been. Now, I think it's obvious she must have been helping the Resistance."

That would have been just like her, Rachel thought.

"One day she vanished and never came back. No one knows what happened to her. They never found a body, no one heard of her being captured or executed. But the fact is, she must have been killed. She would have come back to Zaronza if she could. With everyone gone, your great-grandmother, Letizia, went back to the Bozio area where she came from. The house was shut up and remained empty until it was sold. I think Maria must have left it to Letizia's three children, but none of them wanted to come back and live there."

Another fit of coughing started and Madame Santoni lay back on the pillows, struggling for breath. The door opened and Antonia appeared, red-faced.

"You'd better go," she said. "Granny's been talking too much, I can see that."

Rachel squeezed Madame Santoni's hand and received a gentle pressure in return.

"Could I come back tomorrow and see how she is?"

Antonia nodded. "All right. But I can't guarantee she'll be in any state to see you."

The coughing fit had passed and they could hear the old lady's shallow breathing. Her eyes were closed, her purple-veined eyelids almost transparent.

"I think she's gone to sleep," Rachel said and they tiptoed out.

***

At a loss for how to occupy herself, Rachel sought the car in the marina car park. She sat for a while behind the wheel taking in what Madame Santoni had told her. So, Maria Orsini was an unsung war heroine, or so it appeared. What a life she had led: long periods of inactivity and obscurity, laced with bursts of action and tension, framed by momentous world events.

Starting the ignition, Rachel turned out of the car park and took the road into the Nebbio, up and up into the hills. She visited the chequerboard church at Murato that Raphaël had described to Maria – and that she had never seen – with its frieze of mythical beasts. On the way back, she took a different road that led to the Col de Teghime. Bastia she would leave for another day – or even another visit, for now she was certain she would return. But she wanted to experience what Maria had seen all those times she had taken this route: the day she accompanied Vincentello to see him off at Bastia, never to return; when she left Corsica herself to nurse in northern France; and when, full of hope, she took the train to Corte to search for Raphaël, who was already long dead.

Rachel parked at the col and studied the memorial to the troops who died there during a fierce battle before the Germans withdrew from Bastia in October 1943. She could see both sides of Cap Corse from up there. On one side, Santa-Lucia fringed the bay; on the other, the sprawl of Bastia spread alongside the eastern coast. To the north stretched the mountainous spine separating the two sides of the cape, the peaks swathed in mist. The feeling of coming home spread through her again. She knew she would carry this landscape with her wherever she went, as Maria Orsini must have done.

A cool breeze sprang up as evening approached. She regained the car and took the road back to Zaronza.

Chapter 30

The next morning, Rachel decided to go to Santa-Lucia again to see if Madame Santoni was feeling better. She still had some questions. How did she get hold of Maria's memoir? Who had Maria written it for? What happened to Letizia's two sons, Grandmother Maria's brothers? Each question raised countless others. But, of course, she wouldn't stay if the old lady was no better. She could always come back another day: plenty of exploring to do, anyway.

Passing the café, she noticed it was closed and shuttered. As she stood there, *la patronne* emerged dressed in black and locked the door behind her. She taped a notice to the door.

"Good morning, Madame," Rachel called.

"Oh, hello. I'm sorry, if you want anything I'm afraid we're closed today and probably for the next few days. It's Granny. She died last night."

Rachel stared at her, open-mouthed, a cold fist gripping her stomach.

"I'm so sorry," she said at last.

"Yes, well, she was a very old lady. At least she wasn't bedridden for months and she never had to go into hospital. She would have hated that."

"I'm sure she would have done."

"By the way, did she ever agree to meet you?"

"Yes, I went to see her. She was very kind."

"That doesn't sound like Granny! But then she was very particular about who she liked and who she didn't. Sorry, I'll have to go. There are so many formalities and things to do when someone dies. I can't expect the cousins to do it all."

She hurried down the street, got into a small red car and

drove off. Rachel stood looking after her for a while, a lump in her throat. She had felt an affinity with the old lady. And now her last living link with the two Marias was gone.

***

That evening, after a day touring the upper part of Cap Corse, Rachel gave Pascal and Angelina an edited version of the story Madame Santoni had told her. She was conscious that the old lady had refused to see Pascal, and didn't want him to feel resentful that she had agreed to see Rachel, an outsider. She didn't tell Pascal about the existence of Maria's memoir, but just implied that she was retelling what she had heard. She felt uneasy on that count, too. But somehow she sensed that Maria hadn't written her story for public consumption. Perhaps she had written it for Letizia's children, the nearest she ever came to having her own family.

And now it had come full circle. Rachel might be the last of Raphaël and Letizia's descendants, she and her mother having both been only children. But maybe she had Colombani cousins somewhere: after all, Grandmother Maria had two brothers. Her spine tingling, she realised her quest to piece together her Corsican family history was only just beginning. But even before pursuing that, there was something else she had to do: a mission that would involve a lot of research.

She needn't have worried about Pascal. He was pleased to know a little more about Maria Orsini and her secret lover.

"Well, that's a mystery or two solved. It all slots into place nicely. And so your granny lived in this house?"

"Yes, for a few years, anyway, until she left to continue her studies in France. And then, of course, she married and came to England, so I don't think she ever came back. She must have missed Corsica. From what I understand, people always do – and I can see why. But she must have had her reasons."

"Given your connection with the house and the village,

you're very welcome to stay here anytime you like, even out of season. We'd be happy to have you."

"Thank you. I'd like that. I have a feeling I'll be seeing a lot more of Corsica."

Pascal beamed. "You know, we always had trouble thinking of a suitable name for the guest house. We wanted to give it a Corsican-sounding name so we toyed with things that included Santa Giulia or the ruined château and the watchtower. But we've never found one that appealed, so we just called it unimaginatively the Zaronza Guest House."

He turned to Angelina.

"But now I believe we've hit on exactly the right one. It can't be anything but Osteria Maria."

Epilogue

October 2013, Corse-Matin newspaper report:

On 23rd October 2013, as part of the celebrations to commemorate the liberation of Corsica in 1943, the mayor of Zaronza, Jean-Baptiste Paoli, unveiled the restored fountain and plaque in the central square.

The plaque commemorates Maria Orsini for exemplary services to Corsica and to the French Republic. Recent researches conducted by an English academic, Rachel Swift, had uncovered her role in the Corsican Resistance movement and in helping to conceal Jewish refugees from discovery.

Maria Orsini perished during one of her missions to move a Jewish family to safety. The full circumstances of her death may never be known, but it is clear that her involvement in the partisan movement saved many lives and possibly helped to hasten the departure of the occupying troops.

Madame Orsini also achieved distinction by nursing at the Front during World War I.

Madame Swift, who has Corsican ancestry, said, "I was so glad to find out a little more about this extraordinary and brave woman. She was like an aunt to my grandmother, who lived in Zaronza for a few years, and helped her to achieve her ambitions."

Monsieur Paoli, the mayor, said, "We are glad to honour, at last, a distinguished citizen of Zaronza, whose personal modesty concealed what she did not just for the village but also for Corsica."

Author's Note:

A true story was the inspiration for *The House at Zaronza.*

The main character and her schoolmaster lover, on whom I have based Maria and Raphaël, lived in a village on the Corsican coast in the early 1890s. I have chosen to set the beginning of the story a little later, in 1899. They communicated via a secret letter-drop. Letters written to the young woman by her lover were found in a box walled up in an attic a few years ago, which gave me the idea for the story, but none of her letters has survived. Their relationship appears to have been turbulent, and presumably ended when she was forced to marry a relative for family reasons. Her husband eventually emigrated without her.

The personalities of all the characters are, of course, figments of my imagination, as are the twists and turns of the plot.

I have tried to be as accurate as possible when relating events during World War I but of necessity I have had to employ artistic licence at times. I will be pleased to correct any factual errors at the earliest opportunity.

Select Bibliography

Although Corsica has been part of France since 1769, its history and unique culture set it apart. I have consulted a number of works in writing this story, which might be of interest to readers wanting to know more about the island.

For me, the best account of Corsica remains Dorothy Carrington's wonderful *Granite Island* (London, Penguin Classics, 2008), first published in 1971. I have also enjoyed the lively background provided by James Boswell's *An Account of Corsica, The Journal of a Tour to that Island, and Memoirs of Pascal Paoli*, (London, Dilly, 1768). And Robert Wernick published a more up-to-date view of Corsica in the Smithsonian Magazine (2002), "Corsica - Isle of Beauty, Isle of Bandits".

Books, articles, biographies and memoirs of World War I abound, of course, especially around the hundredth anniversary of its outbreak. I have consulted numerous classic works on the causes and course of the "war to end wars".

Given Maria's experiences on the Western Front, I had to research what it was like to be a French volunteer nurse in World War I. Several general histories provided background information on the development of medicine and nursing during World War I and the organisation of military medical care. Nonetheless, French nurses' experiences at the front are a sadly-neglected topic. I was fortunate, therefore, to discover several memoirs that have helped me to paint a picture of life in a French field hospital:

Bourcier, Claudine : *Nos chers blessés: une infirmière dans la grande guerre* (Paris, Alan Sutton, 2002). Madame Bourcier nursed in a Biarritz hospital before being deployed to Amiens.

Her great-granddaughter found her diaries by chance and published them. I have drawn on this work for the description of Maria's time nursing at Amiens and then at Beauvais in 1918-19.

La Motte, Ellen N.: *The Backwash of War*, 1916. A series of vignettes written in 1915-16 by an American nurse who worked in a French field hospital in Belgium. The book was suppressed in 1918, since it was considered damaging to morale after America had entered the war. It was republished in 1934 and is still in print.

Guinness, May: "The Bombardment of Vadelaincourt" *The Dublin Review*, issue no. 25, Winter 2006-07. A first-hand account of the German bombardment of the hospital at Vadelaincourt near Verdun, published with an introduction by May Guinness's great-grand-niece.

CPSIA information can be obtained at www.ICGtesting.com
Printed in the USA
LVOW07s0541271014

410595LV00001B/3/P